STRANGE PLEASURES

BOOKS BY SEAN WALLACE

Fantasy Annual 1 (co-edited with Philip Harbottle)
Fantasy Annual 2 (co-edited with Philip Harbottle)
Fantasy Annual 3 (co-edited with Philip Harbottle)
Fantasy Annual 4 (co-edited with Philip Harbottle)
The Tall Adventurer: The Works of E.C. Tubb
(bibliography, with Philip Harbottle)
Eric Frank Russell: Our Sentinel in Space, 3rd Ed.
(bibliography, with Phil Stephensen-Payne)

STRANGE PLEASURES

Edited by Sean Wallace

Cosmos Books, an imprint of Wildside Press
New Jersey . New York . California . Ohio

STRANGE PLEASURES

Published by:

Cosmos Books, an imprint of Wildside Press
P.O. Box 45, Gillette, NJ 07933-0045
www.wildsidepress.com / www.cosmos-books.com

CONTENTS

MEMESIS

by Keith Brooke

The townspeople only come out here in daylight. They must feel safer then.

The wild man with the crooked nose stands in the shadow of a high wall and watches them. The kind ones are the worst, he thinks. The ones to avoid.

Two climb out of a low car. The car is all angles and shiny metal. A man, a woman. Well fed. Dressed in bright, clean clothes. They look around.

Crooked Nose edges deeper into the shade. Pulls his ragged clothes more tightly about himself. He shivers — with cold, with fear.

The land is open here, but little grows in the dark, muddy ground. Piles of broken stone blocks dot the area. The same kind of stone that makes this wall. Crooked Nose senses that the piles must be broken walls, rather than walls not yet grown. He thinks about things like this, although he feels sure that real under-standing is beyond him.

"Hey, you over there!"

They've seen him. The shadow of the wall has not hidden him well enough. The man by the car holds a hand aloft, palm facing outward. A signal of some kind. Of friendliness?

The woman, much shorter than her companion, gestures at the car and its rear end lifts up.

"Hey," the man repeats, more softly. "We have food for you. Do you understand? Food."

Crooked Nose just stares. He understands the meaning of their words, if not the precise content.

He wants to flee, but his empty belly argues otherwise. There is a fist-sized rock by his feet. In his head he sees a sudden, brief image of that rock smashing into the face of the tall man by the car.

It is the way, out here on the fringes of the town. It is a hard, and usually brief, way of life.

A shelf has extended from the back of the car and on it the woman is arranging a number of objects. Food, Crooked Nose knows, although it is not the kind of food he would normally eat.

Just then, another figure emerges from behind a heap of rubble. A woman, her tall, thin frame submerged in countless ragged layers.

Crooked Nose recognises her from her shape and the way she moves: awkwardly, no coordination. He thinks of her as Brown Twitch, after the colour of her hair and the way her whole head sometimes jerks repeatedly, a movement he thinks she probably cannot control. Crooked Nose fucks her sometimes, but only when she tells him to. She broke his nose one time when he tried to and she didn't want him. It had been broken several times before that, too, but never by a woman.

He shuffles forward, his hips searing with sudden pain. It's worse now the air is so cold. Sometimes his body is so sore he can barely move. This cold season is probably his last.

Brown Twitch is almost at the car.

Crooked Nose makes his body move faster, grinding his teeth to distract himself from the pain.

This close, the townspeople look scared, the man particularly so. Their clothes are so bright they don't seem real. Their skin is smooth and dark, their hair straight, black, lustrous. Compared to Brown Twitch they look like members of an alien species, although Crooked Nose knows they are human. The real aliens don't come out of the town very often. Their skin is not so dark and they have less hair. They taste of charred bird, even uncooked.

The man's eyes flit between the two deadbeats, as they approach him from opposite sides. In one hand he holds a small gun. Crooked Nose realises he has forgotten the rock.

Brown Twitch hesitates before the two townspeople, eyes fixed on the riches spread out before her. The woman puts a hand on the man's arm, makes him lower it, although he does not put the gun away.

"Go on," says the woman to Brown Twitch. "Have some food, you poor thing." To her companion she adds, "Poor thing looks half-starved, Ray."

Brown Twitch takes a brown square that is probably meat. Crooked Nose thinks it will not be alien meat. He doesn't think town people eat aliens. The aliens would kill them all if they tried.

Brown Twitch fills her mouth in growing frenzy. Crooked Nose forgets the people now. He drags his body as fast as his painful hips will allow.

The two townspeople step clear. The man raises his gun again, scared, despite the woman's steadying hand on his arm.

A square of brown meat. Warm from some heating device, too big to stuff into his mouth. Crooked Nose rips at the meat with the good teeth on the left side of his mouth, feels nauseous with the sudden richness, the eruption of juices flowing across his tongue, spilling out and down his chin.

The first swallow is painful and exquisite. Before the part-chewed hunk of meat has reached his stomach his mouth is full again.

His hand jabs towards another dark block, but Brown Twitch gets there first. For an instant their eyes lock and he remembers the shock and the pain of her fist in his face.

"Steady, steady." The woman's voice, calming.

He lets Brown Twitch have the disputed block, takes a spongy white thing instead, fills his mouth again.

"There's plenty to go around," says the woman. There's something soothing in her tone. Something reaching out to him, reaching into him.

These cars from the town, with their shiny metal and their bright colours, are wonderful things, frightening simply because they are so far removed from Crooked Nose's understanding.

They are quiet, too.

Their wheels on the rough ground make more noise than the whining hum that comes from inside them. It is the sound of wheels that makes Crooked Nose look up from the feast. Another car is approaching.

Crooked Nose grunts a quick warning, then leans over the shelf and sweeps up an armful of the townspeople's offering.

"Please!" said the woman. "It's okay. Do you understand? They are our friends. They have more food. We only want to help you."

Brown Twitch grabs more of the food and turns to run.

Together, they flee, but Crooked Nose rapidly falls behind as the pain flares up in his hips again.

Brown Twitch slows. She is scared and her head keeps jerking upwards as if someone is tugging at her hair. But she waits for Crooked Nose.

He doesn't really understand why she does this, why she does not simply flee. She is faster than him, she could get away easily. But then he has never really understood Brown Twitch: she is beautiful and clever and wise and surprising.

Maybe she wants to fuck him. Maybe that is why she is trotting slowly at his side instead of sprinting for cover as she should do.

Then a sudden explosion of pain in his back sends Crooked Nose staggering to his knees, his armful of food scattered across the poisoned ground.

Brown Twitch falters, stares at him with wide open eyes.

On his knees, struggling to stay upright, he meets her look, shakes his head. This would be his last cold season, then, as he had thought.

"Go," he croaks. "Go . . . food . . . eat. *Run!*"

#

Daylight, bright against the lids of his closed eyes. An echo in his head: the mad jabber of a million voices, a kaleidoscope sequence of images, colours.

The man with the crooked nose feels sick, sore, uncomfortable. He rolls onto his side, vomits, starts to cough on the acidic traces of his last meal.

Opens his eyes.

He's in the corner of a ruined building: four walls standing, but only part of the roof sheltering him from a harsh blue sky above. He feels a distinct sense of misplacement: he does not belong. He struggles to his knees, rubs the cuff of his quilted jacket across his mouth.

He should not be here, but he does not know where else he should be.

He stands, goes across to the broken window. There are more buildings, some ruined and overgrown with creepers, others still in use.

Just then he hears the rattle of wheels on the rough road and he flinches, feels a sudden panic. He does not know why he should feel like this: the car comes into sight, just a Jackson 4Xe, nothing out of the ordinary.

He tries to work out how he knows such things. He thinks about things like this, although he feels sure that real understanding is beyond him.

He remembers little from before this morning — the bright light, the stomach cramps, the vomit. He is a man without a past.

He has a name, he realises. His name is Turner 10B. His friends call him Tenby.

He remembers no friends.

Outside, Tenby pauses, turns tentatively, expecting pain from his hips but there is only a dull ache. The building is low and at some time in the past has been badly damaged. It is overgrown with creepers, just like many of the other buildings in this neighbourhood. There are some shrivelled purple fruits dotted about the creepers, damaged by the cold weather, but that does not deter the blackbirds from gorging themselves.

The house is on the edge of town. Tenby steps out onto the rough road and hesitates again. To his right is wasteland: great tracts of land tainted by the mass destruction of the past, some of the ground so poisoned that nothing will grow, even after so long. To his left: the town.

Tenby turns his back on the wasteland, heads into town.

There are people in the street, and working in the surrounding buildings. They are healthy-looking people, in clean clothes. They work together as if they have all grown up in the same nest, although he suspects that they have not. He thinks nostalgically of his own siblings and their nest father, but the vagueness of the memory disturbs him: no faces, no names . . . he is not really remembering at all. The memory is a shape in his head, a shape with no detail, no substance.

He passes people in the street, their numbers increasing as he heads deeper into the town. There is a vague sense of panic deep inside him, a fear of these clean and happy people which he cannot quite place.

Occasionally someone nods to him in greeting.

When this happens, Tenby looks away, pretends he has not noticed.

In the centre of the town there is a square with grass and shrubs and great, towering pine trees. Tenby sits on a log bench, trying to comprehend, trying to recall.

Birds flit through the nearby branches. He does not know their individual names, but he knows that there are finches and the more agile chickadees. The ugly grey-brown ones are sparrows, he knows that. And the bushes . . . the ones with big, shiny leaves — they are laurels.

He loses track of the passing time as he revels in his ability to attach labels to the features of the world around him. Names give these objects a presence of their own, a substance they had previously lacked. It gives Tenby a growing sense of control, a vocabulary he had not known existed.

At some point he spots a white line across the sky, disappearing into the too-yellow sun. Reflexively, he touches his brow in obeisance, mutters, "Grace of the Father." It is, he recalls, a traditional phrase, invoking the name of the Father of all the Family's nests to protect the travellers on their journey. The white line is the contrail of an alien aircraft.

At the appointed time, he rises from his bench and leaves the square. He feels dispirited, but he cannot quite explain why that should be so.

The bustle of the streets irritates him now, and he feels an instinctive hostility, a need to defend his own small space against encroachment. The anger lifts him. It is as if he remembers in some small way.

He pushes his way through double swing doors and is immediately engulfed by a blanket of warm air, a babble of voices, some vaguely familiar music in the background.

"Tenby!"

A man's voice, deep, mellow, comforting. This man must be a friend because he remembers remembering that his friends call him Tenby.

The man is behind a bar which stretches the length of the room. There is a space part way along and the man is gesturing Tenby to come over and fill it.

Groups of people are gathered around tables, while others stand around a cluster of gaming machines and yet others sit on tall stools, hunched over the bar, exchanging muttered words with the other barkeeps.

Tenby heads for his space at the bar. He sits, stares into the drink that awaits him.

"You're forgetting again, aren't you, Turner 10B?"

He meets the barkeep's gaze. The man is short, bald, with a shiny complexion and wide grey eyes. A plastic box grows discreetly from above his left ear. A communications implant, alien technology which is as much a status symbol as an essential part of his work.

Barkeeps are important, Tenby realises with sudden insight: for people like Tenby they act as surrogate nest fathers, stand-ins for something that most humans leave behind with adolescence.

"Forgetting?" says Tenby. "It's not that I forget, it's that I do not remember. There is a distinction."

"Semantics," says the barkeep, polishing a glass that does not need polishing.

"It's as if I have no past," says Tenby. "My existence has no symmetry: with no past to anchor me I am always tipping forward into the future." Just the thought makes him dizzy, grateful for the solidity of the bar.

"Come on," says the barkeep, sliding the drink towards Tenby. "Drink up and I'll take you through."

#

Daylight, coming in through the windows, rouses him from his slumber. In his head there is a vague echo, memory traces of the voices and images that had been his dreams.

Tenby feels stiff, uncomfortable, but he knows it is just the remains of sleep in his body, that he will feel fine when he can wake fully. He sits, rubs his eyes, then stands and stretches. He feels healthy, an energy in his body that is unfamiliar to him. He looks up, notes that the roof has been repaired, though he cannot recall if it is something he has done or if it has just happened in his absence.

He tries not to think about it: struggling to remember only exacerbates the feelings of misplacement that still plague him. He mutters a brief prayer of thanksgiving to the Father.

One corner of the room has become a kind of shrine, something he has constructed himself. There are candles and blown birds' eggs and tacked to the wall there is a picture of the Father: a stylised figure with spindly limbs, big grey eyes, a bald, domed head with a thick mat of hair sprouting from the back.

The Father is an alien.

Tenby touches his brow reflexively, then backs out of the room.

#

"Tenby!"

It is not just the barkeep who greets Tenby now: there is Lucy who sits at the next stool to him, and Walter and Mathiel who are always playing Top Trump against a machine that never loses, and old Denzel in his seat by the window. These are all Tenby's friends now. He remembers them from day to day and to Tenby that is a special thing.

He sits on his familiar stool, and eyes his familiar drink. He meets the barkeep's look and wonders what the man is hearing in the plastic box on the side of his head.

"Why is God an alien?"

For an instant, the barkeep falters. Tenby can see it in his eyes. Then he shrugs, smiles his too-wide-to-really-trust smile, and says, "Why indeed?"

"I mean it," says Tenby. "Why is the Father an alien?"

"Because that is the way it is," says the barkeep.

Lucy leans over, then. "It's the way they tell it," she says. "They give us their God, like they give us everything else."

Pointedly, the barkeep turns away from Lucy, leans closer to Tenby. "The Father created the first people in his image," he says. "And then he created the lesser races with slight variations. We are not so very different, after all — "

" — is what they tell us," interrupts Lucy again.

There is a tone to her voice that frightens Tenby, disturbing the truths with which he has constructed his world. He is not sure whether or not he likes the feeling.

"What do you mean?" he asks cautiously.

"The reconstruction," says Lucy. "The things they're doing to our heads."

The barkeep leans even closer, slides the drink across the counter. "Come on," he says to Tenby in his most reassuring tone. "I'll take you through."

Tenby downs his drink in one go, then lets the barkeep guide him through the crowded bar to some stairs.

"It's okay," says the barkeep as they walk. "Lucy's just having a bit of a relapse."

They enter a corridor, lined with closed doors.

"Relapse?"

They push through a door and Tenby automatically lowers himself onto a padded bench.

"Hmm," says the barkeep. "The treatment. The rehab. Sometimes it can cause paranoia, but the reaction is only temporary."

Before the barkeep can put the mask over Tenby's face, Tenby raises a hand to stop him. "Why?" he gasps.

"You're being fixed," says the barkeep. "We all are. The aliens are patching humankind together again. We nearly destroyed ourselves with neurological weapons that disrupted our mental functioning. The aliens came along and now they're fixing the damage, memetically reconstructing our minds for us."

The mask slides into place.

"Building memories where there were blanks," continues the barkeep. "Using nanomemetic probes to rewire our brains. It's okay, Tenby, we're making you better."

#

Tenby wakes on a low bench in the corner of his room. He has been doing more work to this place — the floor has been cleared of its debris, there is glass in the window.

He decides they must drive him back in a car or a van after each rehab session, for he can never remember the journey home. He can, however, remember what the barkeep has told him. He understands now that the aliens are rebuilding humankind from the degenerated ruins of its own making. It must be an enormous task, he realises: rebuilding each individual, constructing a human consciousness from its myriad constituent memory patterns. Memesis.

But just then his eye catches the candles, beads and eggs in the corner of his room. Reflexively he touches a finger to his brow, mutters, "The Father of us all." Prayers for an alien god.

The sense of misplacement, of disjoint: how can they know what is human, he wonders? How can they possibly reconstruct us?

He realises that he has been transformed, that the memetically constructed thoughts in his head are some arbitrary cocktail of human and alien.

He remembers the barkeep's words: *You're being fixed. We all are.* And later: *Isn't that what matters? Isn't that what you really want?*

He walks back into town, although it is not his appointed time. The people in the street — all the smiling, healthy faces — are nothing to him now. He is going to confront the barkeep, although he does not know quite how, or even why.

But when he comes to the square he sees two figures on the log bench: Lucy, pale and sobbing, her face buried in the chest of Denzel.

The old man looks up as Tenby approaches. "It's okay," he says.

Denzel never speaks much, but when he does his words have an authority. He is a man who thinks about the world perhaps even more than Tenby does. "She's gotten the shakes, is all," says Denzel. "She'll be okay."

Tenby squats so that his eyes are level with Denzel's. "What are they doing to us?" he asks softly.

"Like the man says, they're fixin' us," says Denzel. "Making up for what they done to us before."

In response to Tenby's blank look, the old man continues, "The wars, boy. The nerve weapons. The memetic bombs. That was when the aliens arrived. They beat us by fuckin' with our heads, Tenby. They damn near wiped us out an' now they're puttin' us back together again. They don't really know who we was, but they're doin' the best they can."

#

The barkeep's waiting for him, Tenby's regular stool free, his regular drink waiting on the polished surface of the bar. Maybe someone has warned him through the plastic comms box on the side of his head. Maybe that's what the thing is for.

"We're only doing the best we can," says the barkeep, eyeing the fist-sized rock in Tenby's hand. "The human race would have been wiped out inside a generation if we hadn't started fixing things — all instinct for survival had near gone."

We. The word jars.

Tenby stares at the barkeep. "You?" he says. "You mean *you* are an alien?"

The barkeep shakes his head. "No," he says. "I am mostly human." He taps the comms box, adds, "I needed more fixing than most, I guess."

Then he points at the rock in Tenby's hand. "You would gain nothing by using that," he says. "I can be reconstructed. Just like you."

Tenby subsides, drops the rock onto the floor. He slumps onto the stool, cradles his head in both hands. "It's wrong," he murmurs. "All wrong. They're building us up by guesswork."

"Informed guesses," says the barkeep.

"Guesswork and propaganda," says Tenby. "We worship their god, we think in their terms. Our heads have been filled with alien thoughts".

"What would *you* do in their position?" asks the barkeep gently. "The damage has been done. They only want to repair us."

Tenby shakes his head. "It's wrong," he insists. "They should just leave us alone, leave us to be human in whatever way we can."

The barkeep slides the drink closer to Tenby. "Here," he says. "This will make it all better."

#

He can't get it out of his head: the wrongness of it all. Every day he tries to classify his thoughts, to distinguish the human from the alien in his head.

And then one day he sees her.

It is cold now. Every morning there is ice on the ground and, even in his house, his breath comes out in clouds of steam.

He is walking through the ruins on the edge of town. He and Denzel have been helping Lucy fix up her place for the winter. Today they should be finished, so long as Lucy is well enough to help them with hanging the window shutters.

And there, by a wall that is little more than a heap of rubble running parallel to the road: a pathetic bundle of rags. A corpse, he is sure, but then it moves, twitches. A head with matted brown hair protrudes from the rags, dark eyes stare at him fearfully. The head jerks again, feebly, as if someone is tugging on the pathetic creature's hair.

There's something happening in Tenby's head and he is not sure what. Perhaps some kind of memory, he wonders?

He stops by the broken woman, crouches so that he presents a less intimidating figure. But still she is frightened, although she is clearly too weak to move.

He reaches out a hand, catches himself thinking that it is the kind ones who are the worst — the ones to avoid. The thought is alien to him.

"It's okay," he says softly. "I'm a friend — do you understand? I only want to help you." He touches her arm and she flinches.

"It's okay," he repeats. "I know a place . . ." Then he catches himself, what he had been about to say. He swallows, starts again: "I know a place where you can get fixed."

GENOCIDE

By Gord Rollo

. . . We wait, in darkness.
A jet-black room, in a jet-black world.
Peter is trembling.
"I hear something. I think they're coming!"
"No Peter," I tell him. "Not yet."
"Yes they are . . . I can hear them. They're coming, oh God, they're com-
ing!"
"No Peter," I try again. "It's still early. Too early."
I touch his hand, gently.
He calms down. A little.
Again we wait, in darkness . . .

Time for us, is quickly running out. You see . . . Peter and I are condemned to die today — this morning, in fact. Peter is taking it much harder than me, his mind fading in and out like a flickering bulb, but perhaps that's for the best. It will be easier for him to go to his death while swimming in the deep calm sea of insanity. I'm actually quite happy for him. I envy him!

Death will be different for me.

Don't get me wrong. It would give me great pleasure to join him in that cool void. To swim with him toward the distant shore of our next lives, but I can't. I've come close . . . believe me, but every time I start running for that frothing surf, something always stops me, pulling me back to shore. My lifeguard or sanityguard if you will, has a name. Its name is . . . Anger, or sometimes . . . Rage, some days even . . . Hatred! *MY ANGER, MY RAGE, MY HATRED!*

Whatever its name, it prevents me from giving in and quitting. So today I will die, but at least it will be with my head held high and proud. My dignity is at least one thing they can't take from me. Not ever!

But why must I die? And my friend Peter? Poor, sweet Peter, who's never harmed a soul in all of his young life. Why must Peter die? The answers escape me. Haunt me.

You see . . . neither Peter nor I have any idea as to why we are condemned to die today. We have neither committed nor been formally charged with any crimes. We were never even read our rights. Apparently, we have none. We are simply scheduled for elimination. Peter is almost beyond caring, but I am still very angry. I seethe at the injustice of it all, but there doesn't seem to be anything that I can do about it.

. . . Except wait, in darkness.

#

. . . We wait, in semi-darkness.

A thin sliver of sun peeking over the horizon like a razor blade slash in the dark throat of night.

Peter is shaking.

"Oh God, they're here. They're here!"

"No Peter," I tell him, "Not yet."

"Oh God, Oh GOD, OH GOD . . . !"

"Easy Peter. Take it easy, it's still too early."

I drape my skinny, bruised arm around him.

He calms down. A little.

Again we wait, in semi-darkness . . .

If my calculations are correct (they're just thin scratches in our cell floor), Peter and I have been held here for forty-one days. Today is day forty-two. Sadly, for us, it will prove to be a short one, much shorter than the rest of the days have been.

They began torturing us almost immediately upon our arrival. Poor Peter was taken away first. I could hear his screams echoing down the corridor. They went on and on and on. He returned to our cell bleeding, with glazed vacant eyes. It was my turn next.

Only so much agony can be registered in the brain. After the pain tolerance threshold has been crossed and re-crossed too many times, the brain simply blocks it all out. By the end of my first session with their needles and their probes and their electricity, my brain had crawled safely away into a dark quiet place. Thank God for small mercies.

I honestly don't remember much about the subsequent torture sessions. I blocked them out too. They were daily and brutal, that much I recall. Worse for me than the pain, is the knowledge that Peter and I are not alone. There are more of us imprisoned here. A great many more. Cell after cell full.

Most of their eyes are as glazed and vacant as Peter's, but not everyone's. There are a few, like me, who still wonder what the hell is going on. They're just as angry and confused as I am. None of them seem to know why they are here either.

There are rumors, though. Plenty!

In hushed whispers we talk, vigilant bloodshot eyes on guard for the slightest sign of our unmerciful captors. Peter never takes part in these talks anymore. He talks only to himself. The general consensus is that war must have been declared — a war somebody conveniently forgot to tell us about.

Genocide.

That's the word I hear a lot.

"They're going to slaughter our whole race," someone on my left whispers.

An old dry voice, two cells down tells me it is happening in other places as well. This house of pain is only one of many. All across the land, we are being herded up and packed into these slaughterhouses. "Death Camps", the old one calls them. A place to be humiliated, tortured, played with . . . and then eliminated.

Genocide.

Could it be true?

Could it?

My mind flashes back to the day Peter and I were captured. Our families had been hungry. Starving. Peter and I took to the streets to beg, borrow and steal — anything to make the pain in our young one's bellies subside. At least for a little while.

We were lucky enough to find some food at the rear entrance to an Italian restaurant. It was mostly leftover scraps tossed in the trash, but we did find a tray of untouched pasta that had gone cold and even a fairly fresh loaf of cheese bread. Discarded trash to the rich people whose supper it had been — life to me and Peter's families.

We thought we had found heaven.

What we had found was a trap.

Stern faced men in dark clothing quickly surrounded us. We fought bravely, but to no avail. That was forty-one days ago.

Why?

God damn it . . . WHY?

The old one with the dry gravely voice says it's because were not like our captors. He says that we're different and they hate us because of it. He also says that they fear us because we are so different from them.

Different? So they have the right to kill us?

Thousands have been eliminated in our captor's fleshy smelling torture rooms and gas chambers since Peter and I arrived. Thousands will probably die after we are gone. They seem to have a scheduled day to die for every one of us. Today is day forty-two. My day — Peter's and mine.

Genocide.

There's nothing that we can do about it.

. . . Except wait, in semi-darkness.

#

. . . We wait, in early morning sunlight.

A blinding sun slowly reaching into our cell with a hand we'd rather not shake.

Peter is silent, his mind thankfully gone from this terrible place.

"It's okay Peter," I reassure him anyway. "They're not here yet." But I know it's a lie. I can hear them talking among themselves at the end of the hall.

I hold Peter close, comforting myself probably more than him.

It helps me calm down. A little.

Again we wait, in early morning sunshine...

It's strange the things you thing about when you know you're watching the sunrise for the very last time. Of course I've been thinking about my family, they are always first and foremost to me. I hope my beautiful wife Heather is going to be okay. Damn these bastards if they ever lay a finger on her. I pray she carries on without me with her head held high and raises our daughter to be strong and proud of our race. I hope my dear little Samantha isn't too young to remember me. That's not too much to ask, is it?

I pray for Peter's family too, and the rest of the friends and relatives we know. Hopefully, God will spare all of them the fate he has chosen for us.

Maybe God doesn't have any say in it.

Who does then? When I think of our captors it makes me want to scream. One second I want to rip their well fed guts apart, the next I find myself praying for their souls. I hate them for what they are doing, but I'm not capable of hating them the way they seem capable of hating me. Like the old dry voiced prisoner keeps telling me — I'm different. Our race doesn't hate someone without a reason, like they do.

They?

Who are . . . *THEY?*

That's something I wonder about. I wonder who it was that has ordered me and Peter do die? Who's calling the shots, in other words? What does he look like? How can he possibly go to sleep at night feeling at ease and justified in what he's doing? I'll probably never know. I do know that it isn't one of the big sweaty men around here that are in control. There has to be people above them. Their boss, or perhaps even higher — who knows just how high up the chain of command the orders come from.

In this poor excuse of a degenerating world we live in, the almighty corporate dollar is usually the boss. Those in control of the money are those in control of the power. Some people will step on and destroy anything and anyone that gets in their way of obtaining this power. Once they have it, they'll crush anyone trying to take it away.

It's really sickening, but quite obviously true.

Peter and I are living examples of this modern greed.

Not for long, though. Soon we'll be dead examples!

They're coming for us now. I can hear heavy footsteps rhythmically echoing off the cement floor, like a grandfather clock chiming out the hour.

The hour of our death.

We are removed from our small cell and roughly taken to the torture chamber at the far end of the hall. The sad, haunted eyes of our fellow prisoners follow along with us.

Our executioners are huge muscular men in pale white uniforms. They tower above us like giants as they strap us down on a large blood stained table. Maybe it's just my fear that makes them seem so large. After all, I am very frightened.

One of them notices me trembling and it makes him smile. He simply walks away to help his partner prepare our death. We watch helplessly, as they fill two shockingly large syringes with some unknown amber liquid. There's not much time left for Peter and I. We look into each other's terrified eyes and pray. Besides that, there's nothing left to do.

. . . Except wait, in early morning sunshine.

#

. . . I wait, in silence.

A paralyzing fear gripping my heart like a thousand slowly tightening cast iron bands.

Peter is dead.

"They murdered him," my mind screams.

They are going to murder me next.

"No!" I try convincing myself, but I know it's true.

I can clearly see them preparing the next needle for me.

I'm trying to stay calm, but my composure is starting to slip. A little.

Alone I wait, in silence . . .

How can they be doing this to me? What have I done to deserve being treated like this? So what if I'm different than them, these people aren't God. I have every right to live in peace too.

Don't I?

The smaller of the two men slowly walks toward me. He has the long needle in his bloody hand. Poor Peter's blood!

I have time to pray for Peter and hope he's moved onto a better place. A place where there's not more pain... no more hate. I say a quick prayer for myself too.

And then the syringe is viciously jabbed into me.

I feel the tip of it enter me just above the base of my long pink tail. My sharp claws are digging involuntarily into the hard wooden table and the whiskers on my face are beginning to twitch spastically as the poison swiftly courses through my small furry body.

Why is this happening?

Why?

Through a haze I see and hear my two executioners talking above me. I see that it says *LAB TECHNICIAN* on the pocket of each of their white coats. They're talking about me . . . saying something about some big cosmetics company any how they're trying really hard to develop new products for them.

That can't be it!

Please tell me that I'm not dying just so some big company can get rich developing a new shade of lipstick. Please tell me that isn't true! Who gave them the right to decide my life was worth so little?

Maybe if I shout out to them, scream my little heart out, maybe they'll begin to understand. I could let them know that I'm more than just some disposable plaything to experiment with. I could tell them that I have feelings just like them. I get scared, I get lonely, and I get confused!

I wonder if they would even care?

I wonder if anyone cares?

My strength is almost gone now. I'm struggling for just a few more ragged breaths. I know I should at least try to make them understand but it just wouldn't do any good. I'm just a little nameless white rat, and my feeble words would never be enough to put a stop to this madness. The corporate heads of business and science that run this world will always carry more weight then the little defenseless animals like me.

Am I in the middle of a quiet war? Is what they're doing publicly supported genocide? I don't know. I just know that it's wrong. There has to be a better way. There just has to be. Maybe someday, someone will find it.

But that day won't be today.

So I wait, like Peter and the millions of test animals before me, for my death. I should try to talk to them, but I won't. I won't do anything.

. . . Except wait, in silence.

MICE

By Dave Hutchinson

The Kid At Juan Carlos . . . The Realities Of Travel In The New Europe . . . "By The Way, Did We Miss That Old Chap?" . . . An Evening With The CIA . . . Viruses Fuck You Up

---

Madrid is the closest you can get by air to where the British Isles used to be without being blown out of the sky. A huge half-circle has been bitten out of Continental European airspace almost as far south as Geneva. Inside this half-circle, nothing larger than a seagull can get off the ground without being incinerated.

We touched down at Juan Carlos International in the middle of a thunderstorm. The 767 bounced once and the engines howled and for a fraction of a second we were in free fall before the wheels touched tarmac again. I screamed and spilled my eighth complimentary — and entirely legal, now we were out of American airspace — Wild Turkey.

JCI is one of those New Architecture things, a monstrosity of tubular composite and wind-singing cable that's supposed to remind the weary traveller of the Spirit of Flight.

Fuck that. My nerves were jangling with the Spirit of our Landing, and I viewed the airport's kilometre-long halls with more jaundice than the architect had allowed for. I went straight to the Arrivals lounge and ordered a double Chivas on the rocks to calm myself.

"Excuse me, sir?"

When you've been panhandled at every airport from LAX to Auckland you learn to recognise that special whining-polite tone of voice, and you either ignore it, or toss some of the local currency over your shoulder, or call the Polizei. This voice was different, though. That and the fact that I was sitting in the executive lounge, where it's rare to find a beggar these days, made me sit up and turn round.

A young man wearing jeans and a greasy Milwaukee Brewers baseball cap was standing behind me. He looked overdue for a shave and a wash, but there was none of the crazy look you sometimes see in panhandlers' eyes.

"English?" I said.

He nodded.

"From Calais, right?"

He nodded again. Out of the corner of my eye I saw one of the security men moving to evict the intruder, but I headed him off.

"This is Mister William Jefferson Clinton, Madrid bureau chief for *Time-Stone*," I said loudly, pointing at the English boy and waving my laminate in the guard's face by way of introduction. "I've just flown in from the Pacific Northwest and I need to be briefed urgently, and if you interrupt you'll be crotch-deep in lawsuits before bedtime. *Capisce?*"

Sometimes that kind of thing works, sometimes it doesn't. All you have to do is sound important and look as if you know what you're doing, and it doesn't matter if you speak the local gibberish or not. This time it worked. The guard looked at my laminate, then at the English boy, and he backed away nodding apologetically. When he was back in his corner of the lounge I motioned the English boy to join me at the bar and got the waiter to draw us a beer. I strongly believe there should be an unwritten Code of Honour for all travellers, no matter of what kind. I hate men in uniforms, too.

We introduced ourselves. His name was John Burton-Seichais, and he'd been hitching all over Europe this Summer looking for work, without any success.

"It's the accent," he said, sipping his second beer. "I mean, of course one speaks French, but one can't get rid of the accent."

His accent was as English as David Niven's, for all that he had been born and brought up on what is — lawsuits at the International Courts of Justice in the Hague notwithstanding — still French soil. I asked him what he was doing wandering around the executive area of Juan Carlos International.

He just shook his head sadly. "I don't know," he said, and started to cry.

Right.Back in the good old days, say twelve or fifteen years ago, there would have been only one way to get through a gig like this. Load up on speed and any other pharmaceuticals you could find, slap a disc into the recorder, and just thrash it out in a wild six-day rush.

You can't do that now. Fucking virus is everywhere. Dope doesn't work, speed doesn't work, a bottle of Wild Turkey costs over two hundred bucks — always presuming you can find a trustworthy connection. And it must be at least a year since I last saw a grapefruit at any price.

I knew it had all gone to shit a couple of years ago, covering Folsom's campaign in the New Hampshire primary. We were standing outside some god-awful compression-board factory in the snow and about ten degrees of frost while Folsom, his speech over, was on his way out, and I found I was out of Camels. One of his staffers, in a rare moment of compassion, offered me one of his cigarettes.

"Tastes strange," I said, lighting up. "New brand?"

"Red Lebanese," said the staffer, sniggering . . .

Well yes. I've gotten higher inhaling next to a burning building. Fucking bastards . . .

The collapse of the drugs culture has been exhaustively documented elsewhere, and it isn't our main topic anyway, but it seems to me that the level of journalism in this country has fallen since those bastards in Atlanta released the virus. It's asking too much to send a human being into some weird situation without any chemical protection at all.

The kid was feeling better by the time we walked down to the Hertz desk in the main concourse, the one in Executive country being clogged with greedheads and minor European aristocracy. I had to get to the main rail terminal in Madrid for my train to Paris, and I don't trust myself on airport courtesy buses after a bad episode in Larnaka that led to . . . well, never mind. What I mean is that I needed a car really badly and the nearest rental desk was almost a mile away across this goddamned modern sculpture that the Spaniards called an airport.

When we finally reached the desk I strode to the head of the queue and held out my laminate, and I said, "I need a car, quick."

The girl behind the desk shrank back, and I thought, Christ, I haven't drunk *that* much. I announced, "My assistant, Mister William Jefferson Clinton, and I must have a car immediately." I leaned across the counter. "Don't you realise there is news happening, somewhere, woman?"

With shaking hands, she produced a form. I signed the car onto the *Time-Stone* tab, grabbed John, and ran out into the parking lot.

The car Hertz gave me was one of those balless electric Nissans, top speed about fifty and no acceleration at all. I weaved it through the traffic and we got to the station with minutes to spare.

By this time John was babbling. "Well, one doesn't . . . no, really, one mustn't impose . . . um, by the way, did we *miss* that old chap?" I ignored his ravings, grabbed his sleeve, and hurled him aboard the train.

We are talking dangerous behaviour here. An Englishman kidnapped by a drink-sodden American claiming to be a journalist. "Well, officer, one moment one was walking through the airport minding one's . . . um, yes, and the next moment there was this absolutely hideous creature who seemed to think one was a dead American president . . . "

Christ, it's harder to maintain an edge out here. Where is the danger? When my Daddy was alive no rational human being would go into South-Central Los Angeles in anything less than an M-1 Abrahams tank packing laser-guided depleted-uranium shells. Now the Crips and the Bloods follow their stock portfolios and set up franchise stands side by side along the route of the LA Marathon. There aren't even any fucking *wars*.

Not that I would consider such a thing. No, sir. A war is a very serious gig indeed, and not one for which I am prepared, either mentally or pharmaceutically. Journalists who follow such things are another breed, another species altogether, lantern-eyed with long sleepless nights of shelling, their postures permanently altered by the weight of their combat armor. They speak a language all their own, intelligible only to others of their species, and they are a dying breed. Today, bereft of even the tiniest civil disturbance to cover, they have begun to fight each other in bloody hand-to-hand combat, one-on-one, with teeth and fingernails, like psychopathic lemmings bent on the annihilation of their species.

And I for one shall not mourn them. Only a sick fuck would follow wars, and your correspondent aspires to greater things.

It's been almost a year since the greedy cash-sucking monsters at *Time-Stone* last called me. We shall have to draw a veil over my last assignment, which got me thrown out of Vanuatu with not much more than my underwear and my laptop, but I will record that when I finally got back to Civilisation my company card had been cancelled and I had to borrow money with which to phone in a death threat to My Friend The Editor.

So imagine my surprise when My Friend The Editor called to offer me a new gig.

"You weren't *fired*, precisely, Thomas," he said when I'd exhausted my supplies of invective.

"You left me in the hands of barbarians, and when I got home I didn't even have a pot to piss in, you slime!" I shouted.

"We want you to go to England," said My Friend The Editor, all the way from his formfitting chair in his formfitting office in fucking formfitting LA. "Do a Centenary piece."

"The only way I'm going to England for you is in a coffin!" I yelled.

"Let's talk about expense accounts," he said soothingly . . .

There is something sick in the heart of even the most incorruptible American correspondent that the words 'expense account' can produce what amounts to a psychic — and in some cases a physical — hard-on, that he can be bought by something as mundane as money. These are the days we live in, though. There is happiness and harmony and plenty to eat for everybody, and the only human rights violations happen between man and wife behind closed doors in those throwback backwoods suburbs in the Alleghenies and Chicago and Munich.

Because, a century on, the entire human race is still scared shitless. The least fart in Dunedin or Magadan can bring on such a storm of fear and guilt that twenty years of analysis won't purge the offender of his terror that he might have brought down the wrath of angels on mankind.

So what kind of surprise can be it be that simple silent greed lurks in all our hearts, even that of your humble correspondent? Damned if I know.

The Crash caught an even million and a half English people outside their country. It happened in Summer, when hundreds of thousands quit the country for warmer climes. The largest percentage were in the fleshpots of the Mediterranean, and there most of them stayed, figuring they had a better deal in Ibiza and Majorca and Benidorm than in a country which had ceased to exist. The holiday spots of the Balearics and along the Spanish Mediterranean coast were almost British colonies by then anyway.

Others didn't feel the same way. They flooded to France, to the Channel coast. They clung to the hurricane fencing the French authorities put up in those early days, and they looked out across the water to where their homes used to be. Then they put down roots.

John was born there. His family had been full-blooded English for almost a hundred years, until his mother had fallen for the charms of a local fisherman.

"Of course, Grandfather cut her off without a penny," he said as the train wound through the Pyrenees. "Marrying a local."

I asked him what it was like to be the product of a mixed marriage, when the Brits in Spain had been Spanish citizens practically from Day One.

"They aren't *English*," he said disdainfully.

There was something almost refreshing in the discovery that English xenophobia has survived a century on the Continent. It must get passed on down the generations, like mitochondrial DNA.

What actually happened is that the English who gravitated towards the Channel Coast as if it was still possible to go through the Tunnel — and some tried, in those early days — found themselves suddenly stateless, citizens of a country which had literally ceased to exist overnight.

Now, one can only stop and speculate what that kind of thing would do to the human psyche. The news networks caught the outward signs — suicides, small neurotic riots, awesome binge-drinking — but nobody knows what really went on in those de-ranged English heads.

Eventually, of course, calm returned. The English did what the English are genetically predisposed to do: they colonised, taking up residence on a stretch of coastline about fifty miles long, westward from Calais. They kept themselves to themselves, in little ghettoes. They never made it very far inland. They wanted to keep England in sight. Just in case.

I was in Paris with the CIA a few years ago. When I say 'the CIA,' I mean a sneaky, wall-eyed little bastard called McIntosh who hammered on the door of my room at the Louis Quinze in the early hours of one morning and demanded alcohol.

"Drank my fucking mini-bar dry," he said when I finally opened the door. He strode into the room. "This place stinks."

I'd been out that day to the fleshpots of Montmartre and I'd scored half a dozen tabs of blotter acid that made me feel giddy with nostalgia, they looked so quaint. I'd gone back to my room and eaten the whole lot and settled back with a Bob Mould disc in my player. The second album, the one where the first track comes up out of a yelp of distortion. The Management can over-ride the room's entertainment set and turn down the volume or shut it off altogether if you disturb your neighbors, but the only way anyone could turn my player down was to come in and beat the fucker to pieces with a claw-hammer.

Which is what I thought was going to happen when this CIA man started to pound on my door.

"Where is it?" he demanded, standing in the middle of the floor and scanning the room. "Oh. Okay." He stumbled across to my mini-bar and pulled the door open. "Jesus, man, you didn't drink any of this yet, you some kind of fucking FAGGOT?"

I told him I was a journalist on assignment. *Washington Post*, I think it was, and he looked at me as if I'd grown horns.

"Fuckers," he muttered, returning his attention to the mini-bar. "Brought down the best fucking President we ever had." I swear there were tears in his eyes when he said this. "McIntosh. CIA."

It's hard to maintain a conversation with an alcohol-twisted Government-sponsored paranoid maniac when you're in the middle of what you thought might be a mildly diverting acid trip, but I said I was pleased to meet him.

"Fuckin' A," he muttered. One of those good ol' boy CIA catchphrases.

McIntosh backed away from the bar with an armfull of little bottles. He backed so far that the edge of the sofa caught him behind the knees and he thudded down beside my disc player.

"What is this shit?" he asked, looking at the machine. He snorted. "Neil Young." He leaned forward and bottles cascaded to the floor. "Neil FUCKING *YOUNG*, MAN!"

There was a definite possibility of something ugly happening. I dug a disc of *Arc-Weld* out of my tote and put it in the player, but he just listened for a while and shook his head. "This isn't Neil fucking Young, man," he mumbled. "'Heart Of Gold.' 'Cortez The Killer,' man. This isn't Neil fucking Young." He shook his head. "Ah, fuck this." He got up off the sofa and the rest of the bottles fell to the floor. "Where's your bathroom? The Company needs your bathroom."

I pointed, and McIntosh stumbled towards the door shedding his jacket and shirt and muttering, "Too dirty, man, too dirty . . ." He went into the bathroom and I heard the shower go on, then some spluttering.

I went in, and McIntosh was sitting in the tub still wearing his pants and his socks, his face turned upward into the spray of the shower, soaping his upper body energetically.

"Who the hell are you?" I asked. The first rush of terror was gone, and a huge curiosity had settled upon me.

"McIntosh," he said, spitting water. "CI fucking A. *You've* been a bad citizen." He waved his arm blindly.

It was only then that I saw the chewed-up remains of the blotter acid on the tiles at the side of the sink.

The next thing I clearly remember is being in the living room, hurling clothes and bits of recording equipment into my tote, gripped by the huge imperative to leave the hotel, leave Paris, leave France, and not stop running until I could see the Pacific.

"Bad citizen." McIntosh was standing in the bathroom doorway, water pouring off him, wagging his finger at me. "Won't be able to do *that* much longer."

"What?" I said, certain he was talking about dragging me off to some *jusgado* in Utah and having my fingers broken by acromelagic guards.

He shook his head. "All you drugs fuckers," he said. "Final Solution."

Which is not the kind of thing you should say to a man in the throes of LSD-induced paranoid flight-response. I tried to make it through the door, but McIntosh was suddenly blocking my way, waving an automatic pistol.

"Tut," he said sadly, "tut." He pointed the pistol at me and a dribble of water ran out of its muzzle. He smiled. "We're going to get you," he said in a conspiratorial voice. "We're going to get all of you. No more coke, no more shit, no more dope. We're going to make you *sick*." His hand fell to his side, and the gun thudded to the floor. "You'll thank us for it, one day."

At which point the Management appeared and two huge men in uniforms hustled McIntosh away.

And I hope that he's still alive somewhere, and running the CIA station down in that part of Tierra del Fuego that the Welsh colonised. Little bastard.

Because I believe that every correspondent gets one Big Break in his life, and McIntosh was mine. Because he was about to tell me about the virus, and with that story I would have been able to retire.

Because a year later the Centers for Disease Control in Atlanta announced that they had released a man-made virus which altered human biochemistry, which made some tiny but important changes in certain receptor sites in the brain.

You could shoot as much heroin as you wanted, and all it did was kill you. You could smoke as much dope as you wanted, and all it did was give you a cough. Coke might make you sneeze, if you were lucky. What none of these substances would do to a person who had the virus was make him high.

The Government called it 'Party-Pooper Flu.' The bastards.

They made sure it didn't affect the receptor sites affected by alcohol.

And then they passed the Second Vollstead Act and outlawed alcohol.

Bastards. Bastards. Thousands of people *died* of the Party-Pooper Flu. Some of them were my friends. And I thought McIntosh was some Ollie North burnout and never wrote the story. Bastards. Bastards. Bastards . . .

"Oh, my word," John said, somewhere around Alençon, and I realised that I had been telling him the story of the Government-sponsored destruction of my lifestyle. "That's *terrible.*"

"Damn right," I said. "Governments always fuck you over, but this time they *gloated* about it. That was the hardest thing to take. Of course, the virus affects the same receptor site that reacts to morphine, so they had to find a new surgical painkiller. Got a big factory, only one in the world that makes it. Better security than Fort Knox."

"I don't understand the bit about alcohol, though."

"Me neither. Maybe alcohol locks on to different receptor sites. Fuck knows. I do know, however, that a number of United States Senators are growing fat and rich on Prohibition. And I'm going to tell you who they are . . . "

(Editor's note: because of the highly litigious nature of the Good Professor's following remarks, they have been stricken from the mass of discs, printout, typescript and scribbled-on napkins delivered to our offices for transcription. The owners of *Time-Stone* would like it read into the record at this point that they have no interest in taking on the US Senate, and indeed fully support the current US domestic drugs policy.)

The Snow, The Snow . . . England Passes . . . John Comes Home . . . I Am Not A Camera . . . God Comes To The Pas De Calais . . . Ships In The Night . . . Colonel Kurtz Was Right

----

At precisely 8.15 am, Greenwich Mean Time, on July 16, 2009, every military and civilian radar in the northern hemisphere went tits-up.

It isn't hard to imagine the sheer terror that overtook the traffic controllers in dozens of control rooms as their screens filled with green and white snow. Thousands of airliners still up there in the sky, and all of a sudden there's no way to direct them, stop them crashing into each other.

In the fifteen minutes that The Snow lasted, thirty-two aircraft did crash into each other. It was a miracle that the death-toll wasn't much higher.

But The Snow did clear. And when it did every radar screen North of the Equator showed an object bigger than Texas moving slowly Westwards over the Atlantic at an altitude of seventy thousand feet.

By the time interceptors were scrambled to investigate, the Object was down to fifteen thousand feet and moving at a few hundred miles an hour.

Most of the fighters didn't make it home. Those that got too close disappeared in hot silver flashes. A number of civilian flights suffered the same fate.

Pictures were beamed back to base. An immense, irregular, roughly circular vehicle was descending through the atmosphere. It was shiny grey and metallic and seemed to be studded with weapons.

The fighters hung back, taking pictures.

I should digress here and make a cultural point. Back in the 1950s a slew of anti-Communist films came out, thinly disguised as science fiction. *Invasion Of The Body Snatchers*, *I Married A Monster From Outer Space*, and so on. I was brought up on re-runs of films like that, and one of the images I most remember is that of the US Air Force. In films as diverse as *War Of The Worlds* (with its flying wing sequence) to *The Giant Claw* (with a very similar flying wing sequence, if memory serves) the USAF was presented as all-powerful, the mighty smiting fist of American Foreign Policy.

What did the USAF do during The Crash? Did they sacrifice themselves hopelessly against the alien invader? Did they fly a perilous mission to attack the invader with the powerful but untested Meson Bomb (unknown outside those long-gone movies)?

Did they fuck. The USAF hung about and took pictures while the invader crashed on Britain. So much for science fiction getting us ready to accept the impossible . . .

The Crash began at 11.26 GMT, and lasted about three hours. The Aliens seemed to have some control of what was an undeniably damaged craft. Maybe they were trying for the huge and still sparsely-populated spaces of Siberia, but they didn't make it.

The Ship crash-landed, very slowly, on England, and in doing so scoured the country off the face of the Earth.

It was raining when we arrived in England. The train rattled slowly through Le Treport, Montreuil and Boulogne on its way towards Calais, the Capital.

Of course, only the English call it England. To everybody else it's still the northern coast of France, and likely to remain so even after a hundred years of legal cases and appeals to the European Union and the UN.

It's extremely unlikely now that any so-called 'English Homeland' will be granted by the powers-that-be. There are only four million pure-blooded English people in the whole world today, people who can trace their ancestry directly back to the lucky ones who were out of the country when the Crash happened. Interbreeding and assimilation have more or less wiped the English off the face of the Earth.

On the other hand, there are five million people in the Continental United States alone who, in the last Census, put down their ethnic background as 'English.' Not a patch on the fifteen million who suddenly unearthed their English roots immediately after the Crash, but not too shabby all the same, and certainly rich fodder for the research sociologists who began to churn out papers and books following the initial upheavals of the disaster.

All the signs at Calais station are in French and English; the kiosks sell *Le Monde* and *Paris Match* alongside locally-produced editions of *The Times* and *Sun*. In the taxi rank outside there are black London cabs, built by a local firm.

The English are everywhere in Calais. Their clothes are subtly different from the native French. They speak a bizarre mixture of BBC standard received pronunciation and Dick Van Dyke Cockney which is known as *Estuary*. They have their own pubs, their own shops, their own currency. Many of the older English have become fantastically adept in the more arcane areas of the Law, those dealing with land rights.

There is a bizarre cultural schizophrenia at work here in Calais. A high percentage of the English work in Paris. At the Bourse or wherever, they are as French as it's possible to be. At home, though, they're English through and through, and the very thought of letting a daughter of theirs marry a Frenchman sends them into fits of frenzied coughing.

It was dark by the time we pulled into Calais Station, and the rain had turned to hail, but John and I had visited the restaurant car and had been fortified by a meal of beef Wellington, assorted vegetables, and several bottles of Beaujolais. I'd slipped one of the stewards some dollars and he had returned with a bottle of Jim Beam, which John and I had made inroads on back in our compartment. I already loved Europe. It had an olde-worlde charm which had entirely vanished from the States: all you had to do was utter the words 'E Pluribus Unum' and somebody brought you a bottle of whisky. I was seriously thinking of set-tling here.

We were laughing as we got off the train, I forget why. John fell over on the platform and I threw my tote at him. "On your feet, you goddam inbred bastard!" I yelled. "I have an assignment!"

"Oh, fuck your assignment you bloody Yank," he giggled, standing up. He picked up my tote and tossed it to me. It hit my chest, knocking me back a few steps, and fell to the platform. "Hey. I say. Want to see the … Um … the, you know, the, er … ?"

I didn't know what the fuck he was talking about, but it seemed like a good idea, and for the next half-hour we tottered through the town laughing and singing. Hail hissed down out of the sky and bounced knee-high off the pavements, ringing on the roofs of cars.

"Here," John said at one point, stopping by a fence. "Here."

"Where the fuck are we?" I said.

"We're here," John said, tipping the bottle of Jim Beam to his lips again. I couldn't remember the bottle being removed from my tote.

I looked about; all I could see was a curtain of hail all around us, and wet buildings dimly beyond it.

"No," John said. "Here." He grabbed the fencing and pulled; it came up in a single curling wing of rusting wire. "Go on, go through."

I went through, and John followed, letting the fence drop be-hind him. We walked on for a few hundred yards more before I realised that the ground under my feet had changed. It had got-ten kind of soft and slithery.

I looked down. "Hey," I said. "Is this *sand?*"

John, a few yards ahead of me, stopped. I suddenly realised that over the diminishing hiss of the hail I could hear another sound, a gentle arrhythmic hissing: waves on a shore.

John extended his arm and pointed. "There."

God will sometimes grant you a Beautiful Vision. You'll be travelling by train through some godforsaken Midwest landscape and all of a sudden a range of hills covered in pines will rise out of the bland sameness; you'll be flying over miles and miles of ocean and suddenly a gorgeous archipelago will roll up over the horizon. You'll . . .

It was like a magic trick, something I would never be smart enough to learn. John pointed and the curtain of hail parted, fractured across twenty-odd miles of English Channel, and at the far end of it a single intensely blue-white light flashed soberly and without any hurry, a light whose source was manufactured under a star countless light-years from the beach where we stood. I thought of the light at the end of Daisy's dock, calling Gatsby to his doom, calling the Dutch settlers to the New World. I could have stood there all night, watching that light, but I passed out. Must have been the jet-lag.

John's family lived down by the harbour, in a section of town called 'Liverpool.' The street looked unremarkable from the outside, a terraced row of apartment blocks built sometime in the middle of the last century. Inside, though, were English-style furnishings, Laura Ashley fabrics, English-language books and magazines, the English Channel on satellite (based in Stockholm, go figure) and a faint but indefinable smell of roast beef and Yorkshire pudding.

Laura, John's mother, was a bone-thin beauty, in her fifties with chapped hands and red spots over her cheekbones. His father, Jean-Christophe, was a big black-haired man who didn't speak much.

"Of course, all I know is what my grandfather told me," Laura said. Her accent was as cut-glass as her son's, perhaps more so. "He worked in Paris and commuted back to London every weekend. That was how things were in those days."

I asked how the Tunnel had altered Britons' view of Europe.

"Not at all, from what I can gather," Laura said. "Perhaps if we'd had longer to get used to it . . . "

I looked across the table. John was trying to cope with his breakfast without necessarily looking at it. Brits never could take their drink. That's something my granddaddy told me. It's in the genes.

Laura had taken us in the night before with an odd kind of calm. It was wonderful to watch a woman, faced with a completely drunk son turning up with an even drunker, jet-lagged and raving stanger, just fatalistically accepting it. Life in France has driven the British into odd patterns of ritualistic behaviour, and the Long-Suffering Wife/Mother is one of these patterns.

"I read there were riots," I said.

"That was all blown up out of proportion by the media," Laura said. "Everyone was very upset, of course, but rioting? No, I don't think so."

"God was here," Jean-Christophe said from his armchair by the fire. His English was very good but his accent very strong. "That's what my grand-father told me. God came here."

"Not God, J-C," Laura said, giving me a knowing smile. "It wasn't God, it was an alien spaceship."

Jean-Christophe shrugged graphically. "*Bof*," he said and went back to his newspaper.

"Father has always been of a religious persuasion," John said.

"Vietnam," Jean-Christophe said from behind his paper. "Korea. Desert Storm. Bosnia. Greater Ingushetia. No more."

Laura looked over at her husband and smiled; John just tried to eat some more of his breakfast. J-C was right, though. No more war. No more nuclear testing. The Crash ended all that.

The aliens have never made a hostile move against us. It's generally agreed that the various aircraft shootdowns were the result of automated defence systems. And impressing the natives never does any harm. But who knows what will piss the aliens off? Who knows what shitstorm they could rain down upon us if they so chose?

So everyone is very nice and loves their neighbour and border disputes are settled with an amicability of almost Byzantine proportions. The United Nations, once a laughably impotent nod at world fellowship, has a lot to thank the aliens for. Now it's the prime talking-shop and arbiter for the problems of Mankind, and it's never wrong because nobody dares argue with its findings.

After all those years of films and stories and novels, it had finally happened. Earth had been invaded by Aliens. And nobody lifted a finger to stop it happening.The human race has dropped its collective head below the parapet like a man afraid to make a noise in case his potentially homicidal neighbour takes offence.

The aliens did not respond to attempts at communication, and made no such attempts themselves. The first expeditions to crushed Britain and the downed Ship met with a similar response as the Air Force jets. A silver flash on the surface of the North Sea or the Atlantic, a vigorous mushroom of steam and wreckage. Scratch one warship, or one trawler, or one yacht. The Ship wants to be alone, and eventually the world powers got the point. And then they started to ponder the wisdom of detonating nuclear devices and conducting wars while in the presence of such power. Shit, even the mean global standard of living has risen since the Crash. Which should make any rational person grateful, but the price may have been too high.

I've talked a little about the psychic shock of the arrival of the little green bastards on the Brits, but the shock was not confined to those most directly affected by it. We're all still shaking, all tiptoeing, smiling and shaking hands and being so fucking ballessly *nice*, and to be honest with you this correspondent would quite happily tell the aliens to shove it and do their worst. Except like the rest of us this correspondent is too shit-scared.

Jean-Christophe lowered his newspaper and looked at me. "You want to go to England?" he asked carefully.

I'm afraid I laughed. Dumb Frenchman must have thought I was a burnout. "Sure," I said. "Sure, J-C."

"Because I know a man who will take you to England," he said.

I don't believe in that Dos Passos bullshit, that Christopher Isherwood crap. I am not a camera, dear reader, and fuck you if you ain't used to it by now.

So let's just say that the next day I was taken to a certain bar and introduced to a certain person, who introduced me to another person, who introduced me to another person, and four days after arriving in Calais I was pitching about on the Channel like a cork in a washing machine, sucking from a bottle of Calvados, screaming into the wind from the deck of a French fishing boat, daring the Sea to do its worst and waiting to be turned into an expanding cloud of vaguely radioactive vapor.

A Word From Our Editor .. A Life On The Ocean Wave ... Bread Of Heaven. . . . The Professor Takes A Little Trip . . .

(Editor's Note: The following, final, section of the Good Professor's report on the hundredth anniversary of the Crash was delivered by post, in the form of a parcel full of scribbled pieces of paper, torn-open cigarette packets and voice-discs, to the American Embassy in Bucharest. It was part of his relationship with this magazine that his stories were a collaboration between himself and the *Time/Stone* staff who had to transcribe the masses of gibberish, rumour, invective and stream of consciousness he was wont to submit to us. However, more than a usual proportion of the material forwarded to us from Bucharest defied the talents of our transcribers; what we have been able to salvage is presented here in what appears to be roughly chronological order. Bearing in mind the failure of all attempts by the United Nations and NATO to approach Britain, by sea and air, over the past century, we are inclined to doubt the Professor's claim that he was landed on the English coast, and his subsequent adventure there must be regarded with extreme scepticism. The continued, and indeed heavy, use of the Professor's *Time/Stone* credit card, in cities as far afield as Warsaw, Rome and Petropavlovsk, leads us to believe that he is still alive and active, though in what capacity we cannot say. All we can say is that, if you're reading this, Thomas, please get in touch. We're worried about you. I didn't mean all that stuff I said about Gonzo Journalism. Really.)

Seasick/hung-over. Bad weather in the Channel. No better in the North Sea. Where are these bastards taking me?

Better today. First view of E/coast from fifty miles off Essex. Shouldn't be this close, UN/NATO lost (how many?) ships and never got this close. Aliens slipping? Not watching so closely after 100 yrs? Amazing. French behaving as if this was day-trip to Rotterdam or something. (Not Rotterdam, somewhere closer, more mundane. Dunkirk? Good resonances – evacuation/Operation Dynamo. Also closer to Calais.)

Boat is usual French fishing boat. They've always gone up and down the Channel, as if the aliens gave craft on this stretch of water a special dispensation, so long as they didn't try to land. Not that there's anywhere to land; Southern England v. chalky soil; simply crumbled under the weight of the Ship. The Ship tilts into the Channel like an impossible ramp, metal edge vanishing into the water, studded with towers and spires and minarets. Towers (weapons emplacements? observation posts? what?) rise out of the water two miles out into the Channel; all tides different now. Miles and miles and miles of it, grey and metal, stained with a tideline now, the waves breaking against it. Corroding it? Impossible to say. Something that size crashing down, no matter how softly, would have to affect the Earth's orbit, at least its rotation. Do they have anti-gravity? Is it still working to some extent?

J-C: "Why are you so angry all the time?"
Me: "Just a throwback, I guess."
J-C: "No one is angry now, Professor. The world is happy. No war, little poverty. Much technological in Etats Unis."
Me: "Have you ever tried to be a journalist in a world where everyone's happy? No? Don't fucking criticise, then."

Me: "Look, J-C, everyone is happy because they're scared. They're afraid to be unhappy. Scared the aliens will rain fire down on them if they don't keep on smiling and don't raise their voices."
J-C: "Pah."

Alain (captain/owner) says we're a hundred miles off the coast of Yorkshire. Boat is bobbing gently, sea calm, weather good. Over my seasickness. Calvados all gone. The Ship rises more than a mile into the sky before us, a ship to carry the inhabitants of a continent in ostentatious luxury, or a hundred thousand little green men a mile tall in spartan comfort. Its upper surface, sculpted and interrupted by towers and spires and minarets, is covered in snow.

What I see: two lines on the horizon, absolutely straight. A dark line which is the Ship, and a white line which is the snow. Glaciers have formed on the hull, and march down to the sea, where they topple in world-breaking splashes into the water. The bergs sometimes drift down into the Channel, says J-C.

The Ship doesn't cover the whole of the British Isles. What happened to the Scots and the Irish? J-C doesn't know. Alain: "Eaten." And a self-satisfied smile.

Aliens have never shown themselves, though satellites have been watching for almost a century. What are they doing in there? Are repairs still going on? Have they given it up? Are they all dead?

Whitby. Bram Stoker country. Crumbly coast but pressure of Ship may not be so great here. Leading edge of Ship hangs out over the North Sea for fifty miles. Sailing beneath it I see more towers and spires hanging down towards us. We sail on in twilight. Tiny lights far far above. Windows? Just lights? Sea very very calm once we pass beneath the hanging shelf of the Ship. Alain: "Fifty years or so." Meaning that the French fishermen have been coming at least this close to the British coast for half a century, when all the world's governments have given up. The French are an insular people, and their fishermen more so. Why tell anyone? The fishing-grounds around the British coast, unfished for almost a century, have become cornucopia (cornucopias? cornucopiae?) Why let anyone else in on the secret? All the time thinking: all those other boats toasted for coming within a hundred miles, and here we are sailing beneath the thing . . .

Me: "How the fuck did you find out you could do this?"
J-C: "We lost many fishermen in the first few months. More than the world took notice of. We stayed away for many years. Then a few captains reported that they were able to approach closer and closer. Trial and error, I suppose."
Me: "Why do you think they're letting you this close?"
Alain (laughing): "Perhaps they are Frenchmen."

Landfall. Pebble beach, backed by cliffs. We land in darkness, though it's mid-morning. The underside of the Ship is a smooth metal sky sparsely scattered with tiny lights, some red, some blue, most white. Far away to the East, between the horizon and the edge of the Ship, is a narrow line of daylight.

The French carry flashlights and bulging AWOL bags, lead the way as we splash up the beach and onto dry land. Odd, etiolated white grasses grow further up beyond the tideline. Radiation? J-C in front. The Ship is two hundred feet above our heads, a vehicle the size of a state resting on the rock above us. Further inland, destroyed cities, crushed towns. England scoured clean and then ground away, as if God had taken a single footstep on the world.

We walk along the line of cliffs until we find a gap in them, a gulley that leads further inland, roofed over by the Ship. We climb up into the gulley and walk up it. At one point we come within a few feet of the Ship and I can reach up and run my fingertips along its underside. Metal feels slick, soapy, *warm* . . .

Hours and hours. Bobbing flashlights behind and in front . . . Air's warm here, almost tropical . . . grass is white; is that normal when daylight's cut off for an extended period . . . ? French chatter all around, voices dull and flat; the Ship above seems to absorb sound. Then lights bobbing in front of us. *Towards* us . . .

Life in England . . . not all dead . . . surviving in hollows and crevices beneath the Ship/grey-skinned (where do they get vitamin D from?)/short, bandy-legged (rickets?) scurvy endemic . . . clothes woven from fibres of white grass, language strangely familiar but hard to understand . . . this is their *Government*? this poor sad collection of survivors . . . miracle they're here at all . . . a century with this immense metal weight hanging above them, pressing down, radiating god only knows what, living by the little lights that shine from above, under the metal sky . . . what in Christ's name do they *eat* . . . ?

Me: "How many are there?"
J-C: "A few thousand. No one knows."
Me: "Why in Christ's name don't they try to leave?"
J-C: "Ah, Professeur. It is le Pain du Dieu."

It grows under the Ship, in rocky hollows close up to the warm metal, big pulpy pillow-sized growths bulging there in the dimness. The Brits use it as a sacrament, kind of a religious cere-mony, although they also use it when they just want to get com-pletely shitfaced . . .

. . . woke up with the floor tilting back and forth under my back, brass ship's lantern swinging from dark beams far above. I felt completely clear-headed and rested. I felt as if I was glowing, very faintly.

Up on deck, J-C and the others were busying themselves with the things experienced people do when they're crewing a fishing boat. We were miles and miles out to sea. Behind us, the Ship sloped up out of the water and curved forever towards the sky. I stood and stared.

"Professeur," said J-C.

"Did we all eat that stuff last night?"

"The Bread of God?" He nodded. "Now you understand why we do not tell the world about Angleterre."

"Jesus, yes." It had been like every good acid trip I'd ever had, like every great orgasm, every fine meal, every glass of twenty-year-old malt whisky, all wrapped up into one package. Total sensory gratification. It must have connected with recep-tor sites untouched by the virus. "What the fuck is it?"

Jean-Christophe shrugged. "Who knows? Perhaps it is a gar-den planted by *Les Etrangers*. I do not know."

"Has any of this stuff reached the mainland yet? It could make you wealthy beyond your wildest dreams."

He smiled at me. "We are very careful, Professeur. If word was to reach the Government, there would be expeditions. Perhaps *Les Etrangers* would become angry and even we might not be able to return to Angleterre." He shook his head. "Non. We all under-stand. It is a thing only for *les pecheurs*. For the fishermen, no?"

. . . how many English know? Do they look out across the Chan-nel and think of the ones who are still there? Are they smugly sit-ting here in Calais and eating the Bread of God and getting out of their heads on St George's Day? A new drug, wild and fine and unaffected by the virus . . . Christ, the man who brought that to the world would never have to work again . . .

No. The man who brought that to the world would die in some back alley, whacked by the Government or by somebody who wanted his action, or both.

On the other hand, I've always wondered what it's like to win the Pulitzer Prize . . .

"We won't run it," said My Friend The Editor.

"Why the fuck not?" I yelled into the receiver.

"Because it's too crazy. Even for you, Thomas. I mean, Jesus Christ. People still living in Britain. Some sort of alien super-narcotic. Come on."

"You little shit," I growled.

He sighed. "Look, send it in. I'll take a look at it and make a decision then, okay?"

"You fucking pussy."

"You're too angry, Thomas. I thought this would be a nice relaxing gig for you."

"It's the way I work!" I shouted.

"You are not Hunter S Thompson, Thomas," My Friend The Editor said. "All this gonzo bullshit is for the old farts. You aren't even very good at it."

"Fuck you, you worthless jar of slime-mold," I snarled. "I'd rather die on my feet than live on my knees."

"Actually," he said smoothly, "I always expected you to die on your knees." And he hung up.

Jesus, there's got to be *someone* in Europe who'll sell me a boat . . .

WOODEN BOYS DON'T BLEED

By Keith Brooke, Lawrence Dyer and D.F. Lewis

Every building has a voice of its own: the creaks and groans of timbers expanding and settling with changes in temperature and humidity, the siren call of the wind in gutter and eaves, the muted hum of the world intruding from without.

I should not, then, have been surprised when Olive Villa began to speak to me in a voice like no other I have known. Understandable? Is that the vaguely patronising term you use? Given my condition, of course. My state of mind. Understandable, yes.

You look at me, at what I have become, and you try to equate what I say with what you know to be true and you cannot — you are forced to filter my words, to separate that which can be verified from what is clearly the demented fantasy of a man who has lost his grip on reality.

"But it's true!"

The more I insist, the less you believe. I see it in your eyes. And so all that I have left to me is my own belief. That, and the imprint of the voice on my mind.

#

It was early evening and I was alone in the house, sitting in my study by the window that looked out over the narrow street. If I craned my neck I could see the concrete balustrade that marked the promenade, and beyond that the dark form of what Lindy

always insisted was the second longest pleasure pier in England.
Most of it planks of timber nailed gap to gap.

Fond memories, then, of Lindy running scared from
Pinocchio in the cinema, of — years later — hand-holding on the
way to school, scratching names in the mellowed bricks of the
playground wall. And exchanging infant vests on the beach,
much to the subsequent irritation of our respective parents who
had abandoned us there to play sandcastles.

My recollections were disturbed by an abrupt difference.
When you have lived in a house for some time you come to take
the noises for granted, yet now I was aware of every creak, every
popping floorboard, every scuttle that may have been a rodent
but was most probably just the wind. Something had changed in
Olive Villa. Or something was in the process of changing.

It was later that day that I noticed the dark line running up
the wall. It ran from skirting to ceiling in one corner, a deep
crack.

Inspecting it closely I could see that the two walls had parted
company, tearing the plaster between them and exposing on
one face a narrow strip of the fabric of the building. It was no
stone or brick that showed behind the thick plaster though, but
brown fibrous stuff.

Like sinews . . .

I pressed my fingertips into the crack to touch it. It was hard
and cold, like slightly-rusted metal. More like the pyritised
wood from below the cliffs. Fossil wood. Questions vied for my
attention. Had there been an earth tremor? Was that the new
voice I heard? Had Olive Villa shifted, however slightly, on its
foundations?

A wave of nausea unexpectedly overtook me — for which I
could not account, having felt fine that day until then. But I resisted the feeling and with firm intent went outside to search for
more evidence of land slippage. On the brick step down from
the front door I had to stop and put a hand on the wall for support as more pain hit my belly. I closed my eyes and again it
passed, and I was able to step down into the narrow street.

The sky was dark and Olive Villa loomed over me, its
dun-painted brickwork heavy and sick with the same depression
I now felt. At my feet the gnarled flints and beach stones — set
into concrete to form a simple border between house and street
— looked monstrous, swollen and bursting with sulphurous

boils. Even the pinched border of dug earth under the casement windows was distended and dry, its surface the flaking hide of some beached carcass left to bloat and mummify in the hot darkness of that day.

A heavy jaw and moistly-downturned mouth thrust into my face — two such sets of features, for one belonged to a dull-eyed man, the other to his dog. It was Bowman — as I called this local man, having once fancied that I heard the name shouted to him — and he was walking his dog, a massively-constructed, liver-coloured beast, as rough-skinned and sour-breathed as I now perceived its master to be.

There was a thump, as if someone had clapped me on the back, though I knew that was not it: more as if the air itself popped. I felt the skin on my face crack slightly and caps of dried mud seemed to fall from my eyes. And I realised I was on all fours in the street, looking up at Bowman's clean white shirt. The sun was shining and Olive Villa was pristine and calm. Bowman helped me to my feet while his dog, which now seemed oddly elegant to my eye, stood obediently by. Bowman had lost the grimy, unshaven look I had seen before and now he was almost refined, a gentleman at leisure perhaps.

"Are you all right?" he asked me, genuine concern showing in his clear eyes.

"I'm not sure." My own voice startled me with an unfamiliarity I could not fathom.

I was sure, though. Sure of my roots. I had been born in this downtrod resort. I actually once lived in Olive Villa as a toddler.

The Villa's garden where my father once built me a swing was now a fish shop. No, an aquarium, is an apter description. I get confused sometimes, and I had only noticed, in later life, that many of the buildings, although bearing their own separate names, also wore other words, the same words, namely Ancient Lights. The lettering was fossilised, frozen meaning, as it were, though, for the life of me, when I was a child, they wore no such labels. How could age encroach so speedily upon such signifiers? Perhaps the cold shadows of winter cast their light too long upon them.

I shrugged. Ah, this town, you'll know it by its nose-shaped peninsula and a tower ever teetering towards the sea's bite.

Sometimes, I can see clearly enough for that. Bowman was a descendant of one of the bravest lifeboat cockswains our community had ever known — but sometimes brave men, like that very cockswain, carried malign characteristics as some variety of demonic compensation. Lindy, by a precarious miscegenation — a miscegenation whispered about and not fully faced — had been linked by blood to Bowman's family.

Walt Disney's Pinnocchio. I wondered what made Lindy flee the cinema in tears, when we were both five years old, and, yes, just like those times on the beach, abandoned in the cinema, by what today — with the gift of hindsight — must be seen as careless parents. I put it down to sadness at the film's story-line. But was it truly as simple as all that? I need to get my bearings in the past, before I can proceed any further with the present, this present moment when I seem to amble along the pier's boardwalk in forgettable confabulation with Bowman and his dog.

#

Olive Villa, to my infant soul, was a huge place. Now it seems smaller. It needs, perhaps, to grow again. Wishful thinking, though, could not actually make it so. Surely.

When I was that ancient infant — with a soul abandoned by an older version that I call myself — there seemed to be figures waiting for me, misshapen by fear, lurking on the landing upstairs, enticing me to trip up the wooden hills to Bedfordshire far too early, even on long summer evenings.

The head at the top of the stairs scared me most of all — it is still there to this day, in fact. Nothing more than a decorative wooden orb sitting atop the post supporting the banister, its round form worn smooth by years of brushing hands and clothes, its polished grain plotting miniature maps across its surface.

But, climbing the stairs to the county of sleep I always sidled by, pressed against the farthest wall, eyes never leaving the wooden sentinel. That newel post of the night. Soon, I knew, it would awaken.

#

"Catch me if you can!" Lindy — six or seven by then, golden hair ever escaping the tight pig-tails her mother imposed — running away from me, satchel bouncing at her hip. Lindy was always so much faster than me. She would have been a fine athlete in later years, if things had turned out differently.

She always let me catch her in the end. Always.

I chased her along the High Street, dodging the pedestrians and the racks of mismatched footwear outside Bleade Shoes. Old Mr Bleade was the local Punch and Judy man. He could twist and subvert the traditional stories at will, his sole intention being to induce nightmares in the children he hated. Or so we all believed.

She darted across the road without a glance, down Newgate Street, which was still badly cobbled in those days — I don't know how she ran so fast over so uneven a surface. I fell even farther behind, slowing more than I had to, so that any onlooker would know that I didn't really care, that I wasn't really chasing.

By the time I reached the sea front I'd lost sight of her altogether. I turned slowly around and it was as if I was standing still and the town and sea were rotating around me. I stopped when I felt too dizzy.

She giggled. Down below. I craned over the metal railing and she was there, smirking, arms wrapped around one of the great wooden columns that supported her beloved pier. She poked her tongue out.

I swung myself over the railing and scrambled down the incline on hands, feet and backside, possessed of a sudden fury. I don't know what I intended, but events overtook me — or rather, gravity did. I lost my balance and tipped forward near the bottom of the slope, tumbling into a heap on the washed-up gravel at the head of the beach.

Winded, I couldn't move for what seemed like hours. As the clenched ache in my chest subsided and I gulped great wracking breaths I became aware of a pain in my left leg, a rawness. I rolled onto my back, made myself sit. I wasn't going to cry. I was determined. I'd been wearing shorts and so my legs were exposed. A six inch graze ran from my left shin to the knee, where white flaps of skin were rucked up, glued in place by blood and sand. I felt sick. I started to sob,
couldn't help it.

A figure, silhouetted against the sky. Lindy. "Blood," she said. "You're bleeding."

Something in her voice made my tears seem suddenly insignificant. I looked into her eyes — she seemed genuinely surprised, curious.

"Why are you bleeding? Wooden boys don't bleed, do they?"

#

Wooden boys don't bleed. As Bowman and I talked, those words rang in my ears for some reason I didn't understand. Bowman — I almost knew him then for what he was. Lindy's second cousin, her great uncle, some relationship of that sort. Some kind of protector, perhaps.

Despite the clarity which might have come from the sun glinting on the sea, I felt muddled. We had reached the shore — in a seaside town all roads, all paths, lead to the shore. The place of spectacle. And when the spectacle is not enough there is always Punch and Judy.

Or Pinnochio, their abandoned son.

"You'll be okay now," Bowman said, as if he knew a secret I didn't.

He left me there on the wet sand. I had no desire to go back to Olive Villa yet, no desire to see what it was straining to become. Its wooden head could remain unseen for a while longer. I watched the small wading birds clockworking the sand. Like toys, they were; toys from another, more precise, age.

I began to walk.

I had no destination in mind, no purpose other than to be away from Olive Villa for a while. Away from childhood memories that nipped like unripe apples.

The air was warm and it wasn't long before my legs carried me to the Naze, that great shrugged-shoulder of slipping cliffs that punctuates the lurching carcass of Essex as it teeters over the North Sea.

The tide was coming in, but still I wanted to walk below the cliffs, to breathe their avuncular calm before I would return to face my life again.

The new concrete steps were cut off by the tide, so precariously I clambered across the peaks of the granite boulders shipped in from hard-edged Norway to protect this corky end of the Naze. That I might fall into the chasms between the head-high boulders did not worry me, for a certain dizzy-elation was setting in now that I was at home with the cliffs, and I bal-let-danced my way across the boulders' crests.

And then I was on the beach under the ancient, crumbling clays and the fiery colours of the red crag above. But something was wrong. My dizziness had increased and now I saw dark clouds filtering across the sky from behind the cliffs, running through the blue like ink in water. I did not want to see this sight, and got down on all fours, falling clumsily to the shingle — almost as I had fallen many years before when Lindy was watching. Why had she ever left me?

My hands, on the sand and shingle, were in something red-brown. I snatched them back and stared. Blood? Had I cut myself? But it wasn't my blood this time. I could see it all over the shore now as the sky darkened further and the waves boomed and crackled on the stones behind me. It was oozing from the brown fragments and finger-shapes which dotted the shore everywhere. The fossil wood was bleeding.

My leg had once been a torn vest. Memories flashed by with-out the need for drowning, although many had drowned before me on this beach, a notorious tidal man-trap which deceived the cleverest weather-fingers of them all. I pointed mine at the cliffs like an insult. When did a single jab of a digit outdo the classic two-fingered gesture we all once made in the ancient school playground? I recalled learning how this wicked manipulation of the waggling handfolk could outrage teachers and parents alike — except my parents never noticed, they were too busy scrimping a living for the three of us to ever really see what I was up to.

A tin bath in front of the craggy coalcliff fire which lit, if not fully warmed, our terraced cottage at Alfred Terrace, when Olive Villa was no longer our domain. The sole toilet at the end of the long snow-driven garden. A battered red tin with compartments where my parents painstakingly apportioned their meagre in-come for the various upcoming utility bills, sometimes raiding one compartment for another in the face of pressing priorities. I never loved them enough for it. Abandonments, like filters, are two-way, after all.

I once two-fingered Lindy. That's when we faded from each other's pathways. Lindy slowly dissolved as a memory and be-came an immediacy I could no longer find.

We had been soul-mates. Now we were so separate. Smalls and separates hanging on a windblown kite tether that many mistook for a washing-line.

Lindy faded back, though. Today. As I delve my fingers, those very fingers of insult and shame, into the red-brown morass of once stony fossils. She hovers beneath the cliffs like a tussock-crowned maiden, made of mud, silty sand and slipping shingly stuff. I can pick her form from any monstrous mess of childhood's scribbled memories.

Ancient light was darkening the very shape into something more than simple imagination's grasping at tangled straws or precarious pick-a-stix. It was a wooden newel-headed puppet of flotsam and driftwood gliding towards me.

"Come back, Lindy," it said, holding up a riven bifurcation.

"Where?" I said, knowing it meant me.

"Olive Villa." The bark of its broken voice was lubricated by visible sea-weedy slime, sown with splinters. A bark worse than Bowman's mastiff.

I took its gnarled manly hand to return to where we once lived, in happy communion with our happy-ever-after past, a past with which the future could never be invested.

#

Every memory has a voice, a distinctive phrasing of sensation, an editing together of incident and accident. Some call louder than others, rooting us in the past, drawing us back again and again, relentlessly.

You're calling me, Lindy. I know it must be you, fingers grasping at my pyritised heart. Fossil emotions. You know how to make me bleed, my love, you always did. Was it really so bad?

DEMON'S EYE VIEW

By Adrian Cole

A familiar is not totally dependent on its master, although a prolonged period away from him can be not only detrimental but also fatal.

To be marooned in some remote region, with only the vaguest idea of where one's master might be, is as unsettling an experience for a familiar as is possible.

Elfloq, necessarily parted from his own dark master many times, was forced to channel his not inconsiderable energies into a constant search for him. The lengths to which he would go to find him were, as this tale demonstrates, quite considerable.

Perched as it was on the very lip of immense cliffs that dropped vertically to unimaginable depths and overlooking as it did an endless stellar void, the erratic architectural jumble that was Fragmarr's Inn had so often been referred to as The Inn at the Edge, that the name had stuck. What was down in the void below its fastness, no one was sure, for its bottom was ever in darkness, an extension of the very night sky above it. However, this usually was an attraction to the residents and guests of the inn, who traditionally came to this remotest of sanctuaries for tranquility, removal from the hurly-burly of an otherwise chaotic omniverse. The sky here rarely knew daylight, a vast stellar canvas, brightened by a rainbow curve of stardust that invited contemplation and relaxation. And the uniqueness of the inn drew to it only persons of exorbitant wealth, while a residence here cost a king's ransom.

Strange, then, to see the main bar of the inn, whose lavish windows enjoyed a prime view of the spectacular heavens, cluttered now with the oddest assortment of beings, none of whom possessed a fraction of the fee demanded by the inn's host. In fact, under normal circumstances, none of the dubious visitors could have afforded the price of a flagon of the inn's superlative ale. Almost a score of these creatures had assembled, enjoying the Fragmarr the landlord's brew as he watched them from the safety of the bar with a disapproving eye. The wizard Gasterpol, who had invited the motley gathering here, had however, hugely recompensed him.

Among the guests were familiars, demi-humans and quasi-demons, for the most part keeping to themselves, looking about them suspiciously, alert for trouble, prepared to bolt on to the astral realm in the blink of an eye. Fragmarr prayed that their business would be swift, for they were far from an ideal mix. Indeed, it would probably not be long before their differences turned into squabbles, if not a fully blown riot.

Gasterpol himself now entered the long room but he merely nodded at the questioning gazes of the assembly, going to the bar and wriggling up on to a high stool, an action which did little to enhance his dignity, hampered as it was by a robe several sizes too large for him. He faced the massive landlord, or rather, stared up at him.

"Surely," said the latter, "your splendid company is now complete."

The minute wizard scowled impatiently. "One left to arrive. But he'll come. His curiosity is legendary among his kind. He'll not be able to resist the call."

As if in response to his confident statement, a shape fluttered down from the high rafters, limned for a moment in the star-glow behind it. It was another familiar, a being no bigger than a child, with membranous wings that it now tucked behind it. Its skin was squamous, its face uniquely batrachian, its expression extraordinarily surly. Cautiously it moved into the shadows, studying the creatures around it.

"Elfloq," breathed Gasterpol. "reputed to be a veritable mine of arcane lore and purloined secrets. More lives than a litter of cats."

"Can't say I've heard of him," muttered Fragmarr, unmoved. "Presumably he will require a flagon — "

the protection of an amnesty in this affair. Some of you may have heard of one particular demon, Qoudamquankhetaxl, whose name I have deliberately abbreviated, for to speak it in full is to invoke horrendous consequences."

To his surprise, Elfloq had indeed heard of this monstrous being, as had everyone assembled. There was no more notorious a fiend in any of the hells and awesome were his misdeeds said to be.

"Yes, I see the name sends a shudder through you all. Rightly so. Well, I bound him. Oh yes, incredible as it may seem, I bested him and bound him. Using my wizards, the greatest of whom you see before you in the person of the esteemed Gasterpol, I had him petrified, turned to igneous rock and set in stone, deep in the heart of my mountain stronghold on Blessed Carrapunta. The most potent of spells, the most diabolically puissant sorcery held him there. But within the stone, he lived yet. And schemed. There were those dark forces beyond reasonable worlds that sought to free him.

"They could not. But like mice nibbling at a cheese mountain, they drew certain pieces of him from his prison. Somehow they purloined vital parts of him, over many years, until now, when they have taken all his vital organs. If I am to re-bind him, as I must, these organs must be recovered. Discreetly."

Elfloq felt a shiver of apprehension. The word resonated, but the sound was not a pleasant one.

"I could, of course, mobilize my immense forces and storm all those secret places where the demon's organs are kept, scattered though they are. But my enemies are far too devious to fall to such an overt attack. They would go further underground and I would be left seeking a dozen fleas in an army of rats. No. More subtlety is required. Not to put too fine a point on it, I need your peculiar brand of skills."

As the monarch had paused for breath, his chest heaving with the effort of making such a prolonged speech, Elfloq stepped forward obsequiously. "Magnificent one," he said, "I bow to your unquestionable reputation, at which the very gods blanch, as I am sure all of us do, but I am no better than a particle of dust in the scheme of things. My master, a being of staggering powers, would be the ideal person to aid you in this noblest of quests — "

"You know where he is, then?" retorted Annarkham sharply.

"Uh, well, not exactly — "

"You have no idea at all." It was a statement. Clearly the king's sources of information were reliable.

"No, but — "

"You could summon him, perhaps."

Elfloq shrank back. Summoning his master was expressly forbidden to him, the consequences being excruciatingly dire. "No, but — "

Annarkham turned his attention once more to the company. "Gasterpol will inform each of you what is expected of you. If you assist us in our endeavours, apart from enjoying the satisfaction of having rebound the frightful demon, Qoudamquankhetaxl, you will be provided with a rich harvest. Discuss this with Gasterpol. I am sure you will not be disappointed." With this, the monarch waved them all away, evidently confident that there would be no dissenters.

Elfloq, along with others of the diffuse company, was not yet ready to take his leave. If Gasterpol really could impart information to him that would help him find his master, he must avail himself of the knowledge. No harm in finding out more.

In the following period of time, that endless night at the Inn on the Edge, the wizard took each of the company to another, far more modest chamber, and spoke to them of their quests. Elfloq bided his time restlessly, back in the bar, keeping to himself. Usually he would have circulated, picking at the brains and knowledge of the guests, for one never knew what useful tidbits would turn up. But this was an unsavoury company. The big barbarian he was especially anxious to avoid, for the bulging brute (whose endless boasts were plainly audible) specialised in reciting imaginary deeds, rather than any based on actual gods or facts.

It was, then, with considerable relief that Elfloq finally joined the wizard for a private conversation. The latter closed the door to the chamber and slid its bolt. A single brazier was set in the centre of the room, its hot coals smouldering. In their red glow, Gasterpol himself looked more demon than human. As the familiar shuffled reluctantly closer, the wizard flung a handful of green dust over the coals. A crackling cloud billowed up and Elfloq had drawn in several breathfuls before he could stagger back out of range.

"Gods of the Abyss, was that necessary?" he spluttered.

"For your protection," said Gasterpol, with what passed for a grin of reassurance.

"You'll excuse me, wizard, but I have yet to find the enthusiasm for this quest. Your eminent master seems of the opinion that you can regale me with precious knowledge – "

"Indeed I can, Elfloq. You are seeking your master, from whom you have been parted for some time. After the quest, I will gladly impart to you both his whereabouts and the swiftest, safest way of reaching him. What more could you want?"

"I don't want to sound distrustful – "

"As for your specific quest," the wizard went on, ignoring Elfloq's misgivings, "it is this. Annarkham spoke of the stolen parts of the demon. We want you to retrieve the most vital part of all."

Elfloq suppressed a shudder, in spite of the baking heat. He did not wish to ponder which part that might be.

"His single, all-seeing eye."

Elfloq was not sure whether to be relieved or appalled. He said nothing.

"Quodam, if I may abbreviate the name further, has but one eye. Yet it is a very singular orb. For he uses it to look inward, studying the demon worlds, worlds which others cannot see. The movements, the strategies, the endless strivings of these creatures, all are visible to the inner eye of Quodam. It is vital to the Binder of Demons that he possesses this eye. Only then can he study his enemies."

"And where would its current residence be, may I ask?"

"It is housed in a tower, on a lonely cinder of a world known as Cinderbaan. Guarded, as one would expect, by winged demons."

"Naturally. And would there be many of them?"

"A goodly host."

"Pardon my scepticism, but you will have noted my small stature. I do have certain minor powers and I know a few dangerous cantrips, but I do not see myself as a credible opponent for a host of demons. Were you, perhaps, thinking of providing me with a host of my own, or some puissant defensive aura?"

"Host? No, no. Remember, the way to success lies in subtlety. But you will not be alone. The eye is crucial, so two of you will collect it."

Elfloq's scowl deepened. "I am to have a partner?"

"Indeed. A warrior without peer. Victor of a thousand battles, destroyer of armies, mocker of hosts, demonic or otherwise."

"Excuse me, but your words have a certain familiar ring to them. The barbarian outside sporting an extravagance of muscles – "

"The insuperable Krazdar! Yes, indeed. No less a warrior – "

"In which case, I will say my good-byes and trouble your hospitality no longer."

Gasterpol raised his brows. "Oh, you are disappointed?"

"He's an oaf! A braggart, a bag of wind, a – a boaster who makes more use of his tongue than that inert lump of iron he calls a sword."

"You underestimate him – "

"I don't think so. I would prefer not to take up your offer – "

"I think that would be unwise. There will be consequences."

Elfloq prepared to launch himself on to the astral and away, but he sensed that this room was surrounded by spells that would prevent it.

"The fumes that you inhaled just now," said Gasterpol, brushing down his thick robe with mock fastidiousness, "were no ordinary fumes. They were thick with spells, conjured specifically for you, familiar. If you do not take up this quest and seek the eye of the demon, your wings will solidify."

"Solidify?"

"Then they'll become very brittle. Then they'll crack and, well, fall off."

Elfloq was speechless, the image horrifying him.

"And further, if at any time, while engaged on the quest, you elect to renege and attempt flight, to no matter how remote a world, the same fate will befall you. It would not kill you initially, but you would lose access to the astral realm and all hope of reunion with your master."

Elfloq's mind raced, but there was nothing to say. He was trapped.

"So, shall I fetch the worthy Krazdar? Time is short and you've both a long journey to Cinderbaan, the world of the tower."

#

Elfloq grimaced, peering through the orange twilight at the panorama below. It appeared to be the vast, sunken crater that Gasterpol had promised would be here on Cinderbaan, this gloomy ember of a world at the very limit of the omniverse. Mist swirled at the heart of the crater, curling up towards its rim like a sluggish tide, lapping over the sprawling rocks and cracked stone debris. Behind him, ducking down among the slabs that formed the upper rim of the crater, the barbarian craned his neck.

"See anything?" he whispered, head bobbing as if to avoid the hidden gazes of the promised defenders of the demon's eye.

For such a celebrated hero, Elfloq mused, the insuperable Krazdar seemed singularly lacking in fortitude. Not to mention brains. And wit. In fact, Elfloq was having difficulty in fathoming why he had been lumbered with the muscular ape in the first place. Gasterpol had, however, insisted that he come. The wizard had personally escorted them through the astral to this world, before leaving them to the questionable business of recovering the eye. There had been little time to get acquainted, though this had suited Elfloq, who was all for a quick strike and getaway.

"It looks like a dozen other craters," he began, but then, as the mists parted, he descried the promised tower. It rose two hundred feet into the frigid air, its side like polished glass, windowless and foreboding. On its upper reaches, a single chamber crowned it like a stone bud, several dark stains suggesting tiny windows there at least. Around this chamber, a dozen or more shapes flapped, swooping and rising like bats. "The tower is there."

"Is it well guarded?" murmured Krazdar.

"See for yourself."

The barbarian dragged himself cautiously across the rock beside Elfloq, hugging it, leech-like. "Demons!" he hissed. "See them? The air is thick with them. Must be two or three hundred."

Elfloq suppressed a groan. Krazdar's eyesight seemed to be another weakness in his imperfect armoury. The familiar's own fear, by no means a small thing, pulsed as he studied the bat-shapes. "Well, that's one way that I can't enter the tower. Unless — "

"Ah, you have a plan?" Krazdar grinned uneasily, looming over his frog-like companion. "What must I do?"

"It's just a thought. If you could create a diversion, draw the demons to you, I could fly up there, snatch the eye and be back here in no time."

Krazdar's jaw dropped. "A diversion? You mean draw the entire host to me?"

Elfloq nodded encouragingly. "But of course! It is why Gasterpol teamed us. Didn't he say? Your power, your fabled blade. And, of course, the glory that will follow will belong to you. Oh, I'll filch the eye, but that's nothing. All the killing — "

"Killing?" Krazdar managed to infuse the word with a real depth of emotion. "Excuse me," he muttered, sliding down off the rock and out of sight.

Gods of the Abyss, how many more times does he need to relieve himself? Elfloq mentally cursed. Krazdar's bladder was proving to be as ineffectual as his brain.

When he at last returned, his brows were knitted in a thoughtful frown. "I wonder if there is another way into the tower. Isn't that a door at its base?" He pointed.

"That's not the tower," replied Elfloq, directing Krazdar's attention to the correct pile. "And I see no door."

"We ought to investigate. The crater floor is broken up. Lots of cover. The demons are expecting an aerial attack. If we crawl across the crater, they might not see us."

"And if we get to the base of the tower unmolested, and there is no door?"

Krazdar paled. "Uh, well, we'll just have to force our way in."

Elfloq screwed his face up, trying to maintain a grip on his patience. "Yes, that would be one option. But if the tower is solid — "

"Solid?"

"All the way up?"

"But, but, we couldn't scale its outer walls — "

"No, no, of course. But I could fly up there. Provided — "

"I create a diversion, yes, you said."

"Well?"

Krazdar fidgeted, avoiding Elfloq's glare. "Uh, could we just check that there isn't a door?"

Elfloq could see that the quivering barbarian would never consent to creating a diversion. A crossing it would have to be. But if things got difficult, he would simply slip on to the astral and back to cover. The guardians, however, would almost certainly have the same astral access.

The familiar nodded and dropped down off the slab into a wide crevice that wound crookedly out into the crater bottom. Hugging the shadows, Krazdar followed.

"Draw your sword," Elfloq told him.

"Why, what have you seen?" gasped the barbarian, appalled.

"Nothing!" Elfloq hissed. "Just a precaution. You may need it." He scouted the bends ahead, creeping forward slowly. When he turned to see if Krazdar was following, he found himself alone. But the big fellow appeared soon afterwards.

"Sorry," he grunted. "I had to — "

"Yes, yes. Now come on. Speed is of the essence."

They zigzagged along a series of cracks and crevices, dropping ever downwards towards the heart of the huge bowl. They had successfully negotiated half the distance to the tower, when Elfloq's finely tuned ears picked up sounds behind them. A muffled breathing, a padding of feet, a shifting of small stones that suggested the guardians of this place were not confined to the skies. Krazdar, however, was blissfully unaware of this.

"Krazdar," Elfloq told him. "Prepare. We are no longer alone."

In his horror, the barbarian almost dropped the huge broadsword. He swung round, gaping at the way back. From out of its coiling shadows, several shapes emerged. Hunched, heads bent forward like scenting hounds, the demon pack flexed its unified talons, preparing for carnage. Their eyes, bulging like those of madmen, red as blood, feasted on the victims awaiting their gruesome ministrations.

Krazdar would have bolted, but terror rooted him to the spot. Elfloq found his back up against the narrowest of defiles in the rock wall and he slid into it, one eye on the barbarian, who seemed now to enjoy the entire attention of the demons. As one, they leapt for him. He reacted from sheer instinct, whirling his blade around his head in an ever-increasing blur, the air whooshing as he did so. Amazingly, as the demons sprang in, totally heedless of their own safety, the blade bit into them, and Elfloq almost choked as two heads sprang outwards in bloody arcs. But even more amazing was the fact that Krazdar's terror drove him to fight with his eyes tightly shut!

The barbarian screamed horribly, but it was no war cry, merely a shriek of fear. Even so, the dizzy spinning of his sword, guided by a sympathetic god, surely, brought pandemonium and slaughter to the demons. Decapitated, cloven in twain, fatally wounded, the entire pack piled up around Krazdar's whirling, demented form. He was still swinging madly and howling at the top of his voice, when a bemused Elfloq approached him.

"Krazdar. Krazdar!" he had to shout for attention. "Stop. Open your eyes."

The barbarian opened one, but closed it again when he saw the bloody carnage about him. Gradually, however, he slowed down, panting with exertion. He squinted cautiously at the carpet of mangled demons. "Gods of Night, Elfloq, how did you — ?"

"I did nothing. You did this."

"All this?"

"You've destroyed them all. But there's no time to gloat. There may be more. This way to the tower." The familiar practically had to drag Krazdar from the battle scene. "Don't tell me," Elfloq snorted. "it was your first time?"

Krazdar, nodding, didn't know whether to laugh with relief or throw up. But he was glad to follow the diminutive figure along the winding trail. They had not gone far when they heard the snarls of more demons behind them, though these were mingled with additional, nauseous sounds. They were feasting.

Without warning, the base of the tower abruptly rose up, its white sides gleaming like glazed porcelain, smooth as ice. A spider would have slithered from that surface, quickly defeated. Elfloq and Krazdar stood very still, listening. They could hear only the distant flap of the winged watchers, but mercifully no other pursuit. Elfloq felt sure, though, that it would come.

He led the way under a last overhang of protective rock to the very wall of the tower, which curved away on either side. It was a far larger construction than it had first appeared, being several hundred yards in circumference. They began a cautious study of it, one eye on the crater floor behind them. But it was a frustrating search. The wall was seamless, not even a hairline crack in it. And certainly no door.

Krazdar looked as though he would sob with frustration. In spite of his bloody triumph over the demon pack, he clearly had no stomach for a second bout. He stabbed petulantly at the wall with the point of his blade. "Cursed wall! Cursed, cursed wall!"

Elfloq was about to berate him for his embarrassingly childish behaviour, when a section of the wall rumbled aside in obedient response to the barbarian's proddings. The reek of ages wafted outwards, but the way in was open.

Elfloq shoved Krazdar into the darkness before the big man could argue. No sooner had the shadows folded them, than the door rumbled shut once more. For a moment they were blind, the darkness absolute, but gradually it eased, the inner wall suffusing its own ethereal light. The hollow tower rose up hugely, its size exaggerated, but nonetheless immense. And around the walls, a stone stairway wound ever upwards towards the chamber of the eye.

"I said there would be a door," Krazdar whispered.

Elfloq motioned for silence, leading the way to the stairs. They had gone no more than a few score of yards up what would be an endless climb, when a new problem confronted them. Or rather, Krazdar. It seemed that another weapon missing from his armoury was an indifference to heights. He began to crouch down.

"What are you doing?" Elfloq snapped. But he saw the problem at once. "Keep close to the wall. Rest a hand on it. You can put your sword away, if it helps."

Ironically Krazdar found the latter difficult, as if he truly believed the blade to be imbued with magical qualities. But he did as bidden, his left hand pressed to the curved outer wall, his eyes fixed on the steps ahead, steadfastly avoiding the ever growing drop on his right. Elfloq would have eschewed the exhausting climb himself, taking to the air, but he was afraid that if he left his quaking companion, Krazdar would lose his nerve altogether.

Time ground to a halt as they staggered ever upward. Above them were only shadows and an all-pervasive silence. There seemed to be no inner protectors of the tower's sanctity. Krazdar had settled into a monotonous routine, putting one foot down in front of another, eyes glazed. There was no questioning his energy, but Elfloq found the climb sapped his. Even so, resting when necessary, they came at long last to the upper reaches of the tower. The infinite stair ended on a narrow platform, above which a trapdoor fitted neatly into the ceiling.

"Shall I break it open?" said Krazdar, who had undertaken the last stages of the climb on his belly. He remained flat to the floor.

Elfloq looked down at him reprovingly. "Probably no need. If you could possibly bring yourself to stand up, I could reach the door from your shoulders."

Krazdar wriggled and squirmed as though he no longer had any control of his legs. Yet, inch by painful inch, he rose to his knees, tottering until he half stood and half crouched. Elfloq swung up on to his back before he could object, regretting it at once as the barbarian wobbled forward to within inches of the platform's edge and the horrifying drop beyond. Elfloq yanked on Krazdar's hair as if steering a horse and the barbarian swung back, finally positioning himself under the trapdoor.

"Straighten up!" Elfloq shouted at him. Krazdar did so, infuriatingly slowly, until Elfloq's head banged up against the door. But it was a simple matter to put his shoulder to it and ease it up. Mercifully it had not been bolted. Krazdar sensed success and gave a sudden heave. As a result, Elfloq bashed back the door, which crashed down in to the chamber above while he went sprawling in a cloud of dust. Had there been any defenders in the room, Elfloq would have been dispatched in the blink of an eye.

But it was devoid of guardians. Elfloq dusted himself down and examined his surroundings. It was a bare place, a simple, circular room, with several windows opening out on to the crater's landscape far below. In the centre of the room, however, was a lone column of black basalt, its top a smooth table. On this rested a singularly large ball of what appeared to be red sandstone. Elfloq examined it, while his companion struggled with some difficulty to haul himself up through the trapdoor.

"Where's the demon's eye?" Krazdar whispered, relieved to be off the stair. He was watching the windows, outside of which an occasional shape flapped past.

"I'm not sure," mumbled Elfloq. "It may be under this stone. Can you see any inscriptions? Try the walls of the chamber."

Krazdar obeyed at once, running his fingers around the stone walls, trying to discern the slightest hint of a sigil or rune. Elfloq was similarly disappointed with the huge ball and its column, so joined the barbarian in studying the walls.

"Gods, have we climbed all this way to be thwarted?" groaned Krazdar.

Elfloq was scowling in fresh frustration, but the barbarian's sudden frightened expression alerted him to a new threat. Swiveling round to see what had disturbed the giant, he gaped anew at the red ball. A section of it had peeled aside like an eye-lid. The ball, or rather, eye, was looking directly at him.

"I think," gasped the familiar, "we have found the eye."

Krazdar fumbled with his sword, uncertain whether to attack.

"Keep still," said Elfloq, himself moving very slowly around the rim of the chamber. The huge eye followed him, but it had a glazed look to it, like the eye of a dreamer, or someone deep in a drugged state. "Of course," Elfloq murmured. "It looks upon the inner world of the demons. It senses us, but is, I think, indifferent to us." Satisfied that they were in no immediate danger, he turned to Krazdar. "And I also think that I have at last come to understand why Gasterpol insisted that you and I team up to steal this jewel."

"Well, yes," said the barbarian. "That's obvious. Your brains and my fighting skills — "

"Your brawn."

"My — ?"

"Well, look at the eye! I couldn't even lift it, let alone fly with it!"

Krazdar shrank back. "Lift it? I couldn't touch it! It's alive!"

"Krazdar, in the name of the gods, why do you think we are here? To steal the eye. Did Gasterpol not threaten you with some dire penalty if we failed? He told me that my wings would solidify and drop off."

Krazdar groaned. "Oh, yes, I had forgotten. He told me I'd lose my arms and legs and — "

"So you'd be forced to crawl about as you just have done on the stairs, for as long as Gasterpol kept you alive — centuries probably."

"But, but, but — "

"Just lift up the eye. Carry it to the window."

"Wait a moment, Elfloq." Krazdar scratched his head as if trying to activate his brain. "If you can't carry it, how do you intend to get it back to Gasterpol?"

"He taught me an incantation. It will bring his astral craft. You get the eye. I'll call up the craft." Elfloq went to the window, careful not to be seen by the winged watchers in the skies outside.

Krazdar approached the huge ball in trepidation. But whatever it gazed at was far, far away. With a sudden dip of his mighty shoulders, the barbarian bent down and gripped the eye in his massive embrace. The one thing he did not lack was muscles, and they bulged as he wrapped his arms about the eye and lifted it from its pedestal. It felt hot as his chest and then face pressed up against it. Swinging it off its base, he teetered for a moment, then stumbled towards the window.

Visions! Weird, wonderful, visions! Brilliant colours, dancing shapes, cavorting, prancing. His head swam, his brain throbbing as the inner world of the demons flooded his sight drawing him deeper.

"Careful!" admonished Elfloq, watching the ragged steps of the barbarian, who was about to crash into the wall. But Krazdar steadied himself and turned to the window. Desperately, Elfloq completed the incantation. Outside he could feel the rush of wings as a number of aerial demons realised that something was amiss in the tower. But another shape was coalescing in the mists out there. The promised craft! Its sleek shape was solidifying. Its blunt-nosed prow was mere feet from the windowsill.

Krazdar began to howl, his head dipping forward, partially absorbed by the eye. He wobbled to the very edge of the sill.

"Steady, steady!" called Elfloq, reaching for him. Outside he was aware of a shape in the prow of the craft, probably Gasterpol himself, hurling spiked light up at a flurry of demons as they clawed at him.

Krazdar's head emerged, eyes wild, lips drawn back over his teeth in an animal snarl of terrible ferocity. He swung the huge eye round, his feet slipping on the ledge as he did so. Before Elfloq could prevent it, he had toppled forward into the prow of Gasterpol's craft. Into it and through it. Right through it.

The gaping hole that was left framed for Elfloq the sight of the barbarian, still clutching the eye to him like an ardent lover, growing ever smaller as he approached the floor of the crater. Elfloq closed his eyes on the disastrous spectacle.

It was Gasterpol's shout of warning that snapped him back to matters at hand. "Defend yourself!" the wizard called, and not a moment too soon, for the demons were buzzing like wasps about them. Elfloq leapt down on to the craft, but this final challenge to its aerial buoyancy was too much for it. Like a leaf caught in a whirlpool, it spun around wildly, heading for the ground, though a little more sedately than Krazdar had done.

Instinctively Elfloq slipped on to the astral, flying from the immediate area as fast as his wings would permit. Satisfied that he had at least temporarily eluded pursuit, he popped back out into Cinderbaan's air, alighting not far from the place where he and Krazdar had first hidden. A movement among the slabs alerted him, but he saw to his great relief that it was Gasterpol. Chests heaving with exertion, they faced each other.

"Can I assume," said the familiar, "that you have a contingency plan?"

Gasterpol snorted with exasperation. "I'll need another aerial craft."

"But the demons will have reclaimed the eye by now. The unfortunate barbarian will be smeared across every rock from the tower to the rim." Elfloq said no more. To his surprise, he felt more than a degree of pity for his erstwhile companion.

"Don't be too sure. The demon's eye is redolent with power. Come with me."

Before Elfloq could argue, Gasterpol had taken both of them back on to the astral. Seconds later they had emerged near the base of the tower, masked from prying eyes by yet another jumble of rocks. But from here they could see the exact spot where Krazdar's impromptu flight with the eye had ended. Demons swarmed about it, masking the grisly result.

Elfloq closed his eyes in revulsion. "Gods, are they eating him?"

"Not at all. Look. The mighty hero lives!" said Gasterpol sarcastically.

Elfloq peered into the gloom below the tower. To his amazement, he saw Krazdar standing amidst a score of demon-shapes, raising high his sword, snarling something to the heavens.

"It's the eye," sighed Gasterpol. "It has both protected and transformed him."

"Into a demon?"

"Temporarily. They seem to be celebrating his conversion. And the eye is intact. We must act quickly. Get as close as you dare. I'll fetch another craft. Use the incantation again."

"But how do I get Krazdar to load the eye on to it?"

"Use your imagination. Remember your wings."

There was no time to protest: Gasterpol was gone. Elfloq swore, but began the tortuous crawl through the rubble towards the demons and their newfound ally. From time to time there were shouts and hideous laughter. Miraculously they seemed to have got hold of some drink and it now flowed liberally. But at least it kept them occupied.

Elfloq, heart racing, squirmed through a last jagged outcrop and found himself no more than a few feet from the demon's eye, which was, as promised, intact. He got as close as he could, for the demons were totally wrapped up in their revelry, Krazdar included. Elfloq edged around the rim of the inert eye, until he could see the big barbarian, several yards away. Krazdar howled at the skies, his voice hoarse, his eyes starting as though they yet looked upon that grim inner world.

"Krazdar!" Elfloq hissed. Again. No response. Not from the barbarian. But unfortunately a number of the carousing demons had heard. Elfloq now found himself the object of their attention. Three of them appeared like mist, standing over him, claws inches away, teeth barred like carnivores.

"What have we here?" grinned one of them hideously. "Unless I'm mistaken, it's food to go with the wine we've opened in honour of our new recruit."

Elfloq attempted to call Krazdar, but nothing emerged from his constricted throat.

"Shall we let the esteemed warrior do the honours?" said another of the ghoulish captors.

"Excellent! Bring him here."

Krazdar was jostled and shoved by a pack of the demons to within a yard or two of the cringing familiar. "There, warrior demon! A feast to enjoy! Demonstrate your fealty to us. Let your sword drink its blood that we may all partake of its delicacies!"

The barbarian acted like an automaton, drawing out the blade and making a few sweeping passes in the air.

"Krazdar!" cried Elfloq, terror lending him speech again. "Krazdar!"

The whirling of the sword increased, and as it did so, the hint of a change came into the barbarian's expression. All the terrors that battle held for him surged up anew, as they had done when he had been beset by the demon pack earlier. And now, just as then, he closed his eyes!

Literal blind panic took over. Within moments, the first demon head sprang from its neck. Elfloq saw what had happened at once. Terror moved Krazdar much more readily than the power of the demon's eye. His brief flirtation with demonic possession had not been to his taste. "Krazdar! Keep your eyes shut!" he shrieked. "Whatever you do, don't open them again!"

The demons drew back in mingled horror and fury. The barbarian was clearly no longer a convert, for his blade swept this way and that, scything into them, chopping them up like so much mincemeat. The air was a bloody blur. Krazdar's eyes were closed so tightly shut, they hurt him. But he had no desire to see again the nightmares the demon eye had forced on him. Foot by foot he carved a path to Elfloq's side, backing up against the huge eye. Elfloq squeezed himself down between the giant's feet, undignified, but safe. As Krazdar mechanically ripped apart the demon mob, including those foolish enough to attempt to swoop down from the skies, Elfloq began reciting Gasterpol's incantation for a second time.

Behind him he sensed the coalescing of another craft, though this time its keel nestled gently among the rocks directly behind the eye. As it did so, the mayhem around the barbarian ceased. Those demons that had not been dispatched had withdrawn to a considerable distance, while the aerial monsters were nowhere to be seen.

"Krazdar!" called Elfloq, rising to his feet and tugging at the giant. "Keep your eyes closed, but put your sword away for a moment. You've swept them all aside, believe me." The giant obeyed, clearly determined to obey, for his eyes were streaming with the pressure he exerted to keep them shut.

"Good. Now. Bend down and lift up the eye. This time it won't harm you. Eyes closed, remember. Good, good. There's another craft. I'll guide you."

It was painfully slow work, with Elfloq nervously watching the surrounding rocks for a renewed demon attack. Gasterpol was in the bow and he lowered a wide plank for Krazdar to climb. Gingerly, as though he were carrying a wafer-thin egg, the barbarian plodded up the plank and into the craft.

"Now," breathed Elfloq, "lower it. Gently!"

Krazdar obeyed. As the eye touched the deck, a scream of rage broke from the surrounding rocks and a score of demons charged forward, realising what had happened. Gasterpol wasted not a moment in getting the craft away and back on to the astral realm. A few winged demons attempted to follow, but the vision of Krazdar standing upright in the stern was enough to keep them at bay until they faded into the distance.

#

Elfloq bowed before the haggard monarch. "I trust, mighty Arrakhan, that you will fulfill our bargain."

"But of course," said the king. "I will have the worthy Gasterpol remove the threat of petrifaction from you. He is a little preoccupied at the moment. I'm sure he will be with you in the fullness of time."

Beside the familiar, the huge figure of Krazdar waited. His eyes were still tightly shut.

"Come, come," said Arrakhan. "I think you can look upon the world again, mighty swordsman."

Elfloq coughed discreetly, an arm on the barbarian's. "Ah, with all due humility, sire, we proceed with caution in that respect. Until we are sure that there will be no repercussions, Krazdar is taking no chances." He mouthed the words demonic possession.

Arrakhan squirmed back into the confines of his throne, mouth working soundlessly.

"Of course," smiled Elfloq, though it was not a pretty sight, "once Gasterpol has lifted the spell on us both, we can remove ourselves in no time at all. In an hour we can be worlds away."

Arrakhan breathed a deep sigh of relief. "An hour? Yes, of course. I will have Gasterpol sent for immediately." And for once the ailing king was as good as his word.

THE BERSERKER CAPTAIN

By Neal Asher

Defeat hung round them like the muggy stink of a week-old battlefield. It was intrinsic in every leaden plodding step they took, in the moans of the wounded in the stolen cart, in the grey tarnish of their weapons and the few tatty scraps of armour they had not yet discarded. Parrick felt there should be more discipline to the march; a straightening of their ragged lines, but he had not the energy to enforce it. He felt the sting of defeat as deeply as every one of the fifty-three surviving infantrymen of his once four hundred strong battalion.

"How much further, sir?" asked Coln, his lieutenant.

Parrick came to a halt and surveyed the rolling countryside, so like the sea they were desperately trying to reach. He looked to the forest ahead of them, with its badly-needed cover.

"At this rate, the rest of the day," he said, then looked back at Coln.

The lieutenant removed his beaten helm, shook his head, then reached up to touch the dried blood that blackened one temple. He had been young and enthusiastic when they had landed here on the shores of Ordanol, Parrick remembered. Now he too was an old man, like his Captain.

"Will the ships be there?" Coln asked, yet again.

"The ships will be there," Parrick replied, forcing conviction up from the hollow in his chest.

"But will there be room for us?"

"Yes, there will be room."

Coln sighed and turned to the men as they trudged past.

"It'll be good to be going home," he said, and rejoined the march.

Would it?

Parrick wondered as he watched his men filing past. Home to the laws of the Priesthood and their damned Clergy. Home to the beatings, the burnings, and the poverty. Was this why none of his men would meet his eyes? The sadness he felt drowned his usual grinding anger. The Glorious Fourth: broken at Habian's pass. When Jurt staggered past, drunk on the stolen brandy he had poured down himself to drown the pain of his beaten back, Parrick could bear it no more, and turned away. It was then that he saw the riders approaching across the grassland.

Now, does it end now?

Coln moved to his side, swore, then turned to the men.

"Riders coming! Form up!" he yelled.

Raggedly the infantrymen drew together at the side of the cart, the few pike-bearers who had retained their weapons moving to the fore. Parrick drew his sword and moved to one side of them.

"Straighten that shield line," he said, too tired to bellow orders.

Coln strode along in front of the line, cracking his sword against any shield that was out of place. Pride drew the line straight but Parrick knew that if this was an advance guard of the Ordanon cavalry they simply did not stand a chance. He watched, as the riders came up out of a dip in the landscape, and waited to see if there were any more. There were only three. Coln moved to his side.

"They must be ours. They would have turned by now, otherwise," he said. Then after watching for a moment, "Looks like they think the hounds of hell are after them. They're pushing those horses too hard."

Parrick nodded. He knew that if these had been Ordanon cavalry he would have ordered an immediate surrender; it would have been a relief to do so. As it was, the tension remained. He had a horrible idea who these riders might be, and he wanted none of them. When they drew close enough to be identified Coln spat on the ground.

"Priest-soldiers," he said.

Had they been of Ordanon, Parrick knew he could have expected mercy. There was no mercy in these black harbingers.

The leader was a thin, effeminate-looking individual. His face scraped of hair, even to his eyebrows, and the long black hair of his head was shaven back halfway. His cloak signified he was of low rank, but Parrick noted he wore *Chothai* battle-armour and was not fooled. The two with him were dressed in the black of Indulgents and were obviously his bodyguards. The three horses they rode were lathered with sweat and clearly close to collapse.

"Well met, Battle-captain!" the man called as he drew rein. He swet his cloak aside to reveal his medallion of rank, then he stared at Parrick coldly and expectantly. Parrick felt a moment of rebellion, then, too tired to sustain it, he went down on one knee and touched his forefinger to his forehead and chest. Behind him his men were down on their faces.

"You men, remain as you are. Battle-captain, you may rise."

Parrick stood and faced the arch-priest barely managing to keep the contempt from his expression. The arch-priest observed him coolly before going on.

He said, "I am Amondius, and I will be accompanying you to the coast."

Parrick kept his face rigid. Amondius; the Red Bishop. What the hell was he doing here dressed like an arch-priest? Why would so arrogant a man want to keep his identity concealed?

"Surely, Reverence, we would delay you?"

Amondius dismounted, his bodyguards did likewise. One of them led the horses to one side.

"You will speak when I ask questions. Otherwise you will remain silent."

Trouble.

Parrick remained said nothing more; too tired for rebellion. Like a good little soldier he would obey this man's orders. The Red Bishop was not known for his tolerance.

It began as soon as they had reached the forest.

"This man is intoxicated!"

Parrick turned and saw that one of the bodyguards had dragged Jurt from the ranks.

"Reverence, he is in some pain — "

"Silence!"

Parrick went on. He could not allow this.

"Reverence, he fought well and has been . . . " Parrick lost the thread. He could not tell Amondius that Jurt's pain was a direct result of the fifty lashes he had received from a Priest-soldier.

" . . . wounded . . . "

Amondius signalled one of his guards to move to Parrick's side. Parrick glanced at the man then back to Amondius as he strode towards Jurt.

"Wait, you can't — "

A fist crashed into the side of his head and blackness took him like a falling wall. He was not out for long, but when he came to it was to shouted orders and Jurt's protests. Without comment or expression Coln helped him to his feet.

"You there, find a rope! I told you two to hold him! Do so, or join him! Where is that rope?"

Parrick stumbled to his feet in time to see Jurt being dragged to a tree and one of Amondius's guards throwing a rope over a branch. There was an ugly muttering from the men.

"No, we made him drink! He couldn't keep up! The cart was full!" Parrick stumbled forwards with Coln coming up behind him.

On his agitated horse Amondius glared at him.

"One more word, Battle-captain, and I will have your tongue cut out!"

Parrick's hand dropped to his sword as the rope went round Jurt's neck. Jurt was yelling now, finally understanding, through his drunken stupor, what was going to happen to him. They were going to hoist him, no clean neck-break, he was going to strangle at the end of a rope. Parrick stepped forwards. Dare he? He ached to cut Amondius from his horse. He took another step as Jurt's yells became a horrible gurgling. He dared not. Twelve years of discipline and indoctrination could not easily be broken.

Jurt was hoisted into the air, his legs kicking and his hands grappling with the rope above him. They hadn't tied him. With his hands free he would fight the rope, try to support his own weight. His death would be more protracted and painful.

"Bastards!" Parrick hissed, and felt he might do something then, but there was a hellish shriek in the forest and a butchering thud that all heard.

A shocked silence fell. Parrick's eyes tracked the arrow that tumbled through the air into the forest. It seemed to take a nightmare age to fall out of sight, and the sound it made as it dropped into the bushes was the dry rattle of knuckle-bones. The stillness was broken by Coln's shout.

"Form up! Form up! Shields!"

Stunned by what he had seen, Parrick looked back up at Jurt as he slowly revolved. He hung twitching, blood pumping from his mouth and the hole in the back of his head. A shriek arrow, and it had gone right through his head. Abruptly the Red Bishop's hangman released the rope and leapt from his horse. Jurt thumped to the ground and the rope slithered down on top of him. Amondius sat with his mouth open for a second or two, then almost fell in his hurry to dismount. The men were shouting as they drew together and formed a shield wall. How well they remembered Habian's Pass where they had lost most of their number to archers. The horses were abandoned. Parrick noted how eagerly the Bishop and his guards sheltered behind the wall. Coln squatted down beside Parrick. His face was pale.

"Sir, shriek arrows are made to scare . . . "

Parrick knew what he meant. The cuts made in the head of such an arrow supposedly lessened its penetrating power, rendering it all but useless as a weapon.

"I would not like to test the arm that drew that bow," he said, and glanced towards Amondius. What he glimpsed suprised him and he turned for a proper look. Not even on the battlefield had he seen such terror. He nodded to himself. So there had been a reason for the Bishop to put up with the inconvenience of travelling with infantry. He looked back out into the trees, and as if summoned, a rider appeared and called to them.

Parrick felt there was something familiar about this man; the long grey hair, skull-like face, and eyes like black nail-heads. The rider was tall and long-boned and hands were big and ugly. His cloak and leggings were grey and ragged, his boots scuffed and worn, and he wore a leather tunic over a shirt of forester's green. On the saddle before him he held a longbow with another arrow already notched.

"I have no score to settle with the infantry of Jardia!" He called to them. "Send out the Bishop and his men and I will let you live!"

Parrick and Coln exchanged glances.

"One man?" asked Coln.

Parrick shook his head.

"Has to be more. Amondius and his men could easily deal with one man. They're trained *Chothai*. There's probably a battalion out there."

Suddenly Amondius was beside them.

"Are you going to sit here and do nothing?" he hissed, his eyes wild. "Get out there and kill him!"

Him? One man then.

Parrick stared at the Bishop for a moment, weighing his words in the face of such fear.

"Reverence, my men are infantry, they would not be able to catch someone on horseback."

He looked pointedly at the abandoned horses. Amondius shook his head and turned away to stare once more at the solitary rider. Parrick felt his guts clench up. Why was he so scared? The rider called to them again.

"I will circle round you. After one circuit I will take a life. Give me Amondius!"

The rider began to move, his grey form only occasionally glimpsed between the trees.

"Have you no bows?" demanded Amondius.

"Infantry are only allowed to carry weapons of hand-to-hand combat," stated Parrick, his expression blank. It was one of those ridiculous arbitrary rules made by the Clergy.

"We must run," said Amondius, his eyes wild.

Parrick glanced at the wounded in the cart.

"If we run we'll be easy prey. Best to stay behind the shields for a while. We'll think of something."

He wanted to tell Amondius to go out and deal with the rider himself. One man, and here the Bishop crouched behind their shield wall as if hiding from a battalion. Amondius seemed to accept his suggestion, for reasons Parrick could only attribute to terror. Again he wondered why the Bishop was so scared.

They watched as the rider made his circuit. When he came back to his original position they waited in tense silence. Abruptly Amondius spoke up again.

"He can't touch us here. Perhaps you were right. Maybe he'll go away."

This time Parrick could not hide the contempt he felt. Clergy. It was their mishandling of the war that had led to disasters such as that at the Pass. He crawled closer to the line of his men. When? When was the rider going to try something? What could he try? Parrick's answer was a loud crack and the *oomph* of someone's breath leaving him. He jerked his head away from a spray of blood as one of his soldiers fell back with his shield on top of him. Parrick moved forward and hoisted the shield upright. The man underneath had an arrow through his chest. A look of bewilderment crossed his face as his mouth filled with blood. He was soon dead. Parrick did not know his name. He looked into the frightened eyes of the soldier next to him.

"It went through his shield. *It went right through Dant's shield.*" *Dant.*

Parrick looked at the shield, at the ruptured wood that framed a neat diamond-shaped hole through the plating. What manner of man could put an arrow through a Jardian infantry shield? He looked down at the dead man. The arrow had also gone through the front of his breastplate, and by its depth of penetration, out through the back as well. He let go the shield and moved back to Amondius. The rider called again.

"After this circuit I will take two lives. I have many arrows."

Parrick did not doubt him for a moment.

"When he's done a half-circuit we move out," he said to Coln, then to Amondius, "if that is acceptable to you, Reverence?" He could not keep the contempt from his voice, but Amondius seemed not to notice. He gave a curt nod. His two guards looked on with taut expressions. Parrick ignored them and turned back to Coln.

"Spear point defensive. We move fast. Perhaps he'll have no time to take aim. It's not easy shooting from horseback."

Coln looked pointedly at the cart containing the wounded.

"Get two volunteers to stay with the cart and bring it on after. We'll have to gamble that he leaves them alone. I think he will. He's not interested in them."

Coln moved away.

"Reverence, do you wish to retrieve your horses?" Parrick asked.

His Reverence did not wish to.

When the rider had done a half-circuit a softly spoken order pulled the men into the new formation with the alacrity of fear. At a jog they set out, eyes directed to where the rider was last seen. When he came, it was from the opposite direction.

The horse was a huge grey with armoured flanks. It crashed into them like an iron-shod ram. Before anyone could react a sword flashed twice and two headless infantrymen fell, jetting blood. Parrick turned as a head thudded to the ground next to him. It seemed to bounce as in the slow drag of nightmare. Every detail of the dying face was clear to Parrick. He looked up at the rider and into eyes devoid of pity, then the flank of the horse slammed him to the ground and he had to scrabble from under its hooves.

Someone was bellowing and tired men crashed against each other as they tried to bring their weapons to bear. As he pulled himself clear of the flailing hooves, Parrick swore in disbelief when he saw the rider reach down and, with one hand, hoist one of the Bishop's guards by the back of his uniform. The man yelled and tried to cut back with his sword. The rider shook him like a child, then cut away his sword-arm as if trimming a piece of wood. Parrick struggled to his feet and cut at the back leg of the horse as it poised to leap. He was too late. The horse was gone. Over the heads of his soldiers. A figure in black clasped to its side, yelling as he waved the stump of his arm.

"He got Garton! He got Garton!"

Amondius back-handed the face of his remaining guard and spun on Parrick.

"Is this how well your men fight!? Pathetic! We move now! Fast! Garton will keep him a while!"

Parrick measured the panic in the Bishop's expression and did not argue the point.

They set out at a run, the formation breaking. It felt horribly to Parrick like a run they had made from Habian's Pass; a rout. As he ran he wondered what the Bishop had meant about Garton, until he heard the screams.

Garton kept the rider busy long enough for them to make quarter a league. The screams grew distant and finally stopped. Parrick choked on his fear. He was coming. The rider was coming.

A soldier coughed and did a front flip in a wheel of blood. The fantastic impact of the arrow had burst his chest open. Pieces of broken doweling protruded between his shattered ribs.

"Who the . . . hell . . . is that?"

Amondius just looked at him.

"Be out of the woods soon!" yelled Coln. Then another soldier went down, spattering the trees as he spun. There came a yell from behind, full of cold fury.

"Give them to me!"

Abruptly Parrick snapped. He grabbed Amondius and slammed him against a tree. The remaining guard kept running.

"Who is that!? You know! Who is he?"

Amondius's gaze fled in every direction. He wanted to run. Parrick held him. His gaze finally centred.

"It is . . . Hadrim," he gasped.

Parrick released him.

The Berserker Captain. . . .

He felt a deep harsh sickness now, and knew that any fear he felt was justified. The Berserker Captain; the greatest weapons master ever known, never defeated, terrifying in battle, the very author of the Jardian defeat at Habian's Pass. Parrick had not seen him; he had too busy trying to fight his way from the trap. But why was he here without his men? Why did he want the Bishop and his guards? He was about to ask, but Amondius pulled back and remembered himself.

"You will pay for this, Battle-captain! Release me!"

Parrick lost his impetus and released his hold. Amondius pushed past him and ran on. Parrick stood there panting for a moment until he caught sight of a pursuing flash of grey. He ran to catch up with his men.

The next arrow struck with the sound of a butcher's cleaver. Parrick saw Amondius' last guard go down as his leg buckled where the bone had been broken. The man hit the ground, rolled, then dragged himself upright and tried to follow on. He fell again.

"Don't leave me!"

"Keep moving!" yelled Amondius.

The infantrymen needed no urging. Ahead was a break in the trees, and beyond that the glittering promise of the sea. Behind them the guard's yells became screams.

"The boats, we have to get to the boats!"

The once-glorious Fourth came out of the trees in a ragged line, up an acclivity, and were at last looking down on the beach. They came to a stumbling halt, the last of their strength draining from them. There were no boats, and there were no ships to take them home.

"Keep moving! Get down to the beach! Tight circle and doubled shields!" Parrick lashed them with his words. They obeyed, all they had left was their discipline, their pride. The circle was made as the screaming in the forest came to an abrupt halt. Forty men waited. Out of the forest and onto the slope above them came the rider.

"*Give him to me!*"

Parrick turned to Amondius.

"He is a great warrior. Yet he comes without his men and kills without mercy. Why? What have you done?"

"Shut up!" Amondius snapped viciously.

Parrick did not shut up.

"What crime did you commit?"

Amondius turned away.

Parrick turned from him and saw Coln looking at him. His lieutenant's hand was on his dagger and Parrick knew by his look that all he had to do was nod and Amondius would be dead. He looked out to the Berserker Captain and saw he was notching another arrow to the string of a laminate bow.

Two shields?

He knew that two shields would not be enough. More of his men would have to die to preserve the life of the Bishop. He frowned in thought. Enough was enough. Abruptly he turned his sword and cracked its pommel against the Bishop's head. Amondius dropped like a wet sack. Parrick sheathed his sword.

"This has gone on long enough," he said to the unconscious Bishop, offered a silent prayer to gods he had ceased to believe in, then he pushed past his men and walked out to meet the Berserker Captain.

The sand Parrick walked on was almost white. What a contrast his blood would make. At every step he expected an arrow to punch him from his feet, but in the end Hadrim lowered his bow and just watched him. Once amongst the sea-thistles and clumps of grass he drew his sword again. Before Hadrim he dropped the weapon to the ground.

He said, "I come to offer to the Empire Ordanon the surrender of the Fourth Shield Infantry."

Cold eyes observed him.

"You have Amondius."

"I do."

Hadrim looked out at the sea.

"Your ships are south of here."

"I wish to surrender, myself and my men."

The cold eyes returned to him.

"I do not want your surrender, Battle-captain. I want Amondius. Give him to me or die. I offer you this simple choice."

"What did he do?"

Hadrim stared at him for a long moment. When he finally replied his rage was tangible.

"What do they always do, these Clergy of yours? While we fought and died at the Pass they brought my people their God. Their God is harsh."

Parrick picked up his sword and resheathed it. That God had been with him all his life. He had seen the beating, the impalings, and the burnings. He needed no further explanation. Without a word he returned to his men. When he got there, Coln looked at him expectantly.

"We go south," he told his lieutenant.

Coln looked down at Amondius.

"Leave him," said Parrick. "There might not be room on the ships."

A BREATH OF MOUNTAIN AIR

By Ron Bennett

It was late afternoon when I reached the pass. It was always the same. I never seemed to time an earlier arrival, however I travelled.

Still, I wasn't worried. Even with the possibility of a sudden mist shrouding the high Yorkshire Pennines, I knew the way well enough. Only five more miles on what in those parts is called a main road, and then the bridle path climb to the inn.

The road wound from shadow to the slant of thin autumn sunlight, at one side falling away steeply to the valley floor three hundred feet below and I paused at what, over the long years, had become a favourite spot.

I unhitched the pack from my shoulders and stretched my arms, exulting in air as cool and as fresh as the waters of the rushing stream I'd encounter a further half-mile along my way.

Far below, on the valley floor, filtered sunlight followed the hide-and seek turns of the river, a distant silver thread sparkling and dimming as it coursed its way towards the village bridge I could have crossed earlier. I restrapped the pack and, dipping my head to avoid looking directly into the westward sunlight, moved on, recovering my earlier rhythmic stride despite the upward slope.

I stopped again at the stream, knowing that the longer I delayed the more I was likely to be caught in the inevitable mist. But, who could resist that inviting cataract? I tasted its water with an eagerness born of lengthy deprivation. Ah, it was good, so good, to be alive.

To be alive and to have returned, striding along this favourite, never forgotten, path. How long away! How long?

Behind me, down the slope, I heard the sound of an engine. Before too long I could see the little vehicle labouring, following my path up the steep slope as though deliberately pursuing me. Should I hide? Or quicken my pace in order to reach the inn before I could be overtaken? I smiled to myself.

What game was I playing?

A lift could take me to the lower end of the bridle path. There was every chance that, for once, I'd avoid the inevitable mist and there was no reason why I could not enjoy the scenery while seated.

I watched the small red vehicle grow in size as it approached to where I stood with arm outstretched, but the driver ignored me, moving steadily past with visor down and eyes screwed up against the low, setting sun.

I strode into the middle of the road and waved in the hope of his catching sight of me in his rear view mirror, but I was out of luck.

I grimaced, but then laughed. What had I lost? The road ahead was still there to be climbed, was still there to be enjoyed. The air was still fresh, the view still magnificent. And who could say that the mist would this time be encountered?

But even as the hope graced my thoughts with its possibility, the sunlight dimmed and the edges of the trees and indeed the hillside itself greyed and became blurred. The very sky appeared to fall slowly towards me, a low ceiling of gray. All about me was gray, gray, gray. The world of color had ceased to exist. I was lost in a small globe of gray mist, a globe which allowed me a small enveloping circle of cloudy colorless light in which all, even my swinging arms and striding feet were but indistinct.

Now, ahead of me I could hear the rushing water of the spring and the stream which fell from it toward the valley floor, a sound dulled by the mist, a sound which seemed to grow louder only as I stood by the bubbling water. I crouched and cupped my hands, almost over-balancing as the weight of my rucksack was once again shifted by the movement. Did I never learn?

But could I be annoyed when alive at such a spot as this? I smiled, took no more than a mouthful of the crystal water, straightened and resumed my walk, marking my position on the road by keeping well to the edge furthest from that terrible drop.

Soon I reached the place where the track left the road and zig-zagged its way to the peak, a track once the original bridle path but now with rough steps hewn for the thankful rambler.

Though deep within me I felt the necessity for haste, a saner voice prevailed and I rested for some moments at each turn in the long rocky stairway so that by the time I reached the summit the gray of the mist had given way to heavy darkness. The inn's lights, diffused by the mist, were as ever a welcome sight. The climb had been enjoyable, and particularly so before the mist had crowded round me, but I was ready for a hot bath and whatever fare the landlord could provide for me.

Though I was heartily welcomed I was not recognised. Why should I have been? How long was it since I had l last ventured here?

"Your room is ready, sir. Number six. As you requested. You must have stayed here before . . . ?"

"Yes," I said. "Many times." I signed his register and took the room key from him.

A door opened behind me and there was a scamper of feet and the snarl of a disapproving dog. I turned and quickly lowered my rucksack as a protecting shield. The beast, an indeterminate black mongrel, still snarling, advanced uncertainly.

The landlord reached down and took its collar. "Quiet, Jess." He drew the dog back into the room from which it had escaped, while he called to me over his shoulder, apologising profusely.

"I'm sorry, sir. Terribly sorry. Don't know what's got into her. She's not usually like that. Even with strangers."

"My cats," I said. "She must have caught the scent of my cats on my clothes. I have two of them. Took them round to a neighbour before I started out this morning."

"That must be it, sir," he agreed. "Though we have two cats ourselves and she's never let them trouble her. Still, 'xpect she's used to them."

I climbed the wooden staircase, its walls adorned with water-colors of mountain scenes, and made my way along the corridor to the room where I'd stayed so many times over the long years. The heavy green drapes looked new and felt crisp to the touch as

I drew them together across the recessed window, blotting out the dark gray outside and the reflection of my tired face and the familiar room behind me. I turned up the heating before unpacking and enjoying the soothing bath for which my aching back and tortured muscles had been yearning.

After a hot meal, satisfactory enough for such a remote place, I made my way, as always, into the small bar with its smoke-stained wood panelling and cushioned bench seating. The mongrel which had greeted me in so unwelcoming a fashion was lying on the varnished boards before the wide grate in which a fire was pulsing its way through recent replenishing logs. I half expected the beast at least to raise its head and snarl at me as I stood at the bar but the heat of the fire and possibly whatever food it had downed, had made it languid and I was by no means sorry for that.

Considering the time of year, the swirling mist outside and the remoteness of the inn, the place was well patronized. The middle-aged couple sitting closest to the fire I guessed to have been the occupants of the red car which had passed me on the road. In the far corner sat two young women, more than adequately clothed in thick jumpers and tweed skirts, clothing more suited to the ramble they'd doubtless be taking the following day; it was only a matter of time before the heat in the room grew overbearing.

The three men of indeterminate age who occupied the table in the centre of the room hailed me as the landlord inquired after my comfort and poured me a whisky.

"On the house, sir. The first one is always on the house."

"Aye, John," said one of the seated men. "The first is always on the house. You might as well make sure a man starts off the way you'd wish him to continue."

The landlord began to protest, claiming altruism and his wish to provide a traveller with nothing more than good fare and comfortable lodgings.

"Come and join us," invited the seated speaker and I took the a vacant chair, ensuring that I was on the far side of theirtable from the fire. And the sleeping dog/

They were pleasant company, local farm workers from the small group of cottages on the far slope of the mountain. One of them I remembered from my previous visit, but there was little point in mentioning the fact to him and over an hour passed in friendly, empty conversation while they learned what I wished to reveal of my background and during which time I provided the obligatory round of whiskies.

A draught of chilling air swept about our feet as the outside door was opened and hurriedly closed. John, the landlord, left to tend to the needs of this latest visitor and our conversation, hardly one of sustaining interest, readily broke off as we listened to the exchange.

Yes, the man's room was ready. He'd been expected much earlier. No, thank you, he had broken his journey to dine in the village. He'd have a drink before he'd go up to his room.

As he walked into the bar the sleeping dog awoke suddenly, raised its head and emitted a howl. At the same time the hairs of its thick coat rose from tail to head, as though ruffled by a strong wind. The dog rose shakily, seemed to rouse itself to wakefulness and moved quickly to the far corner by the two young women, where it cowered by their feet, its teeth bared toward the newcomer. From deep within its throat came not a snarl, but the faintest of whimpers.

"Did you see that!" exclaimed the man sitting next to me. "Did you see that?"

"What? See what?"

"Jess. Her hairs. Didn't you see the way they rippled?"

The others looked across at the dog, but seeing nothing untoward about the lie of its sleek black coat, nor the firelight reflected in it, turned on the speaker and chided him for having drunk too much.

He turned to me for support. "But you saw it, didn't you?"

"I'm sorry," I said. "I wasn't really taking notice."

"My fault, I think." The newcomer threw off his top-coat, picked up his glass and came across to where we sat. He was young, with dark hair, even features and a wide sensuous mouth. "I seem to upset your dog," he said to the landlord. He walked past us and bent to where the dog cowered, his hand half-extended to stroke and placate the beast.

It whimpered again and avoided his touch, wriggling backwards, further under the table where the two young ramblers sat. The young woman whose back was to the wall bent to peer under the table. "I think you'd better leave it," she said.

"It was waking it so suddenly," her companion remarked, the Welsh lilt obvious. "You know. Letting sleeping dogs lie and all that."

"But her hair standing up like that," insisted the man sitting by me. "It was as though she'd seen a ghost."

"And the right place for it." The newcomer announced.

"Really?" The Welsh woman's companion smiled as though she were joining in a game. "What makes you say that?"

"It's just the place for ghosts." The young man returned her smile. "A misty night and a lonely inn way out in the country."

"And an old inn at that," the young woman rejoined. "It must be hundreds of years old."

"Exactly." The young man turned to the landlord. "How old is the inn?"

"Fifteen thirty-five. That's when it were first built."

"Aye," said the eldest of the men sitting with me. "You'll remember that well enough, John."

"You, too, Harry," the landlord retorted. "My first customer. You still owe me for that drink. What about you ladies? Another?"

"Here, I'll take them," offered the newcomer.

"No, it's all right," the Welsh woman said. "The dog's quietened down. I think it's gone back to sleep under the table. I wouldn't want you to disturb it again." She carried the two glasses back to the corner table. The young man didn't appear to be put out by what might have been a deliberate rebuff but perched himself on one of the two stools by the bar counter.

For the first time he was away from the line between the corner table and the door which led out to the corridor and which the newcomer had left open.

Immediately, the dog which we had thought asleep shot from under the table with a loud yelp, scrabbled for purchase on the varnished floor and shot out of the room.

"There!" The man sitting next to me turned to his companions as the landlord walked across to close the door. "I told you there was something strange going on."

"It's the ghost. Like you said." Harry looked across to the newcomer. "She's seen the inn's famous ghost. Why, people come from miles around to see our ghost." He leaned back in his chair and looked over his shoulder to the landlord. "Don't they, John?"

"Now, now, Harry. Don't you be putting ideas into these young ladies' heads. They won't be sleeping a wink all night and when they get back home they'll be blaming it on how uncomfortable they found the beds."

The two young women had the decency to laugh. "I'm sure that'll be far from the truth," said the girl with her back to the wall.

"All the same," Harry insisted, "Jess has never behaved like that before. I tell you, she sensed something."

The middle-aged woman sitting closest to the fire rose to her feet. "All this talk of ghosts. I think it's time we were retiring."

Her husband rose with obvious reluctance. Perhaps he'd been enjoying the talk about ghosts. Perhaps he'd been enjoying the prospect of the two young ladies finding their thick clothing too uncomfortable in the heat of the small room. The pair rose, bade us good night and left.

"Leave the door open, will you?" called the young Welsh woman, "it's getting a little too hot in here."

We tried not to let any disappointment show in our expressions.

"Well, anyway, I'm no ghost." The newcomer put down his empty glass and nodded to the landlord. "But like I say, this seems the right place for one."

"I bet the place is haunted," said the young Welsh woman. "A building as old as this has just got to be. Oh, it's all right. I'll sleep all right. We've walked so far today that I could sleep on a board with nails through it."

"Sounds as though you've been here before," Harry said.

"Hey, steady on," the landlord rejoined as we all laughed.

"Go on," she insisted. "Tell us the truth. The place really is haunted isn't it? You really do have a resident ghost, don't you?"

"Come on, John, own up," Harry said. "If you don't tell her the story, I'll give my version. And then nobody will sleep."

"Oh, all right." The landlord poured himself a glass of whisky, not his first of the evening by a long chalk, and made himself comfortable on a stool close to the newcomer. "Hundreds of years ago a lone traveller took refuge here in the inn. A man of some substance. Very finely dressed. His horse had gone lame a mile or so down the slope. He staggered in here in some distress and told a tale of being followed up the slope by a couple of foul-looking men. Footpads. Robbers. He'd had to leave his horse and had got himself completely breathless running up here. Well, half a dozen of the guests, so the story goes, armed themselves . . . "

" . . . With crossbows and the like," interrupted Harry with a straight face.

"Now, Harry, you're letting me tell it, remember. Crossbows! I ask you. They were armed with pistols. They scoured the hill-side as best they could . . . "

"There was a mist that night, too," Harry interjected. "You forgot the mist."

"There's always a mist," said one of the other men.

"Yes, yes, there was a mist," the landlord said, a little testily. "And the men came back without finding anyone out there. One of them found the horse and managed to bring it up here, but they didn't find any robbers."

"And one of those who came back was really a ghost." The young Welsh woman suggested.

"No, not at all," John said, more gently at this interruption. It might have been the whisky, I thought. "That was the end of the matter for the night. But the next morning when this fellow, the one who'd thought he was being followed . . . when he started out, on a fresh mount, well, half way down the hill he was attacked by the two footpads. They'd had the good sense to stay put in the mist and had huddled together throughout the long night. Needless to say, they weren't in the best of moods. They pulled him from his horse and fair cut him to ribbons. Those who were still here at the inn heard his screams . . . "

"Aye," Harry put in. "Terrible screams. Blood curdling and all that."

"Oh, that's all very well," said the young Welsh woman's companion. "but if the man who was killed came back as a ghost . . . well, he wouldn't be haunting the inn now, would he? He'd be roaming around the hillside."

"Easy for you to say that, miss," Harry said. "You're no ghost. Who but a ghost would know what a ghost would do? Or where he'd do his haunting?"

"It's true enough, miss." John casually poured himself another whisky. "There are times when his screams can be heard up here. They say that he stays the night here, over and over again, and then is torn to pieces the following morning when he goes down the hill."

"Why!" exclaimed the young Welsh woman. "That's no ghost story at all. I know of half a dozen ghosts who inhabit various old buildings in the Black Hills who would give your ghost a good run for his money. Take Faen House for example. Alun Llewellyn owned it, this at the turn of the last century. He was rich and times in the local village were hard."

"Aye, and not only in . . . " Harry began, but a withering look from the young Welsh woman silenced him before he could get into his stride.

"Alun Llewellyn took a young bride. A girl from the village. It was really a case of buying her from her parents. She went willingly for their sakes. But her heart wasn't in it. She loved a young man. A farrier. She would sneak away from time to time to be with him. Of course, they were playing with fire. Alun Llewellyn found out. As he was bound to do, eventually. He had them brought to his manor house. It was as strong as any castle. And so, well away from outside eyes, he had them killed. And in grotesque ways. The young man worked with horses so he was chained between two large drays which were driven in opposite directions. And the girl . . . the girl . . . well, like I said, she'd been playing with fire . . . There's many a villager who hears her screaming still, even though Faen House was pulled down, oh, some time shortly after the first world war."

"Ah!" The newcomer shifted on his stool. He'd been quiet for some time. "Now, that's what you can call a ghost. Reminds me of the time I was in Bulgaria . . . "

"Oh, no!" exclaimed the Welsh woman's companion. "We're not going to go on about vampires, are we?"

"No," the newcomer said haughtily. "At least, I'm not. I don't know of any Bulgarian vampires."

He went on at length about a ghost that was supposed to wander about on some river bank out there. And then it was the young Welsh woman's turn again. She'd said that she knew of half a dozen ghosts tripping about in the Black Hills and she went through them one by one while, from time to time, John replenished the glasses. I noticed that he kept making notes on a pad he kept behind the bar and wondered by how much our accounts would be . . . er . . . padded out when we came to settle them in the morning.

Eventually, we called it a night and went off to our different rooms. And, despite my mind churning through the various tales which had been told, I didn't doubt that I'd sleep well. I usually did, there, and the whiskies I'd drunk would well take care of any tendency towards insomnia.

The mist still hung in the air the following morning, but by the time I'd washed, dressed and taken breakfast, the sun had begun to break through and I breathed deeply of the cool mountain air. No matter how many times I came to the inn, no matter by whatever form of transport I arrived, it always came to this.

As it had to be.

I packed my saddle bags, mounted the fresh horse made ready for me and started down the hillside path to the clump of trees where the pair of them would, as always, be waiting for me.

I hoped my screams wouldn't be heard back at the inn.

IT WAS A LOVER AND HIS LASS

By Barrington Bayley

On the wavering border between the kingdom of Aragon and the fiefdom of Foix, an uncertain region where lords are ambivalent in their allegiances, trimming their pledges to the sways of power and seeking only to preserve their possessions, there are many pleasant woodlands where one might wander for the happy days on end, had the inhabitants the leisure and the inclination to do so. Few in fact ever bestir themselves to such a diversion, not just because pastoral labours are long, but also because it is the habit of country folk to huddle on their acres, and not to be concerned with what lies over the next hill. So it is that these open and easily passable woods lie nearly deserted, and certain of their reaches, secret chambers of the forest seldom trod, become venues for furtive, arcane practices kept far from the eyes of priests.

The tale which follows is of two innocent, harmless people who out of delight in one another ventured further than they normally would. It is also a warning to the incautious, for the world has many snares from which, once caught, there is no certainty of escape.

Eugene Lambert had been born and raised on the demesne of Le Duc Des Esseintes. By some he was regarded as almost a stranger there, for his family had not been resident for long as local people reckoned it. His father hailed from the valley of the Loire, where he claimed to have been cheated of an inheritance by his brothers. Wandering south in an aggrieved spirit, he had eventually settled here not far from Rousillon, which even then was claimed both by the king of France and the king of Aragon. Here at least, he would say, he could begin to understand the form of *larigue d'oc* that was used; any further south and he would have been among mountain-dwellers who spoke an incomprehensible tongue owing nothing to the old Latin. Or perhaps it was meeting the peasant girl who was to become Eugene's mother that had stopped his travels. At any rate he married her, and planted an apple orchard, paying to Le Duc a rent of one-third of the crop, plus two days labour a week in the manor's household fields, a duty which he now mainly delegated to Eugene.

At twenty years of age the son of the northerner had turned into a handsome lad of pleasing manners. While carrying out his father's villeinage in the broad fields he had made the acquaintance of Marienne Vaflard, the seventeen-year-old daughter of Pierre Vaflard, a manorial serf. With her fetching brown eyes and shining chestnut hair, Marienne was as pretty as Eugene was fair, and no one could deny that they made a fine-looking couple. Their courtship proceeded swiftly, Pierre Vaflard viewing the match with approval, for Eugene would one day inherit the tenancy of the orchard, and a man who raises a crop for sale is higher in the social scale than one who merely grows food for himself and his family on strips apportioned to him by his lord. More than that, the formality of consent from Le Duc—for Vaflard was of course required to refer all such family decisions to him—had also been obtained. The wedding was to take place after the harvest.

But it is a rare happiness on which some blot does not fall, and in this case the blot came in the form of Le Duc Des Esseintes himself. One day Eugene paused from his work of hoeing one of the lord's broad fields to drink a jar of refreshing buttermilk which Marienne had thoughtfully brought to him. As they stood together they saw the approach of Des Esseintes, making a casual inspection of his estates. Le Due reined in his horse as he was about to ride by, and Eugene, placing the buttermilk jar on the ground, respectfully bowed his head and touched his forelock, while his betrothed curtsied by his side.

A long, light blue cloak, toggled at the front, almost entirely covered Le Duc. For all the warmth of the day the cloak was topped by a fur-trimmed hood which all but hid Le Due's face.

Eugene had never been this close to a noble before, and he felt nervous. Le Due's eyes were not on him, however. They were on Marienne.

In a resonant, melodious voice, Des Esseintes spoke.

"Your name, girl."

"Marienne Vaflard, my lord," answered Marienne breathlessly.

"Ah, yes. Pierre Vaflard's daughter. Always was a pretty little thing. You are to marry soon, I recall."

"Yes, *monseigneur.*" Marienne grinned shyly, tittering and glancing at Eugene, who blushed.

Des Esseintes leaned closer, enabling Eugene to see his face clearly for the first time. Although easily as old as Eugene's father, perhaps older, he did not bear the marks of age as much. His skin was smooth and glowing. His eyes shone with an almost unnatural light. Important and powerful men were not the same as ordinary folk, Eugene told himself, and he felt awed.

Le Due reached down to chuck Marienne under the chin.

"Then, my dear, we shall be with one another shortly."

At these words the young girl caught her breath and went suddenly pale, all joy gone from her face. The lord did not seem to notice. He smiled, nudged his mount's sides with his heels, and trotted away.

Eugene took Marienne by the hand. "Why, what's the matter?"

"Did you not hear what he said?"

"Why, nothing that meant anything."

He had not understood Le Due's remark, unless he was indicating that he would pay a visit to the wedding feast, which would be a rare honour indeed.

"Of course it meant something!" Marienne's voice quavered. "He is claiming *le droit de seigneur!* Surely you know of it? The right of the lord to spend the first night with the bride, in place of the bridegroom?"

He gaped at her. Then he laughed. He had heard of this barbaric custom from his father. It belonged to the times when lords could — and did — treat their serfs like animals, even to the extent of using their women.

He tried to reassure her. "You are imagining it. Nothing like that has been practised since before King Louis' reign."

"Oh Eugene," Marienne wailed, "this isn't France proper! This is border country! The *seigneur* can do whatever he likes!"

Her head drooped. "The old ways still count here, and he has made his will plain, as plain as day. He means to have me!"

"But I am not even lieged to Des Esseintes," Eugene protested.

"No, but I am!"

And suddenly understanding the situation, Eugene's heart fell to his boots, and his face went gray.

For all the rest of that day the distraught lovers were unable to think what to do or how to confront what was happening. Le Duc's designs had for them the force of inevitability.

A solution which would have been obvious to young people of more urbane communities — that of running away together — scarcely occurred to them. The closed circumstances of their up-bringing, with its constraints and certainties, limited what they were able to conceive of in terms of action. They could not imagine how it would be to face an unknown and possibly dangerous world. Besides, they would have assumed that should they go missing Le Duc would simply despatch his men-at-arms to pursue them and bring them back. They would hardly get beyond the boundaries of his territory.

Eugene said nothing to his father or mother of what had passed. Instead he spent a despairing night and an agonising day in which he was unable to dispel the spectre of Le Duc holding his beloved Marienne in his arms, enjoying her for hour after hour. The pangs he felt were doubly painful, for throughout their courtship he had respected his sweetheart's wish to be a virgin on her wedding night, and they had remained innocent.

But when, next evening, he met her as arranged in the sheep meadow half a mile from his father's orchard, he saw a new boldness in her.

She tossed her chestnut curls. "At least we can make sure he is not the first!"

It took a moment or two for Eugene to catch her meaning, and when he did his heart raced with excitement. He also felt some measure of fright, for he was as inexperienced as herself in amorous matters. Trembling, he embraced and kissed her, then looked about them for a place where they could be secluded together.

"Let us go into the woods."

She nodded. Side by side, hand in hand, they strolled towards the tree line.

It was the height of summer. The evening was hot. Once they had passed into the shade, Marienne suggested timidly, "If I am showing with child before our marriage, perhaps Le Due will not want me."

Then they spoke no more, but wandered on and on among the trees. The wood was like a huge temple alive with birdsong, lit by slanting shafts of sunlight, carpeted with bluebells, the great oaks decorated with fungi and colourful orchids. There was many a pleasant spot where they might have lain down, but instead they continued walking, for despite the decision they had made, despite the crucial act they had agreed upon, each was too shy and nervous to make the necessary move. Further and further they went, the furthest they had ever strayed from their families and their homes, deeper and deeper into reaches they had never seen before, and hours passed while they enjoyed a kind of peaceful paradise.

At length dusk fell, and with it came the realization that they would have to find their way home by moonlight, or else stay out all night — which would, for a fact, besmirch Marienne's name and aid her brave intention of defiling herself publicly. Neither of them cared to voice this thought. Indeed, throughout their long stroll they had unconsciously been trying to forget the world with the trouble it had brought them, and to find solace in each other alone. But now they came to a soft mossy bank, as inviting as any bed, and Eugene decided that they could delay no longer.

She smiled painfully into his face as he drew her down upon the moss. For a while they kissed, and then he began to fumble with the strings of her bodice. She caught her breath and instinctively pushed his hand away. He let it wander down her body, and began slowly to pull the hem of her gown towards her knees.

"No, Eugene! No!"

With a start she sat up, burying her face in her hands.

"I cannot do it!"

Upset by her distress, he desisted, trying nothing to persuade her. They both were weary. Cuddled in each other's arms, their clean breath fanning one another's lips, they fell asleep.

Low, pleasant laughter brought Eugene to consciousness. He opened his eyes. Still clasped in his arms, Marienne stirred also.

A handsome young woman clad in a flowing shift was leaning over them. It was she who was laughing, though not mockingly or with any sense of menace. Rather, she seemed to be welcoming them.

His gaze went beyond her, and his mind stopped with wonder. For the wood, by day a thing of beauty, was now a place of enchantment. They must have slept fairly long. The moon was high and full, and the moonlight that shone through the branches was bright and silvery-cool, outlining everything, causing the dew to shine and sparkle as it bedecked every twig, every blade of grass and every inch of moss. Yet there was no hint of chill; the air was warm and balmy. A silence, a restful hush, permeated everywhere.

Marienne raised herself on her elbows to look sleepily at the girl before them. "Aren't you," she asked in puzzlement, "the serving wench in the great house?"

Eugene thought she must be mistaken. At any rate the girl ignored the question.

"So you have found your way to our society! It is the will of the god. What good fortune for you — congratulations, and welcome!"

Eugene now noticed a small design painted or branded on the girl's forehead, showing a coiled serpent with head raised ready to strike. Seeing his interest, she pointed to it with her forefinger.

"Do you not know what this is? Well, perhaps you would not. This is one of the signs of the Horned God of many names."

"Do you mean the Devil?"

Her laughter tinkled. "Forget that, there is no place for your spoilsport Christ here. The Horned God is the Lord of Nature who brings every pleasure. In his serpent form he supports the world. Even before the Romans came he was worshipped in this forest."

Many gods, Eugene imagined, had been worshipped before Jesus Christ had come into the world, but that was not a subject he had ever interested himself in. In his boyhood his mother had tried to teach him to pray to the Virgin Mary, which had displeased his father who never used the name of Christ except to curse. He had once said there was one thing he liked most about the place where he had chosen to settle: it had no priests, and no church.

Eugene felt Marienne grope for his shoulder and lean against him. Disconsolately, she spoke.

"Shall we go home now, Eugene?"

The other girl laughed yet again. "Poor things! You are like innocent children afraid to do what you really want to do. Here. I have something for you."

She opened her hand and showed them two small objects resting in her palm. They were acorns. With curiosity they obeyed her instruction to take them and lift the caps, which were detachable like lids. The acorns had been hollowed out to make tiny casks. Each brimmed with a shiny liquid somewhat resembling wine.

"Drink," she ordered gently. "It will help you to sleep till day comes. Then we shall see what pleasure the god has in store for you . . . "

Somehow they never thought of refusing. The acorns held but a few drops of the liqueur, which delighted their tongues and burned enjoyably as it went down. The girl withdrew, disappearing behind a leafy bush a short distance away, and they were alone once more.

"How soft the moonlight lies upon this bank," Marienne murmured.

She yawned. A warm indolence and relaxation came over them. They lay down, and in moments were in a deep slumber.

The sun was high end bright when Eugene next awoke. They had slept half the morning at least.

He looked to where Marienne had lain on his left. She was not there. Quickly he sat up. He was alarmed to find, sleeping on his right, a young man wearing doublet and hose similar to his own, even in the same colours.

Mystification assailed him. But wait . . . the clothes were like his, it was true. But the face, framed by chestnut curls, was Marienne's.

The sound of his movement roused her to wakefulness. While she rubbed her eyes Eugene chanced to glance down at himself, and his bewilderment increased. Marienne, it was evident, was wearing his clothes.

And *he* was wearing her bodiced gown!

Had they exchanged garments during the night? No, of course not — why should they? Then he remembered the potion they had drunk. It must have left them senseless.Enabling the woman, aided perhaps by accomplices, to dress them in one another's clothing as a jest.

The thought was indescribably displeasing. He frowned, scratching his cheek.

And his forearm felt, beneath the bodice he wore, the softness of a woman's bosom.

A now familiar mischievous laugh reached his ears. Approaching barefoot on the mossy ground was the girl of the night before. By daylight her silk shift was a dazzling blue: the hue of the morning sky. She carried something in her left hand which she dropped to the moss as she came near. Delight showed in her face. "The Horned God is a playful god always! See how he has favoured you! Come on! Show yourselves to one another!"

At her urging, Eugene and Marienne came slowly to their feet, and retained their sanity during the next few minutes only through the belief that they must be victims of some troubled dream. The woman stepped to Eugene and finished the task he had begun the night before — that of unfastening Marienne's bodice. He stood unresisting, feeling the restraints loosen, the strings go slack. Heavy breasts flopped out.

The woman gave a tug. Gown and petticoat fell to his feet. What he saw, as he gazed down at himself, caused him to clutch frantically at the hair of his head.

That was his, as far as he could tell. But from the neck down, at least, was the body of a woman. A plump-curved, well-endowed woman. His mind stopped, watching in a daze as the girl turned her attention to Marienne.

She seemed equally entranced and unable to resist; in seconds doublet and hose had been stripped off and cast aside.

Eugene, still not understanding what had happened, knew he should not stare at Marienne's nakedness. But he *did* look. Below her pretty head ho saw a young man's body which was lithe and well-muscled. Even then, long seconds passed before the truth sank into his comprehension. That body was utterly familiar to him, for it was *his* body.

The girl stooped to pick up what she had dropped. It was a hand mirror of polished bronze. Holding it up to each in turn, she allowed them to see what manner of creature they had become.

How could a man have a women's body? How could a woman have a men's body? Even more strange, how could they have *each other's bodies?*

"Bewitchment!" Eugene croaked. Beside him, Marienne uttered a horrified gurgle.

"Not bewitchment!" the woman hissed. "A gift from the god! The god brings many changes, and with each change come new pleasures."

Reaching out, she took each of them by the hand and drew them closer together. "Now you must touch one another," she breathed. "Now you must do what it is you long to do."

She skipped back. And in a moment was gone.

A bird sang on a branch over their heads. Stricken, the pair stared at what each beheld.

"What has happened to us?" quavered Marienne.

"What has happened?" Eugene whimpered.

"What can we do?"

He made no reply. The fact was that the potion was still working for them. Their judgment was numbed, making it possible to accept what to normal thinking would have been inconceivable. A wondering excitement stole over them both, so that they admitted a sort of madness in themselves. Involuntarily they reached out to embrace one another. And the embrace was more intimate, more thrilling, than anything they had ever imagined.

They sank to the moss, and there frenzy overtook them.

Decency forbids that what took place during the next hour should be described. One should not look upon the consummation of a love as fresh and innocent as Eugene's and Marienne's. Suffice to say that their intimacy was of the keenest sort, a delirium of impossibilities, and that penetration, when it accomplished — which was almost immediately — was so surprising end so intense that it astonished them both.

At last they lay sated and almost ready to bless their new existence. After a while Marienne raised herself on one elbow. Wonderingly, a puzzled frown on her face, she ran her hand down 'her' muscled chest, stroking 'her' flat belly, toying with 'her' still-swollen phallus.

"No pair of lovers can ever have been as close to one another as this," she murmured thoughtfully.

Then; "Where do you think she goes to, Eugene?"

"Who?" he asked drowsily. Following her example, he too caressed himself, exploring 'his' female body whose curves and clefts were so fascinating to him.

"The woman who did this to us. I could almost swear she is Miranda from the great house. You know I am sometimes called to do kitchen work there. But I suppose it cannot be."

"She went behind that bush over there."

Shortly they rose and looked inquisitively behind the bush. All there was to see was a young beech tree whose branches leaned over to brush the ground, as if resting on the bush itself. Then Eugene noticed that the grass was a trifle worn at that spot.

He pushed his way through the foliage, Marienne following. The beech had acted as a screen, hiding a narrow but well-trodden trail. On both sides the undergrowth was dense, making it unlikely that anyone would come upon the trail by chance.

Winding yet deeper into the forest, the hidden path pulled at them as if by some occult attraction. Besides, it offered the hope of regaining their normal forms. They agreed to follow it and dressed hastily — in their own clothes, badly though these fitted now.

The weeping beech swished into place behind them. Soon they were in a gloomier part of the forest where the tree cover cut off all direct sunlight. At one point they heard a peculiar raucous cry Eugene could not identify, but mostly there was silence. The path meandered, frequently describing meaningless half-circles.

Then, when they had walked for about half an hour, the trees suddenly thinned and sunlight broke through. From ahead came cheerful sounds, as of a crowd of people.

Shortly they emerged into a large sunny grove thronged with men and women, some apparelled in bright colours, but others without any garments at all, and seemingly without shame. The young couple stopped to take in what was to them an amazing scene. At the opposite end of the grove was a dais or platform backed by a brilliant banner bearing a design which, Eugene noted, incorporated the same coiled serpent which had decorated the forehead of the girl who had led them here. To their left, the grove was flanked by a row of gay pavilion tents, while closer at hand were trestle tables laden with food and drink.

Where had all these folk come from, and why were they so shameless? The scene resembled one of the open-air feasts given each year by the *seigneur*, and indeed those were the only occasions when Eugene had seen so many people gathered together at one time.

"Look, Eugene," Marienne said with surprise, "there is Jacques, the *seigneur's* groom. And over there is someone else I have seen at the great house." Understanding dawned on her. "So it was Miranda after all!"

Then Miranda herself came running towards them with en exultant cry.

"I knew that you would come! I have been waiting! But why are you covering your gift? Cast off these rags and show your good fortune to everyone!"

For the second time she reached to divest them of their clothing, but by now the potion she had given them had worn off, and more keenly aware of their circumstances, they resisted. It was no use. They had attracted attention. Helpers rushed forward to assist Miranda to disrobe them of every stitch. In an agony of mortification they stood close together, heads hanging, their unnatural state on display to the crowd.

But instead of jeers and disgust, they found themselves the object of applause and acclaim. "How wonderful!" cried out a bearded man in an orange toga. "What a pleasure it must be!"

"Yes," said Miranda knowingly to the couple, "and you have sampled that pleasure, have you not? I see it in your faces."

They blushed deeply, unable to meet her gaze, while another cried out, "What must I do to be granted such a favour?"

"You must catch the eye of the god," Miranda told him, "and please him sufficiently by your eagerness."

A lilting rhythm suddenly was tapped out at the back of the grove, quickly to be accompanied by a pipe uttering plaintive phrases. Upon which, the people who had gathered seemed to find something else to interest them, and wandered away.

Marienne spoke hesitantly, in a small voice. "Why did you do this to us?"

Miranda let her eyes rove avidly over their exchanged bodies, catching her breath slightly as if she desired them both. She stepped closer and touched Marienne's cheek, making her flinch.

"The god did it," she said quietly. "Pan, Sabbath — he has many names, for all mankind knows him one way or another. He is a playful god and ever loves to bring changes to people. For what is pleasure without change? As one pleasure grows tiresome, we must find another."

"Please change us back."

Miranda threw back her head and chuckled. "Only the god can do that. It was no accident that brought you here. He has seen into your hearts and read your secret desires. You have but to accept his mastery, and you will know joys unimaginable." She smiled, aware of the tingle of anticipation which her words aroused in them, whether they wished it or no.

"You poor dears, you must be famished — come and eat! No, don't bother with clothes — you don't need them here!"

She tossed her head and waved them on when they tried to recover their garments. Reluctantly they left them piled where they had fallen and followed her to one of the trestle tables. Here they sat on a bench together while Miranda served them with her own hands.

What food! Breast of swan seethed in almonds and smothered with buttered asparagus. Vegetables casseroled with herbs and rough red wine. A delicious fruit which they had never seen or tasted before, which they ate covered with cream. And all washed down with an invigorating wine which made them light-headed.

"Everyone is so pleasant to us here!" Marienne exclaimed.

Miranda laughed and poured more wine into their goblets. It made Eugene drawl as he spoke. "Tell us more about this marvellous god you talk of," he said.

"You will learn. You will be instructed. Better than that, this very day *you will see him for yourself.*" Her eyes flashed. "You have come in good time, for here in the sacred grove he chooses to reveal himself in physical form. The thrill of it!"

Eugene drank. The tabor sounded again, tapping out a foreign-sounding rhythm, and the pipe skirled its weird tune. For some reason he began to feel less strange about having Marienne's body, or about her having his. Could this come to seem natural?

A sigh, a moan, went up from the company. Miranda let out a hiss.

"It begins!"

All eyes were turned to the dais, but at first there seemed to be nothing. Then the air over the platform shimmered and swirled.

With a clap like thunder, a figure appeared.

And what a figure! Twice the size of a man, partly human, partly bestial, sporting massive antlers which magnified every slight motion made by a dignified, majestic head. That head was hard to make out. It possessed three faces, one looking forward, one to either side, each resembling a different animal recast into nearly human semblance. The body was massive, gleaming with colours as if covered in oil or bird's plumage, despite that powerful muscles rippled on it.

The god was naked and sat cross-legged on the dais, hands resting lightly on his knees. His phallus was erect and truly enormous, the tip on a level with his middle ribs. Eugene noticed that Marienne modestly looked aside at the first glimpse of that magnificent organ.

The crowd, however, mooed its appreciation of the apparition. The sight should have been hideous; instead it radiated an unearthly beauty. Three pairs of eyes turned this way and that to regard everything in the grove, their pupils brilliant horizontal strips, and to have those eyes fall on one made one tremble. More than that, a powerful heady perfume emanated from the being. Carried on the light breeze, it seemed to imbue all it reached with erotic desire, for those in the crowd began to grope at one another, pulling off each other's garments where there were any. Soon an orgy was in progress.

What by now could be shocking to the eyes of the lovers who had stolen into the wood the night before so as to enjoy one another unseen? They declined to take part themselves, and their innocent minds could scarcely have conceived of the acts they witnessed; yet they watched with shivering excitement, their eyes darting here and there about this feast of depravity.

After a while, the Horned God uttered a low, musical bellow, at the same time making a gesture upon which the lewd activity stopped immediately. The debauchees fell back, hurriedly tumbling and crawling, to create a roughly circular space before the dais. The god studied the gathering. He pointed twice, once to a man, once to a woman.

Slowly those designated came forward, though whether their faces expressed trepidation, anticipation or stark fear Eugene could not tell. Side by side they stood facing the god, and Eugene was incongruously reminded of a bride and groom about to have the wedding sacrament performed.

The Horned God raised his hand and described a complicated motion. A whisper ran through the gathering.

"The sign of change!"

The couple turned to one another and stepped closer, holding out their arms for an embrace. As their faces came together they put out their tongues. Somehow they seemed too large for human tongues, as they began to *lick*.

The couple were *tasting* one another. Here was where the magical change had been wrought. The tongues grew longer and broader, and longer and broader still. They became ever-expanding cloaks of pinkness which writhed and coiled. Like snakes or snails they twisted slimily around one another, wrapped themselves around faces, necks and shoulders, grew yet further, each to enfold an entire body.

On and on proceeded the strange coupling, with slick slapping sounds, while the changelings looked close to fainting with pleasure.

The god faded slowly from view, leaving the dais empty. Emerging from the trance into which the scene had put him, Eugene discovered that he sat alone. Miranda and Marienne both had gone.

Looking round the grove, he thought to glimpse a figure — naked male body, chestnut hair — disappearing behind the line of pavilions. Anxiously he rose and hurried after her, picking his way through the crowd which still raptly watched the tongue-play. But when he rounded the nearest tent and looked along the line, Marienne was nowhere to be seen.

A rustle of cloth alerted him. Miranda was beckoning from the entrance to the pavilion, holding aside a linen screen. Thinking she was showing him where to find Marienne, he went up to her.

Her lips brushed his ear. "Your instruction begins," she cooed. "You may ask questions."

Deftly she ushered him into the tent. It was hot inside. The sun beat on the tent fabric, providing a suffuse mellow light and over-heating the enclosed air. Marienne was not there. Instead there was a man seated on a tabouret, clad in a loose robe which covered even his feet. His skin was swarthy, his hair ginger and tufted, his eyebrows pronounced and lifted at the ends, giving him a piratical look. Yet his face was undeniably intelligent. Gracefully he gestured Eugene to a cane stool and began to speak in a soft, clear accent which identified him as coming from the far south.

"Your heart has made a pact with the Horned God of many names," he said seriously, once Eugene had seated himself. "With Abraxas, Ialdabaoth, Cernunnos, Pan, Nature, the Voluptuous One, with the power which men and women secretly call upon to grant them their hidden desires. Your heart has led you to the sacred grove. Those unfriendly to the god never find it.

"Now the time has come for the world to be explained to you. You will not understand, but listen just the same. Later you will hear it all again, in more detail, and little by little you will come to understand it.

"The world was made by the Horned God. Once there was no world. There was only the god, and even he did not exist then in the form in which you have just seen him. He was the great serpent without end, his tail in his mouth, before all worlds, and there was no experience of anything. There was just nothing. Until the serpent stirred, and wished to create pleasure and enjoyment. So he whirled and coiled, and generated a garden paradise filled with creatures so that there would be gratification of the senses. And he changed himself into the Horned God, so that he too could take delight in it.

"That garden is our world. It was made for the experience of pleasure, and for nothing else. Whatever denies pleasure denies the Horned God and so denies the very purpose of existence. Of course, this is not whet you have been raised to believe. Priests and rulers have taught you that It is wicked to be carnal. They have told you that you must be dutiful and obey their laws and commands. This is because a false, lying god entered the garden and set himself up in opposition to the true god. His authority is what the priests preach. Yet the truth is that all woe, all frustration and suffering, come from him. Only in places like this, where no king holds sway, does the Horned God now show himself."

Eugene looked down at 'his' body; at what he had become. "But why has this been done to me? And the people outside, with the big tongues — "

A lascivious chuckle escaped his teacher's lips. "Come, you have enjoyed it, have you not? Pleasure is the only thing of value, young man. Go wherever it leads you! And it will lead you to change. Change begets pleasure, change is the essence of pleasure. Change and pleasure belong together, because they began together when the great serpent roused himself and mutated into the Horned God. Up until that moment, when he lay unmoving in himself with his tail in his mouth, there was no pleasure. There was no sensation at all."

The sybaritic tutor leaned towards him. "In lust and pleasure animals produce their young. Without this, life would vanish! It is change that brings the different kinds of animals into being. Where do you think they came from? Do you imagine they flashed into existence out of nothing? That would be absurd. I will tell you the truth of it. The god takes animals in rut, in heat, in passionate mating, and moulds new, different animals in their wombs. That is how there come to be so many different kinds." The swarthy-skinned man's voice became intense. "So do not be afraid of change. Wallow in the flesh!"

"But — do we change back?" stuttered Eugene.

"Oh, at first you always change back. Later, you may not want to — *as I do not.*"

Rising to his feet, the teacher cast off his robe. Eugene blinked to see his naked form. From the waist down he was more goat than human, sparsely covered with coarse hair, knees bent the wrong way, the feet not feet but elongated hooves. More astonishing than this was his sexual organ. It did not match the tree-trunk massiveness of the Horned God — what could? — and necessarily was more slender. But it was long, and furthermore was lengthening and rising even as Eugene stared at it, flexing and lunging with a snake-like life of its own, the foreskin peeling back to bare a crimson head which swelled and searched the air. Almost, Eugene fancied he saw a little tongue come licking out of it.

The satyr set his gaze on Miranda, who throughout the lecture had stood silent near the wall of the tent. In a moment her shift was off. He took hold of her and turned her back to him, then bent her over so that she presented her plump buttocks. He seized her haunches in strong hands. It seemed impossible that his prolonged member could enter in full, but enter it did, to the hilt, and Miranda gave vent to a groan of that could have been of pain or appreciation, but which was more probably both. In a daze of venery, Eugene watched as the satyr jerked his hips and Miranda rocked to and fro, her cries growing louder.

Throwing back his head, the satyr howled.

Something was dripping from Miranda's mouth. Something white, viscous like honey, dribbling in copious gobs. It was phallus honey, thick male love fluid that had come surging from her throat, its spunky odour mingling with the smell of trampled grass and hot tent fabric.

How could this be? How could sperm find its way from a woman's womb to her mouth? With startlement Eugene realized that it could not be 'her *woman's* orifice that had been entered. It had to be her *other* opening, her 'dirty' opening. From there the emission could spurt through her entrails, invade her stomach, gush from her lips.

He had not quite been able to believe it when, during the orgy, he had thought to see a man perform this travesty of the sexual act *upon another man*. He stepped back, felt for the portière that screened the entrance, and stumbled through it.

The air outside seemed mild after the furnace heat of the tent. From within, there continued to come Miranda's gasps and spitting sounds.

Suddenly Eugene urgently wanted Marienne. He cast his eye along the stand of tents. What prurience, what wantonness, was taking place within those gay pavilions? Was Marienne herself a participant? Was she at this moment using his body to enjoy herself with others?

The thought stung him to jealousy. He crept to the neighbouring pavilion, gold in colour, fingered the portière and listened. At first he heard nothing. Then a smooth, melodious voice called out.

"Come within."

Unthinkingly he obeyed. In the centre of the tent a cloaked, hooded figure watched his entry with interest.

"Ah yes. The orchard-keeper's son. I heard of your gift. Delightful!"

The hood was thrown back to reveal the man's face. Eugene gasped in recognition.

Le Duc Des Esseintes!

How unnaturally smooth was his skin, how bright were his eyes! They glowed with pleasure at the sight of the boy-girl.

"How kind of you to bring me the body of your betrothed," he purred. "The body which it is my right to pillage. Her body, your face — a charming combination! Let us wait no longer! *This* shall be your wedding night!"

Eugene whimpered. His legs felt weak, too weak to move, and he stood paralyzed as the lord came closer. Le Duc murmured reassurance on seeing his fright. "What, are you so coy? Do not worry, it will be more interesting than you think. I, too, have a gift from the god — a small one, but it is permanent. See, I am hermaphrodite."

The blue cloak fell to the ground. The *seigneur's* plump pale body was a man's, and the male organ was slowly swelling, but from his chest grew incongruous breasts. They were not full and voluptuous, like Marienne's which Eugene now bore. They were small and pert, the nipples tiny; the breasts of a young girl undergoing puberty.

Le Duc fixed Eugene with a leer, caressing first one breast then the other, brushing the little buds with his forefinger. Eugene made an effort to turn and run, but a musky perfume had reached him, the same as that given off by the Horned God except that this time it seemed to emanate from De Esseintes, for it grew stronger as the *seigneur* took a step nearer. Eugene realized that he would not be able to resist his advances. A croak broke from him, a croak of revulsion in which there was buried a trembling, unwilling delight. Le Duc was taller than he, and placed a fondling hand on his shoulder. His lips reached down for the side of his neck.

A shriek came from behind. *"Eugene!"*

Marienne had entered the tent. Le Duc raised his head and fixed her with a stare.

"Begone! I am your lord and this is my right! Later, perhaps . . . "

His offer went unheard. As he spoke Marienne snatched her lover from his grasp and hauled him out of the tent.

"We must get away from here!"

"We must get away," Eugene repeated in a babble. The irrestistible perfume seemed to be seeping through the portière. He was seized by an impulse to return to Le Duc and offer himself. Had Des Esseintes ventured from the tent he might even have done so. But Marienne was physically the stronger of the two, and she dragged him out of range of the musk.

They were immediately confronted by Miranda, who had emerged from the first tent Eugene had entered. Still naked, her breasts were heaving, her eyes half-closed. She clutched her arms to her chest and writhed, as if she could still feel the satyr's lengthy phallus engaged in her rectum.

"Pleasure!" she crooned. "Why are you so frightened? Pleasure is the meaning of life!"

They went to edge round her. Suddenly she lunged forward, throwing her arms around Eugene's neck and kissing him full on the lips. For a moment he stood and allowed the kiss, enjoying the sensation of her breasts pressed against 'his'.

Then her body convulsed. She vomited up a prodigious quantity of rich semen which splattered into Eugene's mouth and over his lips and chin. He pulled away retching and spitting, wiping his mouth with the back of his arm.

Marienne grabbed his free hand and urged him into a run. Miranda's mocking laughter followed after them.

"There is nothing else once you have truly tasted pleasure! Whet will you do now?"

Frantically they fled across the grove, where the orgy was still in progress and the couple who had initiated it lay on the ground wholly enwrapped in each other's tongues. In a minute they had found the trail by which they had come, had snatched up their clothes from where they had been thrown down, and had plunged in panic down the path in terror of being pursued.

But soon only silence lay behind them, and realizing this, they slowed their pace.

"I left the table because I could not watch any longer," she told him. "I thought to hide myself in one of the pavilions. But, oh, Eugene, there are such thing's there!"

He made no reply. Dusk had fallen by the time they pushed their way through the foliage of the weeping beech tree to find themselves once more by the mossy bank. The moonlight was not nearly as bright as it had been the night before, and they decided they would not be able to find their way home in the dark. Indeed, how could they go home? Besides, they were weary. And they were also together, and alone, and the memory of so much lasciviousness was still fresh. So they sank down again upon the soft bank, and repeated what had happened earlier that day, enjoying their exchanged bodies long and ardently.

Eventually, they slept. Awakening at dawn, their arms round one another, they felt a returned familiarity which caused them to inspect themselves anew.

No longer were they creatures made up of each other.

They were themselves.

"The god has released us!" Marienne sighed. "Thanks be!"

"Released us? Or taken back his gift?" Eugene pondered. He regarded the hidden entrance. Eventually, he supposed, Le Duc and the others would emerge from behind it and make their way home. Or were there other paths to the grove?

"Who would have thought our *seigneur* leads such a life," Marienne mused. "What goes on in the great house, I wonder?"

They fell to looking at one another, still naked from their frenetic exertions. For the first time Eugene could see Marienne's body *as* hers, and she, his. No words were spoken between them. They looked, and touched . . . so that within a few minutes they were enjoying the coupling of a man and a woman as nature intended. The sun slowly ascended until it cast slanting shafts of light through the trees, and only then did they desist. They dressed themselves and set off, picking this direction and that, losing themselves for quite a while, but in the end arriving dirty and bedraggled in the sheep meadow from where they had set out.

Eugene looked at his betrothed. She was downcast. A shiver went through him as he thought of the double physical enjoyment they had both known. In his heart rose a fierce longing to have that double pleasure again. At least, he thought, they could have one half of it — and though he doubted that their parents would allow either of them out that evening, he said, "Shall I see you later?"

She turned to him sorrowful and dispirited. "Oh, dearest, we must not see each other any more. And we must not marry. Do you not see that, painful though it is?"

His expression showed plainly that he did not, and she went on, "Only by remaining forever apart can we resist the lure of what lies in the secret grove. The pleasures to be had there are piercing, but the price is terrible. You did not see within the other pavilions, as I did, where people who have worshipped the Horned God for a long time take their ease. They are turning into animals, or into something worse, into indescribable monsters. If you follow the Horned God you descend into your own bestial nature, which lies in all of us, and there is no escape.

"Who knows," she reflected, "perhaps that is where all the world's animals come from. Perhaps they were people once."

She tossed her head. "No, dearest. We must never touch one another again. The attraction between us is too great, and it will lead to that *other* attraction."

Eugene's heart began to grieve, and he protested, but in the end he saw that she was right. Destruction as human beings would be their lot if they stayed together.

Perhaps, too, he recognised that in marriage she would be the stronger partner. For in contrast to his timorousness when she had resisted him that first night In the forest, he recalled with what force and impetuosity *she* had *taken* him — had, in effect, taken *her own* maidenly virginity — once she had the use of his masculine body.

And so each went home to worried families. Having spent two days and nights lost in the forest with him, Marienne suffered a sullied reputation from then on, though this was mollified to some extent when she called off their betrothal. As for Le Duc Des Esseintes, he paid them no heed at all whenever he chanced to ride by, and neither did the call to the great house, so much dreaded by them both, ever come.

Or was it dreaded? Eugene and Marienne studiously ignored one another in the fields thereafter, but It is a fact again that neither married, or ever looked again for a sweetheart. For his part, Eugene's thoughts would turn again and again to those two days in the forest. And whenever — which was often — he was tormented by desires he could not assuage, he would dream of searching the woodlands, of seeking out the hidden trail and once more entering the secret grove. It seemed impossible to him, sometimes, that the day he dreamed of would not arrive. And always, in his dreams, he would eventually meet Marienne there. But who could say if they would even recognise one another by then, so altered might they have become.

CAVISO GAMO

By L.H. Maynard & M.P.N. Sims

When he was young, still at school, he remembered painting a sunset in art classes. Nothing special, he had no talent, but the teacher put it on the wall for the parents' evening so that the other boys' parents could comment on it, as his parents would have done, had they been alive.

It was a painting he had started casually, as befitted his temperament, and yet he had added to it, layer after layer, until even a heart as phlegmatic as his, as carefully defended, began to whisper emotion. He thought back now to that afternoon and how the art class had seemed to stand still in time, so that no matter how long it took him, he would be able to complete the picture.

He had ladled on as many colours as he could find in his palette at first. All the cliché colours of all the bursting suns he could see in his mind's eye he slapped onto the grey paper. Layer after layer, colours merging into each other like faulty memories. Yet as he added more colours, and the new oranges blended in with the old reds, so the pattern of the rays of the sun took on a life of their own. As russets were painted over yellows so the texture on the page grew, and the dappled effect added shadows. The paint began to dry in places and the depth of the colours began to expand, with the darker colours complimenting the lighter ones, the reds fading into the whites, as night seemed to be actually approaching in his picture. As he added more paint and the sunset was taking a physical shape now on the paper, so heavily was it applied, so it did seem as if the painting was becoming reality, as if the encroaching night was waiting impatiently to be drawn onto the page. To be added to the scene as naturally as the sunset will slip away as darkness becomes king.

His heart had been defended as if by a castle wall since early childhood. The death of his parents, the disappearance of his brother, the misery of his upbringing, all had conspired to lock away in the highest tower of his soul the pure thoughts that would mould the boy into a different man.

The sunset painting had intruded into his thoughts after so many years, and it was if he could still see, still feel, the mound of paint he had created, and the vivid way it had encapsulated all the sunsets, all the end of days he had known. The real sunset, the one he could see from the Air Africa window, was a copy of the one he had painted. It was just as vivid, like a raw scar in the blackening sky. It was what had triggered his school day memory, clearly, but it was remarkable nevertheless how true to the image he had painted this real life image was. A different continent, a different life, and yet each was linked by the colours and feelings they projected.

As the aeroplane slowly banked ready for descent, the remarkable colours dodged behind his field of vision, to be replaced by the imminent impenetrable black of night that truly surrounded them. The seatbelt sign was on and the passengers were tensed waiting for the rush of fear and excitement that was the landing. It had been a long, uneventful flight, not unlike most of the annual trips he had made here.

The elegant cabin staff had been efficiently helpful, and the people sitting next to him politely aloof. He was already eager to be there, in his mind was already inside, and no amount of human courtesy would compensate for still having a few days travelling to endure.

They landed safely, noisily, and the lines drew up behind the slow, unsmiling immigration officers. Paul White was already standing outside the cave, frightened to enter, but anxious to be engulfed nonetheless.

The cool rarefied atmosphere of the plane was a distant pleasure. Here in the airport reception space the first reminder of the Africa of his dreams taunted him. The heat was as a beggar in the street, slightly uncomfortable to experience, and seemingly as unrelenting. The humidity clung to his clothes, soaking them within minutes, so that he stood there casually dripping, the damp clothing emphasising his tourist status, his sense of not belonging. It was so hot he felt it like a tight band around his head, pounding in waves upon his shore of resistance, frothing sweat into his eyes, causing soreness, instant discomfort.

The noise was another reality he had forgotten. Everyone seemed to want to speak at the same time, loudly, and expressively. The local language was a mixture of tribal patterns and modern colloquiums so that even had he been able to recall some of the guidebook dialect he had failed to learn he would not have been able to penetrate far into any meaning. Even the women had deep voices, bass rhythms that spoke of history and troubles, of ancient kings and rites of the night that haunted the new century. Voices echoed all around him, bouncing from the damp glass ceiling, reverberating along the body crushed corridors and seating areas. There were no discernible words so far as he could tell. Merely layers of sound laid one on top of the other like the layers of paint he had been remembering from his past. Voices lay thickly upon one another, the cadences blending as one, the volume seemingly rising as each moment passed by.

"Passport." The voice was thickly accented, arrogance spoken and reflected in the watery eyes. The large hands, black with pink undersides, flicked the pages of the document idly as the eyes never once left Paul White's face.

Paul tried to stare back neutrally but he knew the man was waiting for the first sign of insolence, and then he would silently signal to a colleague and the police would be called to open a small side room for the Englishman to explain himself. This was a country where the past was in control, and the present felt incapable of interference. The future has been stillborn.

The wary eyes flicked over the fading ink on the stamps from previous visits, took in the annual dates. Never exactly the same month, never quite the same length of stay, but a general pattern that revealed he was a frequent visitor, a fact that might need an explanation.

Just then a squabble broke out near the baggage reclaim. Two local men were staking ownership of a well-worn attaché case that threatened to burst open as they tugged and argued over it. A movement in the crowds of people showed where the soldiers were approaching.

"Take it." A now impatient official thrust Paul's passport at him. The ensuing argument, and its resolve was clearly more interesting than the reasons why a white man approaching middle age should want to re-visit this troubled country.

Aware of the dangers of delay or apparent disagreement he took the passport and slipped it quickly into his jacket pocket. Then he picked up his small suitcase and moved to the exit. He glanced back into the crowded airport lounge, but flinched away from the sight of raised rifle butts. The doors closed behind him and he stood in the naked heat of the equatorial evening.

His dreams had ladled on as many colours as his memory could find in his thoughts at first. All the cliché colours of all the Africas he could see in his mind's eye. Layer after layer, colours merging into each other like they might be real. As more colours were added, and the rich oranges blended with the deep reds, so the pattern of the recollections took on a life of their own. As greens mingled with yellows so the myth grew, and the only intrusion was the shadows. He tried to add more colour with each memory, but the shadows were taking on a physical shape by now. He knew there was colour to this country and this continent, this vast landscape of peoples and animals, this assortment of landscapes and mood, but all he would find now was the darkness of the other side.

Although he knew it was nearly nightfall he vainly hoped against perception that he might rediscover the colours he had once known. He shut his eyes and waited. All around him he could hear movement, of cars, of people, and of indistinct shuffling that he knew existed elsewhere. He could feel the choking heat as a constant companion. In his mind he could see the colours of the carnival, the purples, the pinks and reds, the blues, greens. The fabrics of the markets worn by the people, silk, cotton, linen, flowing and soft, showing movement even when the body was still.

Then he opened his eyes and all was blackness. The sunset was gone, the colours were sucked dry, and all that was left was the noise of the night. As well as his memories and the task ahead, and neither were a welcome diversion.

He hailed a taxi and explained where he wanted to go. The driver nodded and drove him through narrow streets that were almost deserted. Dust flew up from the wheels, coating the pinching doorways of the houses with sheen of grey. Thin dogs sniffed at corners as if looking for the people who were suddenly absent from the streets. Despite being so near to the airport Paul might have been a million miles from any vestiges of civilisation. The buildings had quickly changed from the Westernised apartment blocks and offices to a more simple, basic and indigenous, series of dwellings. Wood smoke rose from cooking pots at the front of some of the houses but no one stirred the contents.

After a couple of miles the taxi stopped and the driver turned to the rear seats, his hand outstretched. Paul knew the intimation. The driver had gone as far as he intended. If the journey was to be completed it would be alone and on foot. It was what he had expected. Not many ventured to the house any longer. If he wanted to see Felix, he would do so without company, as he had done for all the past visits.

As the taxi drove back to the city Paul trudged on through the darkness, the persistent sounds of insects in the bush his only companion.

The reality was in stark contrast to his earliest memory of the journey. As a boy his parents had believed in developing the minds of their two sons to the fullest. Travel was encouraged when the concept was still something new and raw. Africa was a wild and reckless place to be, and the excitement of the unknown was as real as the heat, the dangers as diverse as the region itself. His father had heard about a ceremony that took place once a year, a kind of pagan fertility service was how he described it to their mother, though neither Paul nor his elder brother knew what any of the descriptions meant. Their guide was a man called Felix, a tall, seemingly honest man of Zulu stock, who promised them they would be able to witness what they imagined would be a tableau of dance and performance. It didn't happen that way. In that both reality and memory concurred.

The house was even more dilapidated than he remembered. The earthen walls bowed inwards as if the night was trying to fold up the house and carry it away. The roof sagged as if out of guilt for what lay within, and for what had been allowed to happen.

Paul smelled it as soon as he put his head inside the open front door – a kind of dissolution, an odour of decay and of dank disuse. There were two men sitting in the bare room. One was stroking an unidentifiable animal on his lap while the other was staring into space and smiling. This was Felix.

"Surely it is not that time yet?" he said without removing his attention from the ceiling.

Paul set his bag down on the mud floor. "A month earlier, but it is the time."

Felix said something in an ancient language to his companion and the animal slithered off the man's lap and scuttled away into another room.

"Who is this?" Paul said, attempting to stay calm but knowing he was failing.

"My eyes."

And then Paul saw that a kind of blindness had overtaken this man whom he had known for so long. There would be a tale to be heard first, about pirates pricking out his irises with needles, or of slavers applying hot irons to his pupils to guarantee his silence, but the whiteness of the eyes spoke of cataracts and nothing more. Paul felt a pleasure to think there might be some suffering because it was long overdue.

"I still need to go there." He knew he sounded as if he was pleading but so near to the time he had no choice. There was too much to lose if he didn't enter the cave.

"Celeste will take you." And Felix seemed to sink into his chair, the height, and the proud heritage, melting into a pool at his feet.

In contrast Celeste stood and gestured to Paul to leave the house.

"Wait," Paul began, but the hands pushed and insisted, until both men were standing outside the dying house.

Bloated shadows emerged from the trees and sank into the walls. Rustling movement slipped from the tall grass and entered the doorway. For a few moments there was frenzied activity inside the house. Skin being slapped, then torn. Hair being ripped, and bones cracked. Then there was a single scream of such depth that Paul shrank away from the sound, trying to hide within the night itself. Smoke began billowing out in formless shapes.

Paul ran to the house, brushing off the restraining hands that reached after him. The source of the smoke was what was left of Felix. The white-coated eyes were open and staring, though no longer alive. The head was hanging down on the chest, the throat and neck all but severed from the torso. Blood dribbled down the chest, mingling with the pink sacks of the lungs, which had been drawn out through the jagged and broken ribcage. Neither leg possessed a foot now, but the stumps were pushed back at an excruciating angle, forcing even wider the gaping wound at the groin. The fingers of each hand were severed at irregular points, the remains crushed and weeping.

Back in the gloom of the open night Paul picked up his bag and gestured at Celeste with open palms.

So many years ago when he had been a boy the expedition, as their father labelled it, was a great hit. The chance to see at first hand the wild animals they had only read about in books, and seen once at a cramped zoo. The opportunity to show off skills learned in scout camp; how to erect a tent, tie knots, survive in the wild.

The jeep was bumpy but that was all part of the fun. Felix then had been a young man, full of enthusiasm, even if plagued by a devious nature. His fee for acting as guide was reasonable and the chance to see real African culture was invigorating. Their father was full of stories about big game hunters, and lions, elephants all manner of exotica. If their mother were hesitant the boys would not have been aware of it.

They reached the place after two days of driving through increasingly dense bush. They were all tired, though Felix seemed infused with a new energy now they had arrived.

The ceremony took place, so it seemed, in a large cave, the entrance to which was shielded by two thorny trees. It was important he told them to be seated on a flat rock in the far corner, as that would give the best, and most private view. He would wait outside as he had seen it all before.

Paul's parents let his elder brother take a position at the front, while he, still tired from the journey, and very young, leant against his mother. He probably slept, at first, but later, when he was the only one to emerge from the cave, he never slept peacefully again.

That would be the case now, as he sat beside Celeste in a modern version of the jeep, and started to relive the first journey, back to the cave, and his memories.

Modern vehicle or not it still took two days hard travelling to reach their destination. The first day they drove steadily, heading west, until they made camp beside a thin river where they could wash and drink. The food was already packed on the jeep and when Celeste left before dusk, with a rifle on his shoulder, Paul knew they would be eating small game for supper.

Somewhere, not so far away, he could here the low rumble of a lion's roar. It concerned him, but without too much fear. They were in inhospitable territory now, open acres of shrub, dotted with patches of tree cover, long grass and bare earth. The presence of wild animals was expected. There was evidence of zebra, perhaps a giraffe, and certainly the recently killed carcass of a gazelle on which the hyenas were feasting was within sight on the far bank of the river.

It was almost satisfying to be here again. The reality of the African bush matching the tributaries of his memory, allowing him, for a brief moment, to live in the present instead of in his mind.

Celeste returned with a small rodent slung over his shoulder and began to make up a small fire. There was no attempt at conversation, no stories as there had always been with Felix. Paul knew that even though this journey, and the occasion was so familiar, this time it would be very different. Possibly because the guide was not the same, but possibly instead because Paul was at last different.

When they had found him, wandering in the shrub just outside the city limits, they had not understood the language he spoke. His English was barely formed, so young was he, and the ancient babble that had intruded into his mouth was so old that no one had ever heard it spoken before. The questions about his parents' whereabouts were asked of him but not understood so they remained un-mourned, except in memory and nightmare. He could not make them understand about his brother, and the bond between them weakened every year, so that while once he had come back to find him, now he tried to forget.

Celeste rose early the next day, the last day, and beckoned for Paul to hurry.

"What's the rush?" he asked, wanting to add that it was his journey, his memory, and he would dictate the pace.

The scrawny little man shrugged, defiance and acceptance in equal measures. The yellowy eyes slipped away from Paul's face, as he busied himself with packing the belongings back onto the jeep.

The terrain became increasingly familiar as they neared the cave. Sometimes memory held the upper hand, as they reached a landmark he was waiting for, and sometimes reality triumphed as an image was not the same as it should have been according to his recollection.

Too soon they stopped near two thorny trees that were bent horizontal to the ground as if being held open and away from the black entrance. There were no leaves on the trees, yet there should have been at this time of the season. With a feeling of dread Paul realised that the trees had died since last year's visit.

Celeste waited by the jeep while Paul approached the cave. When Paul looked back at him the little man stared blankly as if neither of them was actually there at all.

Just as Paul walked into the cold embrace of the cave entrance Celeste called out, "Good luck." Spoken in perfect English, the words had as much finality as "goodbye."

When they were a family they had run into the cave, excited and daring each other to be the first into the darkness. They had tried to spook one another with stories of ghosts and demons, not knowing that their reality was to be far worse.

The flat stone where it had been suggested they sit was a little damp, but they expected a cave to have moisture. That the moisture was dark was probably due to it being bat droppings or something their father had said, and they all laughed and shivered.

When the whispers started they thought it was just the beginning of the ceremony, which it was, in a way.

Memory and reality merged seamlessly for Paul now as he walked calmly into the interior. It was as dark as he remembered, and the floor was even more slippery. There was a rippling backdrop to the silence that might have been caused by bats, but he knew it wasn't. It was like coming home in a way that was unlike any other for him.

The flat stone was still there, darker and damper now, as the years had progressed. The years he had spent returning to recapture one moment was nothing by comparison to the centuries the stone had lain in silent witness to the rituals and secrets. He sat upon it and waited.

Outside Celeste had gone. He had been replaced by his true guise. Wearing his new form he entered the cave.

Paul thought back to the family adventure all those years ago. The first indication that something was wrong was when his brother jumped off the rock and fled into the shadows. Out of polite courtesy, or simple fear, Paul never knew, but his parents remained seated and silent. After all they were on holiday, and this was a local festival of sorts. Their son would be safe, surely. Then the shouting and the movement began. It all got too hectic for the small boy that he was and Paul closed his eyes and tried to obliterate the memory before it had even formed. It was like an abortion of experience. The feelings remained through the years, the revenant of memory, the unformed reality, but never the completion of actual participation. Each year since he had made his pilgrimage to visit his parents, and to search for his brother, without actually trying to do either. He was fumbling for his memory. If he could turn it into reality he might be able to change it, to stop it.

The whispers began. Not a language he could understand or a volume that he could comfortably hear, but it was sound that now, as on all previous occasions, sent a serpentine shiver of fear along his body.

Eventually the movement started. Slowly at first, then gradually increasing in speed and tempo, strangely shaped shadows began to pulse in a rhythmic dance. An ululation crept into the cave as the sounds increased and diversified, with voices and animal noises interspersed. A crescendo of sound washed over the flat stone, draping heavy black shadow over his legs, pinning him there. He had tried to move in earlier years but had found the shadows moved with him, effectively holding him in position. Now he just accepted it and sat and waited.

Gradually the shadows that had disgorged from the blackness beyond his vision began to soak into the walls of the cave. Some hung on rough fingers of rock, twitching, as though cloaks hung for wearing later. Others partly submerged into the walls, so that half their shape was flopping out over the grey rock, softly breathing. The majority slipped directly into the stone walls, leaving dark stains as evidence of their entrance.

The emptiness in the cave was filled by a single figure. Paul sat up, finding the shadows around his legs had gone. The appearance of this figure was new.

At first it walked on two legs like a man. Then without warning it snarled like the beast it was and dropped to all fours.

When it looked up at Paul he knew from the yellowed eyes that this is what had presented itself to him as Celeste. Then he saw something else behind the eyes and reality began to subjugate itself to memory as his lost brothers face swirled around his mind as a kite in a violent storm.

The beast loped across to a mound on the cave floor. With disgusted fascination Paul saw that the mound was in fact the shape of two bodies, or what had once been the bodies, of two people. The shapes were entwined, as if with affection, but although curiously preserved, almost as if embalmed in some way, there was an incompleteness about them that was unnatural. When he saw what the beast was doing he realised why.

There was no memory intact with this image; this was a victory for the reality of the moment. The bodies had been gradually broken over the years, the fresh state somehow maintained, and they had been eaten in very small pieces, almost as though the feasting had prevented their memories from vanishing completely.

Paul watched in abject and defeated horror as the misshapen beast carved out a slice of flesh from the leg of what had once been its mother and licked it with furred tongue.

As if in celebration the shadows fell from the walls, and rose up in triumph from the floor, sloping down from the ceiling, joining the ancient ritual. At the height of the frenzy Paul saw what had been his brother look up to him and what passed between them was as enigmatic as the eternities, as elemental as agony.

Never before in all the years of his pilgrimage had Paul witnessed any of this. He knew now for sure that this would be his last time. When his parents had rushed forwards to join in the frantic dancing of what appeared to be local men and women Paul had held back, eyes tightly shut as his mothers hands trailed away from his. When he heard the shouts and the screams he glanced up only occasionally, just enough to fuel all the unending nightmares he had suffered since. When he had woken he was out of the cave, and the trees were crouching in defiance across the entrance.

This time, as he rushed outside, the trees were lying flat on the earth, ripped at the base of their trunks by a great force. The jagged teeth of the trunks were gaping white, bright and unreal in the glare of the sun.

The jeep was on fire, crackling flames lighting up the sky like the sunset remembered from his youthful painting. As he had started the painting, so casually, so he thought he would be present at its ending. The colours of the flames rested on top of each other as if deliberately trying to climb higher. The reds, ochre's, blues from the petrol, the yellows and oranges, all ascended, layer after layer, providing a balance to the darkness he had just left in the cave.

Only the darkness was with him, despite the sunlight. All around him lithe shapes swarmed with feline grace, others with Neanderthal cunning, more with distended limbs, and mutilated bodies that came neither from reality nor memory but somewhere beyond, where the sunset has slipped away and the darkness is king.

Some of the shadows roared, and the echo of their sound was like a bellow of rage.

The memory of what it had been like as a small boy in the cave the first time all those years ago crowded into his head, as a stabbing pain. He fell to his knees and wept at the wasted years of searching, the setting aside of reality for dreams. Wept for his parents and his brother, but mostly for himself.

The shadows had formed into a crude hunting pattern, tracking the prey, silently now, slinking closer, alert and determined. The leader broke away from the pack and moved as close to the man as it could without actually touching him. Then it slashed out and felt the gloriously soft skin as it yielded.

The sunset was a distant memory before the reality of the pain subsided.

'TALES FROM THE SPIRED INN'

GRANNY

By Stephen Palmer

Translator's note: Because of the difficulty outsiders have understanding reveller speech and writing, I have translated this story, the Third Tale From The Spired Inn, from the original bio-rec audio files. The story was told to me during the annual Evening of Cemetery Culture, held on Vert Day in this, the final year of Kray.

It is my sincere hope that something of reveller mores can here be conveyed to you, the reader. Revellers of course are by their nature unpredictable, even chaotic. The tribes of the Cemetery, on the other hand, stand out as being the most stable social group in all Kray. To many this is an incomprehensible contradiction. But my tale shows how their fierce pride – their narcissistic desire to shape the world in their own image – creates from a filthy rabble the sort of social cohesion that our rulers in the Citadel only dream of. Such cohesion brings life, long life, but it also deals out death, because it is so uncompromising. There is no contradiction here, rather the reverse.

Qmeela of the Spired Inn.

#

In a glade of tombstones and yews three people stand. One is Dieffery, of medium height and build, noticeable because of the yellow tattoos on her scalp, opposite her Kyne, tall, imposing, wearing black clothes to match her dark expression. Third is the grandmother reveller, wearing gown and slippers and a brimmed rain-hat.

Drizzle drifts down as granny coughs to clear the phlegm from her throat, spits, swallows a pastille, then speaks. "This is a duel to the death. I accept no alternatives." Here, she glances at Dieffery, and the look in her eye is not kind. "By the end of today I want a result one way or the other. It's about midday, now. You can do what you like as long as you stay inside the Cemetery. If you leave, you lose, and your life is forfeit. I've got trackers all along the Cemetery wall ready to follow a coward. Got it? Apart from that, no rules."

Granny looks to them both.

Kyne nods. But Dieffery is frightened, looking nervous, and she tries to peer into the mist swirling around the edge of the glade, as if for other enemies. "As long as it is a fair fight," she says.

Granny croaks a laugh. "Ain't no such thing as a fair fight." She points to the east. "Off you go. I'll send Kyne the opposite way. Ten minutes and the duel is on."

"Wait a moment," Dieffery says, "are we allowed to use any weapons?"

"Yeah."

"Any weapons at all? Including anything we find lying around in the Cemetery?"

"As I said," the reply comes, "ain't no rules. If you don't see that now, it's too late. Now off you go."

Kyne sneers. "You're dead," she tells Dieffery. It is the first time she has spoken. Dieffery, pale, makes no reply and Kyne turns to walk away. Dieffery shrugs then walks in the opposite direction.

And granny grins.

#

When Geleshen and Dieffery took their daughter to the Spired Inn, they were unprepared for its welcoming atmosphere. Its location in the north of the city and its proximity to the Cemetery meant all the rumours they had heard were bad, tales of strife and violence, raid and counter-raid.

It was early evening. Through rain, the lamps of the Inn were hazy aquamarine orbs, its roof hidden in low cloud. Geleshen glanced at his wife and said, "This must be the place."

No reply.

He walked up to one of the windows and peered in. Three fires roared, there was a bar and many alcoves set with tables and chairs; only a few people drinking, but that did not imply danger. Geleshen returned to his wife and said, "Follow me in. It seems quite cosy."

Dieffery muttered, "A coffin is cosy to a dead woman."

"Now, now, there's no need to be glum. We've made our decision and we are sticking to it. We can't call it off the night before, can we?"

Dieffery looked elsewhere.

"Besides," Geleshen added, "our daughter comes first. Don't you, Marashary?"

"It's what I want," came the reply, in a small voice. "I love him and I must be with him."

"Then follow me inside."

Geleshen opened the front door and walked into a hall. Indicating the green zone, he let them take off their boots and place them in the antiseptic buckets provided, following suit, then waiting for them to hang up their coats and inflate their slippers before opening the door into the common room and striding in. He put a big grin on his face, though it felt like enemy territory. He wondered if he ought to make an effort to speak like the locals. No. They would feel patronised.

Behind the bar stood an old woman, hunched over gleaming tankards; dusty vest and thinning hair. This might be the owner. A dozen other locals raised their gazes to satisfy their curiosity, then returned to their drinks and games of chess.

Geleshen walked forward. At the bar he said, "You must be Dhow-lin."

She nodded once.

"I am Geleshen." He indicated his wife and daughter, introduced them, then said, "You are expecting us?"

Understanding changed the expression on Dhow-lin's face to one of pleasure. "Ah, got you." She looked at Marashary. "This is the lady, then?"

Geleshen nodded. "My daughter."

"Then welcome to the Spired Inn."

The atmosphere relaxed. Dhow-lin prepared hot drinks, told a serving lad to show them to their rooms, even introduced them to some of the locals. One, a dark-skinned girl called Qmeela, made conspicuous efforts to befriend Marashary. Geleshen was pleased. In this place they would need friends.

They passed a quiet, if difficult night. Sleeping was not easy. Though the inn was peaceful — none of the fights they had expected — all three of them felt on edge, aware that tomorrow would be the most perilous day of their lives. At least, of Dieffery's life. But Geleshen, sitting alone at the window while his wife and daughter dozed in their chairs under woollen blankets, recalled the effort he had put into preparing weapons for the duel. Hope was strong. Where there was cunning, there was always hope. Alas that tribal code necessitated the duel.

Dhow-lin cooked a proper breakfast when morning arrived, courgettes and potatoes in a butter sauce, garnished with parsley; tea and honey biscuits to follow. The Goddess only knew where she found such luxuries.

And so they turned to their own preparations. Geleshen wore a one-piece jumpsuit of grey cotton, black boots and an antiseptic hat, Marashary white breeches and a white tunic. Dieffery, in recognition of the forthcoming duel, wore body armour under a leather jerkin, cotton breeches and lace-up boots. Two holsters on a belt, each home to a black weapon.

Dhow-lin had been left a map by the grandmother reveller. They departed the Inn, following Morte Street to the Cemetery wall, passing underneath a gate, then making for the cluster of tents marked on the map. Geleshen could not be sure, but it looked as if they had been drawn with green algae. A symbol for death.

#

Kyne decides her plan will be to strike as soon as possible, killing Dieffery quick so that everyone can have as much time as possible in the Spired Inn afterwards. She likes the dooch there. She likes the baqa and she likes the mootsflosser. Besides, she has an important speech to make and she will need courage out of the bottle.

Rain is falling hard from dark clouds leaning in from the south. That means Dieffery will be confused. Because Kyne knows the Cemetery like the back of her hand she expects an easy task, but just in case — she did not like the look of the two hand-guns slung from that belt — she readies her laser rifle. Clunk. Snap. It is energised and ready to fire.

She stands with the Cemetery wall to her back. She can see the dark shadows of yews, a mausoleum; mist and rain all grey and smelly. Perfect conditions.

And she knows what Dieffery will do. Because Dieffery is in an environment never encountered before she will first want to find a hide, somewhere safe where she can watch for a while. Granny sent her east for a good reason — not fifty yards away from the starting point lies a ruined mausoleum. Dieffery will be there, scared, watching.

Easy.

Kyne moves down the Cemetery wall until she sees a single holly bush. She strikes out west, following a green glass path into the heart of the Cemetery, then heading around in a circle so that she approaches the ruined mausoleum from the unexpected eastern side. Laser rifle pointing ahead of her. Still raining hard.

The ruins loom up before her, a single hulk of green-grey set in curtains of rain, and she grins, knowing the time is close. At the back of the ruin is a hole where recently a window collapsed, and through it she will sneak.

Something small and black passes across her face. She looks to her right.

Dieffery!

Dieffery is stalking her.

Another shot, and this time it rips through one sleeve; fractional miss. Kyne runs forward, slips on wet grass, and so saves her life as a cloud of autonomous bullets fall out of the sky and slap like so many beetles into the ground.

Luck has saved her.

She runs like mad. Got to get away!

#

From the tent encampment a reveller usher led the trio to the Shrine of Eskhthonatos, the shovel-headed harridan of the underlands held sacred by the Cemetery revellers. It consisted of a green grove, holly trees to one side, laburnum to the other, between them two sets of wooden seats separated by an aisle. At the far end of this aisle Geleshen saw the grandmother, dressed in a black raincoat, behind her a twenty-foot effigy of Eskhthonatos: square head, clawed hands, hunched over like an old woman. Hideous, bulging eyes that gleamed like rubies.

Revellers sat relaxed on the right side of the aisle, two score or more, many drinking mugs of tea. Dieffery was led to one of the seats on the other side. These were empty.

Geleshen waited at the rear of the Shrine with Marashary at his side. What tore his heart was the sight of his wife sitting alone on her seat, head bowed, not looking at the grandmother or the revellers, as if steeling herself for the task ahead. Geleshen felt his guts churn in sympathy. Was his daughter worth all this? He glanced aside to see her expectant face, and he knew he must go on, for she was his only surviving child and she had to have what she wanted, at this time of all times.

Damn her, though, in the name of the Goddess, and damn Bansusen too.

A trio of grimy women began to play music — fiddle and zither and flute — that bounced jolly from one melody to another, causing the revellers to put down their mugs and sit up straight. Geleshen took the arm of his daughter and led her between the seats, looking straight ahead to where the grandmother stood hunched as if exhausted, lighting a stick of incense and poking it into her coat lapel. He tried to keep his bearing as noble as possible, but it was difficult in the presence of these rapacious low-lifes.

He stopped before the grandmother. To his right Bansusen stood up, and Kyne, the supporter. He found himself grinding his teeth. Now he was here, he did not want to go on, not even for Marashary's sake.

The grandmother began her pronouncements. She held no book or screen before her, the formulary clear in her memory. Dhow-lin had told Geleshen that the grandmother boasted of enforcing many ceremonies in her time. Enforcing: he did not like the sound of that word.

"In the sight of Eskhthonatos I bring you, Marashary of southerly parts, and you, Bansusen son of our dear Korydiya, together before me, that a deed irreversible be performed."

Geleshen closed his eyes. The rain stank of rotten fish and he felt sick. Standing up was all he could concentrate on.

"Being a ceremony blessed by the Lady of the Underworld, who made us all from clay and sea-water and bodily fluids, molding us in her mouth and spitting us into the city of Kray. Being a pact agreed by both parties. All hail. This morning I say you, Marashary, though you be an outsider, and you, Bansusen, do you both swear to do reveller right before the sight of the other?"

A faint "I do," from Marashary.

One stronger from Bansusen, who was smiling.

"And are there any here who know anything that might stop me from joining these two-"

Geleshen heard himself shout, "Yes!"

For a moment he did not realise he had spoken, so sudden was the feeling, so loud the cry. Then he opened his eyes and saw the venemous gaze of the grandmother locked into him.

"Yes," he repeated.

"But you are the father," she said.

Marashary had disengaged herself from him. He ignored her as he replied, "There is something you do not know, something that means this ceremony can't continue." He paused. He had no idea what to say next. All he could think of was the vileness of the revellers, their pillage, the murderous street-gangs, the constant battles . . . "The Temple of Youth," he said.

That was it. The way out. Everyone knew the depth of the enmity between revellers and the girls of Youth. Now everybody was looking at him, the revellers muttering curses at this mention of their foe.

"There is something you must know," he said in a firm voice. "Marashary was once a convert to the Temple of Youth. You must know this in case it is revealed later, and we are all shamed — "

"Father, no!" Marashary cried. She ran behind him and took Bansusen's hands in her own. "Bansusen," she wailed, "he's lying, honestly, it isn't true — "

Bansusen said, "Quiet."

Silence fell.

Bansusen glanced at the grandmother, then told Geleshen, "Do you really think we didn't check that out first? Do you think we would risk even a sniff of Youth in our precious Cemetery? You are a fool, Geleshen. You mock us with your false claim, you shame us. You are nothing more than a worm. Nothing more." And he looked away, hugging Marashary.

Geleshen bowed his head, shutting his eyes once again. The ceremony was going to be completed. His moment of madness had made it worse.

#

Kyne does not expect to lose, nor does she expect to be offered chances by the unpredictable woman from the south. The duel is taking an unexpected turn. She has two choices. Either she can continue alone and keep pure her reputation and her honour, or she can accept a small diminution of honour in order to send the woman to the worms.

It is time to call on help.

She runs due south for five minutes.

The mobile shrine has been placed between a pair of tombstones so tall they seem like holes through the mist into the chthonic world. Inside the mini-yurt Kyne finds her two aides, the sisters Bzajia and Aqadizia, crouching low, armed with laser pistols, their eyes glinting in the light of a steel glow-worm. She hunkers down beside them and describes what has happened so far. She has to tell them twice because they refuse to believe her.

Then they make plans.

"We have to set a trap," says Kyne. "Is that twin grave still open by the white marble steps?"

They know where she means. "Yes!" they reply, glee animating their faces.

Kyne pulls out a second set of clothes from the slim-pack on her back. Turning to Bzajia — not as strong as her sister, but more cunning and more courageous — she hands over a black sack dress, a pair of pull-on boots, and leggings similar to those she is wearing.

"Disguise yourself as me," she tells Bzajia, shrugging off her own dress and pulling a grey coat from the slim-pack. "We'll lead the woman down the steps." She turns to the other and says, "You prepare a natural cover for the grave. The woman will walk over it as she follows us two. She'll fall in and then we'll blast her, all three of us so there's no chance of return fire."

"Blast her!"

"Kill her!"

"Right," Kyne affirms, spitting and grinding the mucus into the earth to show her contempt for the enemy. "One of you's got the Felis optical?"

Aqadizia reaches inside her tunic while Kyne buttons up her coat. A green hat is the final touch. Taking the IR monocular, Kyne indicates its front lens, telling Bzajia, "I'll use this to track her in the mist, and when I find her we'll begin the trap. You follow me. Make sure the woman can spot you, but keep out of range — you know the score. Soon as we're down the steps, I'll run off and you follow. The woman will have to cross the grave to enter the western zones, because of the fallen yew blocking the path. Soon as she's dropped, fire."

"Fire!"

Kyne turns to Aqadizia. This sister is the better shot. "You'll be behind the woman," she says, "so you fire soon as you can. We'll add." She nods once. "Right. Time to go. Soon as this southern no-brain is dead we'll call granny on the radio."

#

Now it was time for symbolic exchanges to be made.

Kyne rummaged around in her black sack of a dress and produced a varnished eyeball. Geleshen had been warned about this by Dhow-lin, but he still felt the return of nausea the moment he saw it. The eyeball was fixed to a ring of coiled pubic hair taken from Bansusen, made — he had been assured — with loving care over a period of three days. The eyeball had been taken from one of the Cemetery totem poles. Revellers, who tore the dead from their graves, did not bury kith and kin, they coagulated the heads into immense columns and left the bodies to be eaten by vermin.

Geleshen had tried to imagine what it would be like in the Cemetery. Now he was here, just the word made his stomach turn. He felt like sobbing and running away.

But he could not. If the revellers took offence, his life was in peril.

From his pocket he took a ring of simple silver, which he gave to his daughter.

The exchange was made.

Duel time.

The grandmother coughed, spat, then with a forefinger gestured at Dieffery and Kyne, indicating that they should follow her. Geleshen watched his wife pass before him. She glanced up once, her expression one of both fear and hope; fear because of their circumstances, hope because of the preparations they had made, because of their strategy. It took all Geleshen's self-restraint to stop himself reaching out and pulling her back.

Too late. She was gone — three figures vanishing into grey mist between the holly trees. Two would return and then the ceremony could reach its end.

Two would return.

The grandmother and which other?

#

Dieffery is lost.

Her problem is how to locate her enemy without being spotted. If she hides, her enemy has to come to her but she will be trapped. If she wanders, she is at the mercy of the Cemetery. And those who live in it.

How the grandmother expects all this to be over by evening is a mystery. It could go on for days.

Then a stroke of luck. She is peering out into lifting mist from beneath a bush when she sees the black shape of Kyne in the distance, half shadow, half trick of the light. She stands upright and creeps out into the open. No sounds nearby, just the drip-drip of raindrops falling from foliage. All she has to do is follow until she has a clear view.

But Kyne is running, and Dieffery hurries to keep up. They cross a wide patch of grass before reaching a path of marble steps, where Kyne turns left, to make downhill.

Dieffery pauses to point her second weapon at the departing figure. Then she throws the black pistol to the ground and says, "Begin". A replica of herself struggles free of this soft device, like a kitten in an amniotic sac, first a miniature, shiny wet black, then, after a few seconds, a full-size duplicate wearing identical clothes. But although this is a machine made by the sentient mechanician Majaq-Aqhaj, it will only last an hour or so before the power cells in its belly run out.

"Follow the black figure you just saw," she says. "When it stops to hide or prepare weapons, or to dig in the earth, pounce. It's a woman. Kill her."

"I understand." The voice is poor, synthesized, metallic.

Dieffery hastens away. She must let the replica do its work.

The replica is equipped with optics superior to human eyesight. It will find Kyne. Dieffery follows at some distance to the right as the replica takes the marble steps two at a time. It is a long path leading down a shallow hill, and she, on wet sod, slips three times as she negotiates the mounds and open graves. She has to keep her noise to the minimum: not easy in this appalling place.

She stands alert at the bottom of the hill. Through a curtain of mist she sees the replica stepping off the path where a yew has fallen and blocked the way. Then a crash, a cry, and the replica vanishes into a hole. Stunned, Dieffery flattens herself upon the grass, expecting trouble.

From behind the yew two figures emerge, then a third from the path. They run towards the hole, weapons raised. Dieffery can only stare.

There are two Kynes.

A second of panic, then a second of furious determination. Dieffery pulls out her other pistol, flicks the autonomous bullets out of the chamber and back into her pocket, then takes a single red bullet, which she kisses, then loads. Geleshen was only able to acquire one of these.

One intelligent bullet, but two Kynes — a black one and a grey one.

The three revellers are firing into the hole as the replica climbs out. Dieffery notices that it is trying to grab the ankles of one of the Kynes as the laser beams make charcoal of its plastic flesh.

Dieffery has to choose. Surely the replica would try to grab the fake Kyne if that was who its finder-seeker inspected? The other one has the correct face but the wrong clothes. This other one has noticed artificial skin and metal bones — she has stopped firing. Dieffery aims and whispers, "Get that one," as she pulls the trigger.

The replica falls back into the pit. The intelligent bullet speeds through an arc. Kyne is hit. The other two stare, look around to where Dieffery is lying, then flee.

But Kyne is not dead yet. She manages to turn as she falls, firing at Dieffery. Just missing. Dieffery rolls, stands up, runs, dodges, as Kyne crawls away from the pit towards the yew. The autonomous bullets are back in the hand-gun. Dieffery fires. A slow black shower emerges from the pistol muzzle, to land on Kyne's head. She drops.

Dieffery waits.

#

Two figures emerged from the mist, the grandmother and . . . Dieffery. Sure the revellers would cheat, Geleshen found himself first amazed, then ecstatic. He ran forward to hug his wife — both of them weeping, unable to speak yet communicating their joy and relief — while the grandmother walked on at the same pace, to stop before the effigy of Eskhthonatos and sign for calm. After a minute Geleshen noticed that the revellers were waiting. He led Dieffery back to the aisle, then sat with her in the front seat, leaving only the grandmother, Bansusen and Marashary standing.

The grandmother spoke. "In the sight of Mother Clay, this afternoon, witnessed by us all, I declare the end of our ceremony." She paused, lowered her head and seemed to sigh. "For this woman and this man it is done. Let nobody declare it otherwise."

Marashary turned to Bansusen, raised herself on tip-toe, and kissed him. As the rain intensified, pattering against innumerable leaves, and the thunder rumbled far out across the sea, the couple walked back down the aisle, followed by Geleshen and Dieffery, the revellers — a chaotic, chattering horde — and the grandmother bringing up the rear. As custom required, they walked slow as slugs to the western gate of the Cemetery, where the grandmother threw decayed leaves and clods of soil to bless the couple, the revellers broke out into song, and Geleshen, despite the horror and the macabre moments, felt glad to see his beloved daughter smiling.

He turned to the grandmother. "Will you be joining us later?" he asked, in what he hoped was a conciliatory tone of voice.

For a moment she seemed lost in thought, before she replied, "I will." Then she grinned and added, "For it is not quite over yet."

So the noisy throng followed Morte Street to the Spired Inn. This part of the day was something Geleshen had been told nothing about. He walked into the common room and stood amazed. All the chairs and tables had been pushed to the edge of the room, creating a huge space lit by candles, leaving the outer parts enshadowed. The bar twinkled in the light of a hundred tiny lanterns. The reveller trio had been joined by local musicians — percussionists and flute players, even a belly-dancer — and already the atmosphere was alive.

Geleshen relaxed. He would get drunk, wake tomorrow with a hangover, then with his wife return to the south of the city.

Soon the common room was a swaying, bouncing menagerie of drunken revellers, shouting locals, musicians standing on tables to play their solo passages, communal dances that everybody, young and old, seemed to know. With Marashary and Bansusen ordered to dance alone in a clear space so that everybody could jig and prance in their wake, the whole inn seemed to vibrate under the impact of hundreds of feet. After ten minutes Geleshen found himself exhausted. With Dieffery he retired to sit at the far end of the bar, where Dhow-lin, quiet, almost aloof, stood preparing bottles of dooch and uz.

Qmeela, the girl who had befriended Marashary, joined them, sitting next to Dieffery. "I heard what happened," she said.

Dieffery nodded. "Someone had to lose the duel," she replied, adding, "If that was the way they wanted it . . . "

Qmeela shook her head. "I don't understand. You are the outsider family, joining them. How come you're sitting here now?"

"I don't follow," said Dieffery.

Geleshen added, "What do you mean by 'joining them?'"

Qmeela said, "When somebody from outside the Cemetery becomes part of their tribe, they have to prove they're better. It's a matter of pride — didn't you see the expression of determination on Kyne's face? If there was no duel, the two families — the two traditions, if you like — might be perceived as equals. The Cemetery revellers won't have that because their whole world, in which they survive because they're the best, would collapse. Their moral codes may be twisted-"

"They are twisted."

"— but they're codes granny keeps to the letter." She shrugged. "Cemetery revellers don't permit themselves to lose."

Geleshen frowned. "I accept that everybody has their own way of trying to survive," he admitted, "but we were better prepared than them, and that was why my wife won."

Qmeela turned to Dhow-lin and with a puzzled expression on her face said, "You know what I mean, don't you? How can Dieffery have won?"

Dhow-lin stopped pouring alcohol to glance at Dieffery. She shook her head, then walked away, flicking a cloth over one shoulder as if in a gesture of resignation.

A hush fell across the common room. The grandmother had arrived, and for some reason, possibly a perverse sense of respect, Geleshen stood up to greet her. Conversation returned to the room. But the grandmother ignored her kin and walked straight to Dieffery, to ask, "Are you enjoying the evening?"

Dieffery's eyes were watering. "To be honest," she said, "I'm feeling rather queasy. I expect it's bugs in the dooch."

From the other end of the bar Dhow-lin called out, "It ain't bugs, not this time."

The grandmother said, "Know why I'm a grandmother? Because we survive to be old. We survive to see our grandchildren. That's why we're the best." Emotion twisted her face. "Ain't nobody older than me in this city."

Dieffery tried to stand up, but instead fell to the floor.

And the grandmother grinned.

#

Dieffery is watching Kyne's body for twitches, flickering eyelids, any sign that life might still be in her. But the woman is stone dead and not faking it.

She has won.

Despite her fears — her terror — she has won. She must have had the Goddess on her side.

A few minutes pass before a figure emerges from the mist and Dieffery realises the revellers have been tracking Kyne on a location screen, possibly even monitoring her vital signs. It is granny. She has arrived to admit defeat. She was in communication with Kyne all the time. Nonchalant, granny moves the body with her foot, then kneels to retrieve all the useful odd-ments, dropping them into her pocket. Quite brazen. Dieffery sees this woman for the vile thief she is.

"So you won the duel," says granny.

"I won," confirms Dieffery. She wants to use the word 'cheat', but the ceremony is not over yet and there is a risk of rubbing salt into a wound.

Granny grunts, as if displeased with her lot. "Seems bad to me," she mutters, "but luck is luck, and there ain't no tinkering with it." Then with a deep intake of breath she lifts herself out of melancholia, takes a small bag from her pocket and offers it to Dieffery. "Sweet?"

Dieffery accepts with grace. The sweets are blobs of boiled sugar. They have an unusual flavour.

THE PLANTER

By Lauren Halkon

It is autumn and the forests burn with the sun's stolen flame. Once there were as many people as there were trees. Now there is one.

She walks down the mountainside, breath steaming and curling before her in the brittle air. A shapeless bag rests across her back and her clothes are plain, functional. Her pace is swift, yet comfortable, the long, ground-eating lope that comes from many years of travel. Her face is a flat, emotionless expanse. It has been a long time since life walked its bitter plains.

Rocks clatter beneath her feet as the ground sheers away beneath her and she half-slides, half-falls, the rest of the way. She lands softly in a cloud of dust and stands still for a moment, looking out across the soon-to-be-sleeping world. The thought of a sigh eases past her lips and she turns her gaze back to the trail, does not look away again.

She has walked this land for an eternity and more. Always looking, always seeking. A way to fulfil her promise. Never finding. The Tower of Silence is full of forlorn and misplaced hopes and she knows that she will never replace them. She has taken them all now. And all have failed.

Night closes quickly around her and soon she is walking by the light of the moon. It is the same to her.

Her footsteps take on a hollow ring and she stops, blinks, looks down at the ground, sees the glimmering stones of white that once paved a city like so many others she has visited, so many others in which she failed to find that which she sought.

Something that might have been a laugh fills the blackness. But there is no humour in it, only a sad irony. She reaches up a hand to her bag, strokes the material, soft and pliable from many years of use. A beloved familiar in a land devoid of any other.

She moves on, eyes alert for any movement. Old habits die hard. The ruins rise high above her now. Empty, broken windows, shattered walls, bent and crooked posts, all that is left of a race that thought itself better than it was, better than it could ever be. Stars cough and choke behind the claw remains, stone murdering a sky it had once, so long ago, venerated. She feels the bag growing heavy on her back, remembrances of past and future lives.

A sound echoes through the emptiness. High, mad. Her head turns, zeroing in with none of her earlier detachment. Her stride lengthens, becomes a jog, a run, a sprint. If she were not so tired, perhaps her eyes would sparkle, her breath come a little faster, as it is she barely flickers a lash.

She rounds a corner. Hollow, rusted containers roll and clatter away from her slapping feet. Loud in the silence that has swallowed the sound that drew her here.

She sees why.

Two old men, deformed, skin mottled and sagging, hands knobbed claws, eyes dark holes, stand poised over a small creature, a creature that lies motionless before them, waiting for their hands to descend.

She keeps running. She has seen their kind far too many times. The old, old men. Senile, deranged, lustful, greedy. They have murdered a world for their sins.

She skids to a halt; they look up, eyes slits beneath folds of skin. For a moment, no one moves, eyes study, brains work, then she looks down at the creature at their feet.

Her gaze snaps up. The old men back away. Something about her scares them now. Maybe the memories of a thousand other of their kind speak to them of the fate that awaits them.

She turns to the creature on the ground, picks it up, slings it over her shoulder and walks away.

The two old men totter out into the middle of the street. They stare after her. Wind whistles through them, cannot be bothered to toss their stick-like hair.

#

Her pace is slower than usual now that she carries a burden. She had thought they were all gone, but this creature, and those old men back there, prove that even she can be wrong. She moves the creature around to her chest as she walks, to better see it. She cannot decide what it is. It seems human in form, yet its limbs are small, scrawny even, its skin mottled black and white, its eyes too big, bearing no iris, just endlessly contracting and widening pupils in a sea of white.

It regards her solemnly, round, smooth head bobbing loosely with her movement. She returns it to her back where it fastens small arms around her and seems content to stay.

#

She makes a fire that night, just because she has someone with which to share it. She puts the creature on the ground and wraps it in her coat. It will not do for it to catch a chill before she reaches the Tower of Silence. She has not been there for a long time now. She wonders if the birds will remember her. She scarcely remembers herself these days.

She sits down across from the creature, wondering if it will begin to cry for food like all the others, but it does not, merely sits and stares into the flames.

After a while this behaviour disturbs her, though she cannot say why, and she moves closer to the creature, looks into its strange eyes for the answer.

It blinks when her face replaces the fire and begins to wriggle. She almost backs away.

An arm emerges from the cocooning coat, springing exuberantly into the air before sailing gently down to touch her cheek.

The eyes glisten, the skin around them crinkles, the mouth beneath grimaces.

"Look." The creature's hand turns her head with surprising strength. "Can you see them dancing in the fire?"

She looks. Thousands of flames lift their hands to her, sing to her, leap for her.

"It's alive," the creature's melodious voice comes from behind her. "It always has been."

#

Snow greets the resumption of their journey. Early. Too early. The land shrinks beneath its icy touch. The mountains sadly surrender to the featureless mask, the trees hold close to leaves that can no longer shelter them. It has been this way for a long time. She remembers vaguely the slow, endless turn of seasons, the comforting familiarity. Lost now in a time that changes with the blink of an eye.

The creature sits, silent again, on her back, next to the bag, humped beneath her winter cloak, fingers sharp as the wind digging into her flesh.

She feels neither. A memory of last night's flames keeps her strangely warm.

Her boots imprint her presence on the snow; here and there she spies the skitter-splayed marks of birds, the large, deep pits that promise a deadly predator. But nowhere does the poignant sole of humanity mark the earth and she stops for a moment, turns around, casts her gaze over the solitary trail she has created, sees the snow spiral down, already covering it over, erasing her presence as she has erased so much already.

She reaches for the creature, pulls it from its place, sets it on the ground, begins to walk again.

The creature looks at the snow with wide eyes, as though it has never seen it before. Then its eyes crinkle and it bends over, plunges inviolable hands deep into the grainy wetness. Returns with its prize.

Something thuds wetly against her neck, drips steadily under her cloak, dribbling down her back, tickling her. She reaches up a hand, touches the ball of melting snow already falling apart between her fingers. She is confused, looks up at the sky. Large flakes of tattered cloud float downwards. None are like the balls she has found.

Another hits her; she hears a shrill, excited cry, the creature bounds past her, white balls flying from its hands. She ducks, looks down at the ground, looks for a long time, sees the marks, the human soul, where the creature has gone, pulls her cloak more closely about her and follows.

#

The creature is stronger than its small frame suggests, but still she thinks it wise not to travel through the night. The Tower of Silence is close. Perhaps they could reach it that same day if they continued, but she has waited a long time for this and one more day will not hurt. She does not build a fire this night. The snow has stopped for now and the creature does not seem to feel the cold. Besides, she has already learnt that lesson.

She walks across the top of the crag they climbed today. Sits at the very edge, stares out over a land encased in brilliant sheens, sweeping curtains of snow growing drunk on the moon's light, greedily intensifying, shimmering, blinding. Yet all she can see is the darkness in between.

The creature pads softly to her side and sits. It does not speak for a while and she forgets it is there.

"You can see the whole world from here."

She regards the creature from a corner of her eye. It moves closer, lays its head in her lap, looks up at her out of vastly dilated pupils.

"Can't you?" It lifts a dappled hand, points randomly. She looks again, afresh.

The world spreads before her. She can see for miles. All glows for her. She can indeed see it all. For this is all that is important. This that surrounds her now. Holds her now. Cradles her now.

She lays a hand on the creature's head. Feels its life pulse eagerly beneath her touch. Returns her gaze to her world.

#

Their journey is almost at an end. The Tower of Silence looms before them. The creature is fascinated by it and runs on ahead. She wishes she does not know what she knows. That those old men have infected her creature, that it is dying even as it embraces life, the only one she has ever found, and she struggles against what she must do as the creature climbs the side of the circle and she reaches up and spins the Tower of Silence once more.

#

A watery sun watches her gather. The birds still circle. She wonders if it is a sign. She wonders if the tears she sheds are also a sign.

#

Two old men crest a rise and stop in sudden fear and wonderment. A vast structure lies before them. A circle with walls as high as the mountains they have travelled to get here, to follow the woman who took their prey. They look at one another, then back at this behemoth. As though by some unspoken agreement they start forth at one and the same time and soon are climbing those walls, voices high and cackling, reason long since absent from minds that have destroyed so much.

It takes them a long time. Wasted limbs wave and flap, ragged clothes tangle and trip, but soon their fingers fold over the top and they heave themselves up.

She stands in the middle, a lone hub, and laid out around her are millions of skeletal spokes, human bodies, bones dead, bleached and pitted, limbs outstretched, sacrifices in silence.

The two old men scream, hands held to their eyes, not wanting to see, not wanting to know, it is what they have done, all their fault, the endless death, and her laughter is bright as the vultures swoop down and tear them apart, dead flesh that walks, useless, forever.

#

She knew they would follow her and now it is over and her job will soon be done. Of the billions of bones she carries only a few in her bag. Her precious creature, sole lover of life. She has planted futile others, but she thinks that this time, this time it will be different.

THE MAGPIE

By Sarah Singleton

He dreamed of magpies again. Scritch scratch, their nailed feet hopped upon the roof tiles. But the town upon the hill was far away.

The cell was always dark, but with the night came a cold stone breath from the earth. A diurnal sigh, the exhalation of the ancient slabs of rock and river, under the tower.

The air played icy fingers across his skin, his body like a soft purse, his soul embroidered in the fabric of flesh, twisted about the knuckles of bone, the sinews. A soul stitched upon a network of nerves.

How fine the mechanism of his fingers. How supple and silken the material of his skin. They tried to unpick his soul, to tear it from the purse of flesh, rending the spirit from the substance, thread by fragile thread. Despite his screams, he did not speak. Blood spilled from his mouth, but the words held tight. He could not tell them what they wanted to know.

He slept, and dreamed again. He walked in the orchards in the slopes below the town walls. Apricot and almond trees blossomed. Katherine held out her white hand.

"Remember," she said. "Remember Edmund." Her thin face was grave, the soft fold of golden hair visible beneath her linen cap. A paper lay folded upon her palm. Then it quivered, flapped — transformed as he watched into a white dove, wings in a clatter, as it rose into the blinding white of the sun.

But he woke again, suddenly, as he always woke in this place. Senses strained — were they coming for him? His limbs ached, in anticipation of another beating. The cold floor, through the thin layer of dusty straw, sucked the heat from his body. White spots still burned in his retina as though he had indeed looked up into the sun. In this place, how vivid and bright his dreams had become.

He had ridden from Oxford, along the rutted highways to Maumesbury, high upon the hill. His father had given him the roan mare, with a blessing. He had completed his first year at the university, learning a little Latin and Greek, dabbling in mathematics. Now he hoped he had secured an appointment as secretary to a Wyltshire squire, William Shallow. Shallow had attached himself in a minor capacity to the court of Elizabeth, and Edmund held into hopes he might make his own advancement in Shallow's trail.

The long hours of darkness were drawing near. The mare plodded through the mud, her hooves leaving watery pockmarks in the thin, pitted grass beside the deeper ruts of the main thoroughfare. Distantly he could hear the clamour of geese, and the shouts of two boys herding sheep towards the town. The clouds burned coldly purple, as the sun descended. Edmund could see, rising above the houses, the humped back of the broken abbey.

An old man was riding a pied horse on the far side of the ribbon of mud, keeping pace.

Edmund was startled, his hand leaping to the head of his bodkin. The land spread emptily away. He hadn't seen the man approach. The stranger nodded. He was well dressed, in black with a warm fur collar. Edmund nodded cautiously.

"Sir!" the man called. Now eight hooves ploshed in the moist earth. "Sir, will you deliver a letter to Catherine Shallow?"

Edmund was puzzled. He did not answer at once.

"How do you know me?" he called back. The wind rose. His clothes did not keep out the chill. "Who are you?"

"Tell her I shall not need long. Tell her to trust you."

"Trust me, sir?" Edmund kept his hand upon the hilt. "Why should I tell her such a thing?"

"Can she trust you, Edmund Larkham?" The man held out the letter, with its thick wax seal. Irritated, Edmund consigned the mare to the trough of mud, to take it.

The man dropped the letter into his hand, turned the horse and cantered off. Too soon, he disappeared.

William Shallow lived in a house in Westport, just beyond the old Abbey. Edmund was received by the steward and the mare was taken to the stables behind the house, where the gardens dropped away to the swollen river. The house was very dark, a single tallow candle burning in the wood-panelled room where he was told to wait. A fire blazed, a pool of hot yellow light sending shadows flickering over the walls. Edmund eased his feet from wet boots, draped his cloak upon a chair by the fire to dry. Beyond the door he could hear the maids laughing.

He woke to a clatter of pewter plates, the young women carelessly setting the table. The chamberlain carried in a joint of mutton, dishes of cabbage and barley bread. Candles multiplied upon the long table, driving back the darkness to the walls, and a woman dressed in a blue linen dress took her place at the head of the table.

"Is he sleeping?" a child asked. A little boy of about eight or nine, sitting at his mother's right hand. Edmund lifted his head from the table, blinking.

"No, Mistress Shallow," he said, rising clumsily to his feet. "I've come to meet your husband. I have an appointment."

"The secretary, yes. We've been waiting for you," she said. Edmund stepped closer, and bowed, sweeping off his hat like the gallants at the university. Catherine smiled. The warm light played upon her face, the golden eyelashes, the tiny mouth, the skin very pale and delicate, dark around her eyes.

"I have a letter for you," he said.

"A letter? Already? See how earnest our secretary is," Catherine said, turning to the boy. Dark and dour, he did not resemble his mother.

Edmund dipped his hand into the pocket of his breeches and drew out the letter.

But when he placed the paper in the table it dissolved into a handful of black and white feathers. The boy laughed.

"Mistress, I —" he stumbled. "The letter. I had the letter."

The boy laughed again, the sound of his young voice sounded very cruel, so Edmund wondered if some trick had been played, perhaps as he slept.

"The gentleman said he would not need long. He said you might trust me," Edmund said, recovering his dignity. He stood up straight. Catherine held his gaze, her face very gentle and even.

"Then I shall trust you," she said. "Robert, be quiet. My husband is in London. You shall serve me in his absence."

The house was still. Catherine said grace, and the small household dined.

The man sitting behind the table placed his hand upon the papers. Edmund was seated upon a stool, to face him. His feet were very cold. A broken tooth nagged. His throat was dry. One candle burned in a pewter stand. It was hard to make out the limits of the room, beyond the small pool of quivering light.

"I am thirsty," the man said. He poured water from a jug into a wooden cup. He lifted the vessel, and drank. He wiped his lips. Edmund did not know the man's name. They had no names. But Edmund, looking sideways, thought he had seen him before, outside. He called him Fish, for his flat, greyish eyes. Now Fish stared. Then he poured another cup of water and passed it to Edmund. When Edmund drank, his broken mouth began to bleed again but the flesh of his throat seemed to soak up the water like a desert.

The man stroked the papers. "You see what I have here?" A second man, some lowly clerk in dowdy black, emerged from the darkness and sat at the end of the table, taking notes.

"Yes."

"It is your own work."

"It is."

Fish lowered his eyes, rifled through the mismatched pages.

"I have read the work," he said. "You are a playmaker."

"Yes," Edmund said again.

"You say you arrived in Maumesbury on All Hallows. Tell me again when you wrote the play."

"During the summer, at the university."

"Yes, yes. I remember now." The fish man frowned, stroking his chin. He was richly dressed, in green velvet. Some badge of office glinted dull gold in the folds of his thick coat. Edmund sighed, wearying of the performance.

Fish pondered again. Then he lifted his face, something cold seemingly snapping into place.

"What do you know of Catherine Shallow's profession of faith?" Fish said. Edmund had answered the question before, time and again.

"Shallow is a servant of the Queen, serving in her court. Mistress Shallow spoke a grace that night. What else can I say?"

"What were the words of the grace?"

"I can not remember. What does it matter?"

The clerk scribbled. Fish was quiet again, for a minute or two. The he stood up abruptly and vanished into the shadows. A door opened and closed.

The clerk and the man guarding Edmund remained as they were, silent. Edmund did not address them. He waited.

He waited a long time. His mind and body grew numb.

At last, the unseen door opened again. He felt a curious and contradictory sensation of fear and relief. Sometimes a blow was easier to bear than the endless anticipation.

Fish sat down again.

"I do not understand," Fish said. "You tell me All Hallows, but we have reports you stayed at the Angel in March, and subsequently took a house in Abbey Row. The woman signed a paper. She said you stayed, sometimes for several days at a time, during the summer."

"Before the night of my arrest, I had never been to Maumesbury, as I have sworn to you a hundred times."

Fish fluttered his fingers on the play again.

"The Magpie," he said. "Scribbled over the summer months, at the university. It is not, you will forgive me for saying, a very good piece of work."

Edmund nodded, barely.

"The tragical history of a sorcerer, who can transform his bodily shape to help him seduce a young woman," Fish said. "I have read it all, every word. It is sensational, too many murders." Momentarily the man's thoughts seemed to drift from the present.

"I like a romantic comedy," he said, almost wistful. "Some light matter to lift the spirits."

Then —

"Did you know of the colleges in the north of Spain where the English heretics are hiding out, where they take their holy orders for the priesthood?"

"I have heard of them. Who has not? At the university, we heard rumours."

The clerk scribbled. The guard sighed heavily, scratched noisily at his thigh. Edmund could smell him, sweat and meat. How intimately he knew the man, the strong hands, the fingers rimed with grease. But the other man, the fish, was fastidious and clean. The questions made no sense. They jumped, from one disparate spot to another. Edmund tried to make connections. He struggled to assemble the larger matter. His hands were shaking.

"This is taking too long," Fish said. "We need your help. We require some kind of resolution."

Edmund looked up quickly, anticipating a new direction. But Fish stared over his head to the guard.

"Take him," Fish said. The guard pushed Edmund to his feet.

After the meal, Catherine requested Edmund to take a letter to the Angel Inn. He wandered the streets of the town, in the night. The broken abbey, one nave still intact, served as the parish church. The tumbled stonework had been broken up and dragged away. The huge entrance, now out of kilter with the standing remnant of the church, was carved with vines and faces. Arches, sapped off, jutted from the north wing.

At the Angel he asked for Robert Bowen. The young men came drinking here in the endless winter evenings, the stone floor slick with spilled beer, and filth from boots. Edmund introduced himself, the sea of faces taking him in.

"Larkham, you are a scholar?" Robert Bowen, flambuoyant, tucked the note away without reading it. Then he dropped a thick paper into Edmund's hand. Edmund wiped the moist slick from the table and lay the paper down, peering at the soft print in the hot tavern twilight. Then he pushed it aside.

"Bowen sir, you are a fool. They'll break the press."

Bowen had set up a printing press in a small house in Abbey Row. He scattered pamphlets like chaff. Bowen sat beside Edmund, close upon the bench. Beer had sweetened his breath. Confidentially he stretched out his hand to squeeze Edmund's arm.

"Edmund," he said. "You are a coward. You have the heart and stomach of a rabbit."

"When the tyrant abbey was pulled down the people of Maumesbury caroused in the streets, I hear. The abbey wielded power like a monarch."

Bowen sneered, his speech slurred, but his grip was still tight. A black-haired, whey-faced pretty boy, with a pearl ear-ring and velvet coat. Edmund recoiled, repulsed. And tantalised.

"Mistress Shallow," Bowen said, confidentially, "she will show you where the priest still celebrates mass, in a chamber underneath the house. A passageway links it to the old abbey."

Bowen's loud whisper had stilled the conversation at the table. The other men stared. Then Bowen began to laugh, shaking his head.

"You bloody fools," he shouted. "Look at your goose faces. A pox on the Roman church and all its servants. I am the Queen's man. Elizabeth!" he shouted. "Elizabeth!" Excitedly he scrambled to his feet, and onto the table. Cups slopped.

"God save Elizabeth!" he cried, patent boots dancing in the beer. The youngbloods laughed and jeered. The older men shook their heads.

Edmund drank until his cold body warmed through, until his face was moist with sweat. His mind grew hazy, laughing with Bowen, a quick, slim flower who jumped and shouted, ready with a sonnet, or a bawdy rhyme, his hand upon the breast of the flushed girl who brought the beer.

Later, when the doors were closed, Bowen gripped tightly on Edmund's sleeve.

"Come with me," he whispered, serious now. "Come." He looked around, at the dark figures stepping through the filth on the street, hurrying through the night to their homes.

"Larkham, this way. It is time. I've been waiting for you."

Edmund followed Bowen, anticipating a reply to Catherine's note. They walked through the grounds of the broken Abbey and beyond, to Abbey Row. Inside a small house, flames crackled in the fireplace. A woman brought spiced wine and the two young men drank again. Edmund fell asleep, briefly, lulled by the drink and the heat.

Some time later Bowen woke him up. He didn't speak, but beckoned Edmund to follow. Stupified, half-dreaming, Edmund struggled to his feet. Bowen took him through the house, down stone steps into the scullery, revealing another door behind a wooden panel. Bowen carried a lantern, but his body often blocked off the light so Edmund stumbled in the dark. When he tried to speak, Bowen raised his finger to his lips.

Beyond the door in the panel a low tunnel led away. Pitted stone lined the tunnel, odd fronds of anaemic moss and lichen illuminated by stray beams from the lantern. Edmund was afraid, then, as Bowen darted on, slightly stooped in the tunnel. He tried to speak again, but Bowen shook his head and urged him to follow. Edmund was pursued by some nagging concern, something he should have remembered. What was he doing? Had Bowen mistaken him for somebody else? The tunnel was not long. It finished at a small, heavy door bound with black iron. Bowen fiddled with keys, wedged the door open and went through, to a circular chamber. Vaulting fanned out from a central boss decorated with a golden sun. Bowen lifted the lantern, lighting cracked blue paint between the stone ribs.

"Sit," Bowen said. He flashed the light upon a wooden bench at the rear of the chamber. His childish face seemed older now, the waxy skin threaded with lines around the eyes and mouth. Thousands of books and unbound manuscripts stood upon shelves at the back of the chamber.

"Why have you brought me here?" Edmund asked. "Where are we? Who do you think I am?" The drink was clearing from his brain now. The chamber was cold. He was affected with unease, afraid he had been lured into some kind of trap.

"An old chamber beneath the abbey," said Bowen. He was looking around, flashing the lantern. "Don't worry. Everything is prepared."

"Prepared for what?"

"Just wait. We must wait."

He did not understand the dreams. As the stitchery of his body unravelled, perhaps the subtle links of his mind were also tearing apart.

He lay in bed with Catherine. She rubbed her face into the soft, warm skin of his belly. She was laughing, her small hand pressed between his thighs. Long strands of pale golden hair glittered in the candlelight, curling over her white back. The perfume of rosemary sweetened the linen sheets. He stroked the nape of her neck with his fingertips.

"Magpie," she said. "Keep my secret."

Edmund woke, in shock. His bruised body heated, prickled by lust. He shook his head. No. So vivid. The imprint of the woman's fingers still tingled on the flesh of his thigh. Had he harboured a secret desire for her, for Catherine? They had met so briefly. The dream burned.

But the cell door opened and the guard dragged him out again. He screamed as they hauled him down the stairs to the darkest room, but now one part of his mind stood apart. The dream held him still, two places at once.

Fish was sitting by a fire. When Edmund was brought before him, Fish gestured calmly to the machinery.

"I am sorry it has come to this," Fish said. "It is a barbarous practice. But these are dangerous times."

As Fish quietly explained the workings of the mechanism the guards fumbled with straps of leather and rope about his wrists and ankles. Then they stood back.

"Tell me what you know of the abbey," the fish man said. He blinked, rubbing his eyes. Fat fingers of smoke drifted from the tallow candles. The dowdy clerk waited, pen poised.

"It was corrupt," Edmund said. "Her majesty's father, God rest his soul, undertook to reform the religious houses, and Maumesbury Abbey was the greatest. Its lands stretched from Cornwall to York. Henry ordered the abbey to be torn asunder. The monks were pensioned, some of them living openly thenceforward with their wives and children. Now it is nothing. A ruin."

Fish didn't seem to listen. Then he looked up.

"Maumesbury was taken apart, stone from stone," he said. "Among the general herd of lazy, corrupt clerics, sucking the blood of the state, a second monastery existed. An order within an order. Cloaked within the confines of the religious house a sect of heretics flourished. Do you understand?"

Edmund nodded. Fish continued, "The hidden number held views contrary even to the Roman church. They were reputed to be sorcerers. They practised magickal arts. They could alter their shapes, like witches. They could take on the forms of beasts. Do you believe this?"

Edmund hesitated. He did not know the answer the fish man required of him. His limbs began to shake.

"I am not setting traps," Fish said gently. " I want to make you free." He stood up, walked to Edmund and gently stroked the hair from his face. His skin tingled, the faint contact over the bruises and broken skin.

"The inner order fled. Some we caught. Others made their way to Spain. But some still lingered, caught among the broken bones of the abbey. Hiding out in the passageways and tunnels under the hill, some protected by sympathisers in the town itself. Yes," he whispered. He brought his face so close to Edmund's he could smell the cooked spiced beef on his breath.

"Catherine Shallow, " he said. " Catherine Shallow."

The lantern flashed, the stone ribs reeled about the blue domed ceiling. Edmund put his hand to his face, pressing his fingers against his eyes. His skin burned. Curiously he felt himself totter, stepping back, and back. He anticipated the impact of the stone, but the cell wall seemed to fall away with him. Then — the wall rose to his back, cradled him.

Bowen watched, closely.

"I read your play," he said. "The Magpie. The Oxford printer, he gave it to me." Bowen lifted the soft sheaf of paper from an untidy pile upon a table. "It is strange," he continued. "I am a magpie too. A thief. A hoarder of gems. A black and white marauder."

Edmund 's eyes watered. Bowen had changed again, the black hair of the flash boy threaded with white. A blind spot in Edmund's memory blinked out. The man on the horse, by the trough of mud. The rider with the letter of feathers.

The pathways of his mind converged at some hitherto unexpected point, several disparate routes meeting up to offer a new vista. Before he could speak, Bowen stepped in.

"I was instrumental in your appointment to the Shallow household," he said. "Perhaps I was curious to meet the playmaker who had so pertinently cast me in his first work."

"I am here," Edmund said. His heart beat so fiercely it echoed in the stone drum of the room. "Why do you want me, Bowen?"

(In the panelled chamber, sitting besides Catherine Shallow, Bowen tears up a letter with a fat seal, dropping the pieces into Edmund's dish of stewed mutton. Then he plucks feathers from his hair and stuffs them into Edmund's pocket. Edmund dips his bread, mopping the sauce, chews ribbons of paper where the arcane codes of magickal transmutation are inscribed. This is magick, then, not the alteration of the external instrument but the blinding, the skew, in the agents of perception. The dish of paper altered not — no, the boy watches him eat the letter . . .)

"Why do you want me, Bowen?" He asked the question again. The inside of his mind has become an unfamiliar place, empty cracks opening up in the hindmost parts. Elsewhere, locked doors have opened. The letter had tied itself into a heavy knot, down in the pit of his belly.

The cycle of day and night had become confused, now. Long hours Edmund drifted. He dreamed when awake, thought when asleep. The boundaries of his mind had fallen apart. Fish picked through the garbage, turning over the pebbles of his thoughts, still trying to prise out the secret.

Often he sat in the cell, beside Edmund, to talk with him most gently. He told Edmund about his own family, his service for the queen. He shared some small confidences, wheedling, as though a show of kindness might work where cruelty has failed.

"We are hunting for a man called the Magpie," the fish said. "A priest of the Roman church. A heretic. He has slipped through our fingers. Catherine Shallow sheltered him in her home and he has travelled about the country stirring up dissent, firing opposition to the Crown. We can not find him."

The fish laid his hands upon his lap, staring at the palms. Briefly he looked like a boy, about to weep.

"Help me," he pleaded wearily. "Where is he? Where is the Magpie?"

Edmund shook his head, and the guard stepped forward, about to kick, but Fish lifted his hand, indicating restraint.

"I have statements suggesting the Magpie is a man called Robert Bowen. Do you understand me? You say that is not your name, and you are not the Magpie. But I have a dozen signed testaments, from the people in the town, affirming you are Bowen."

Edmund shook his head.

"And yet you say you have made a play called the Magpie, written by Edmund Larkham. This is no small coinicidence."

The words filtered into a dim but active space in his mind. Edmund understood the double bind into which he had been tied. He tried to speak, but a seal like a lead weight closed his mouth, froze the words in his throat.

"The Magpie moved among the heretic order within the major body of the Abbey, which closed its doors more than five and fifty years ago. The Magpie must be a venerable old man. A greybeard of eighty, or more.

"You are not the Magpie. You tell me you are not Robert Bowen, and I say you are not Edmund Larkham. So who are you?"

The brute guard lifted his foot again.

Bowen had aged again, rubbed his face, became young. Edmund heard a strange singing in his blood, which surged about his limbs in a kind of storm. He struggled under the enchantment, the notes and orders of the paper spell digested into the lining of his stomach, touching his heart and spleen.

Bowen pirouetted, discarding his cloak, his shirt and shoes. Edmund struggled to retain the last threads of his sense of self but the fingers of his mind were plucked away one by one and he fell away, and away.

An indefinable space opened, and closed. Then he was walking along Silver Street, staggering across the gulley in the centre of the road where the foul sluggish water trickled. The stars flamed and dazzled, high up, above the broken line of the roof tops. A man and woman approached, the woman shod with wooden pattens which clopped on the slick paving.

The woman drew back the shawl from her head, revealing the fine golden hair fastened back. She nodded, putting out her hand to touch Edmund's shoulder, patting him. Her face was black and white, chequered with shadow. She spoke with her companion but Edmund could not hear what she said. They lead him back along the road to the Angel and the man took him inside.

Later the Queen's men came, thrusting into the pub. First stunned silence, then hasty panic when the men began turning over tables, pushing the drinkers against the wall, searching for someone. Edmund was seized. One man lifted a torch close to his face, nodded, and he was hauled out. They tied his hands behind his back, hefted him on top of a horse, and headed off through the night. The pace was breakneck, the horse stumbling and struggling in the mud. They rode for hours, stopped near dawn to change the horses. Edmund was tugged from the horse to the ground, pushed back on a fresh mount. His bare hands hurt from the cold. His breath puffed white in the icy morning. The red sun ahead of him, a pot, blood-red. Huddles of sheep lay on the frosty grass. He felt a peculiar indifference to this unexpected turn of fortune. Like a dream it carried him. He was playing a part. At mid-day the riders pulled in at a great house, surrounded by woodland. He was dragged to a cell littered with straw, wrists still bound, where he lay a day and a night until the man with eyes like a fish had him untied, and the questions began.

Edmund no longer knew who he was. Bowen's dreams drifted through his head like tantalising ribbons, memories of events Edmund had never been a part of. So real, the flash of scent and sound, the orchards below the town, Catherine Shallow's rosemary-scented sheets. Maybe Bowen, now, was heading for Spain. Maybe he was travelling to the north of England to seek other Roman sympathisers. Maybe he lay yet in Catherine's bedroom, or sought an entrance to the Queen's court, to spread his influence, to work magick. Like a gem, like a piece of broken glass catching a random piece of glass, he had been scooped up, fitted haphardly into another man's picture.

Perhaps he had been forgotten now. He thought days had passed, and weak from his wounds and famished close to death he felt the bonds tying him to his wretched mortal frame had frayed to breaking point.

Then the sound of the door woke him. A candle and a trencher of beef porridge appeared on the floor. He crawled over, spying a white glint, also, on the floor. A polished mirror lay beside the food. His stiffened fingers struggled to pick it up. Dimly in the candlelight the mirror flickered bright and dull . . .

He throws the polished mirror away with a hoarse cry. He has seen himself, first the swollen lips, the bruises, the broken front teeth. Beyond the tapestry of bodily damage — he can not see his own face.

Later the door opens again. Edmund has tried to eat, pressing the porridge into his mouth with his fingers, where it sits upon his tongue because he can not swallow. Men enter the cell, three perhaps. The fish man has a companion, a superior. He is deferential. He kneels beside Edmund, lifts his head.

"See, this is John Dee," Fish says. "The Queen's own servant. You are honoured."

But Edmund can not shape words. Fish drops him, careless now.

"He is beyond us," Fish says. Dee, dressed in the grand style in furs and velvet, sends Fish out of the cell. Then he crouches, strokes Edmund's hair.

"It is nearly over," he whispers. Edmund looks up, at the silk embroidered tunic, scenting rose-water, spying upon the man's cuff the birds embroidered minutely. Beneath the man's russet cap, Edmund sees his own face. Dee peers through Edmund's eyes.

Dee draws out a black feather, clutches Edmund's face and stuffs the feather past his lips and into the back of his throat. Edmund chokes and struggles. Dee stands, watches Edmund retching. Then he turns and leaves the room.

Edmund has changed once. This second time, the fabric of his bodily form is already unravelled, it is not so hard to knit itself anew.

A pot of flesh, stirred up and stirred again. Choler, phlegm, earth, air. One man contains a world in miniature, a microcosm. One man holds a multitude, the beasts of the field, the birds of the air. He is Bowen, Shallow, Dee. The fish man and the guard.

Pied wings clatter. He hops, to a sill where the sky shows. He flies up, and up, to the yawning heavens.

(Thanks to John Bowen, historian extraordinaire)

WINTERTIME ON FRASCH

By Chris Butler

1

Someone hoists me out of my chair, my legs flailing, spins me round and slams me back against the wall. Desperately I try to focus. He is twice my size and his tail is as thick as a Feyl tree. It is Preservationist Gort. He wraps his tail around my throat and squeezes.

"What was that you were saying?" he sneers.

I try to speak but the pressure on my throat prevents me. Gort never was too bright. After a moment he relaxes his hold a little.

"I said that I believe only in things that have been proven to be so."

He breathes in sharply, as if preparing to blow out a flame. "On Frasch, the summer lasts thrice as long as the winter, and life lasts thrice as long as death," he says quoting from scripture. "Those who live by the traditions of the society shall be reborn into the society in the summer after death. Do you wish to be reborn, girl?"

"I apologise Preservationist Gort. I meant no offence."

"If you cannot think of your own future, think then of your father. I pray you do nothing to shake his faith."

I quote back to him from the same scriptures, "Our world is a pendulum. It swings through summer. For a moment the pendulum slows to complete stillness and winter settles upon the tribe-lands. The world gathers itself, swings back into summer, new life blooms and the Yanintow are welcomed back into the world."

"You speak with passion, Balette," he says, and relaxes his grip a little more.

"I know my scriptures. I meant only that if we are to continue the engineering advancements of recent generations then we must be open to new ideas, and we must pursue those ideas with scientific rigour."

Dismissing me he pushes me back in the direction of my table. "I shall have words with your tutors. Perhaps they do not place enough emphasis on the importance of our long-held beliefs."

I sit back down, quietly sipping my drink. Yes, I think it is true, our world is a pendulum. I have the proof of it here in my pocket on the back of an envelope.

2

I hear a pounding at the front door. It is the Preservationists; pounding is their way. They trudge into the house in their heavy boots. The floorboards recoil from them, as do I. The doctor examines my father again. He confirms that the end is nearing, reporting unsteady fluctuations in my father's heart, hormonal imbalances, increased blood pressure, imminent renal failure.

"Do you feel the migration urge, Kalin?" Gort asks.

"Yes," my father replies. "It grows strong in me now."

We are instructed to commence the mourning. In truth the preparations have been underway for some time. My mother is nothing if not efficient.

I wish I could believe that we each possess a soul, through which we are reborn in the summer after death. If we carried memories of our former lives into the Now then I would believe. But if, as I fear, our life experiences ultimately count for nothing save the enrichment of those immediately about us, then surely that is where our priorities should lie. So when Father says he must take himself away to prepare for the end of his lifetime, forgive me for thinking that I would much rather he stay with us, and spend his final days in our home.

My mother wears her mourning clothing. She prepares the Ending of the Now feast, her sisters supporting her as sisters must.

There will be more food than I have ever seen. Food enough to sustain a thousand for a week. Or a family through its darkest hour.

Away from it all, I sit in my favourite part of the garden. The stars are bright tonight and the weather remains fine though they say winter is only days away now. It will be my second winter, I confess I do not clearly remember the last. I recall that there was snow and that I shivered with the cold. Last winter I did not lose my father. I believe this winter will be colder than the last.

"I might have known I would find you out here," he says.

I look up at him with tears in my eyes. "Where else would I be?"

"I hope you do not feel ... excluded from the celebrations."

He sits down beside me and I do not feel excluded. "I try to participate for your sake, but it is difficult. I do not wholly agree with the old ways."

"I know," he says smiling, "and I know that I have said it many times, but I feel the need to tell you once again how very proud I am of all that you have achieved in your young life."

"I have not always been certain that you approved of the path I have chosen."

The moonlight danced on the pond and reflected in my father's eyes like new ideas trying to find acceptance. "The old ways ... have served our people well. You would be wise not to abandon them in your rush for new technologies and ideas. They have sustained our people in more ways than you know."

"How do you mean?" I ask.

He seemed to be choosing his words carefully when he replied, "Ages of wisdom support our beliefs. We would be little more than Haal if we were to abandon the accumulated wisdom of our race."

His words seemed strange. No Yanintow would ever compare himself either directly or indirectly with the pathetic Haal that live away from the tribe-lands and have achieved no measure of civilisation. There is far more than mere custom separating the Yanintow from the Haal. When I looked again in my father's direction to question him on this he was gone.

The celebrations continued for many days and I will carry fond memories of dances we shared, and laughter and singing shared by all. But there were no further opportunities for the two of us to speak in the way that we had for those few minutes in the garden.

Perhaps I risk everything now simply because I have unfinished business with him. A conversation to complete. Maybe I have just grown tired of "old ways" whose creation I did not participate in, and whose meanings, I sometimes feel, are deliberately withheld from me.

"Where are you going, little Ballette?" Preservationist Gort demands of me.

"I need some time to myself, oversized Gort."

"Impudent whelp," he sneers, his eyes seeming to shrink back into his skull.

"What, do you think that I would follow my father?"

"Your kind would take us in directions that should not be travelled. But no, I do not think you would be so foolish."

The most cherished of the old ways is the sanctity of the migration. My father left us this morning, leaving the tribe-lands as he came into them, without any of the possessions accumulated over his long life. He travels out into the forest alone, there to perish. Five summers of wisdom lost to us forever.

In the Observation Centre, Gort's team monitor the transmitters implanted beneath the skin of each of us. They will watch to ensure that no one attempts to follow my father. If I openly tried to I would be swiftly apprehended.

"I have no particular direction in mind," I tell him. "No doubt you will know my destination even before I do."

"Information is power," he says smiling.

"But hard to control," I say, wiping it from his smug face.

I travelled for a day out to the east in order to avoid suspicion, then began to circle round to the south to follow him. I did not have the courage to cut my own transmitter out from under my skin. In retrospect I am glad because it would have lacked finesse. Instead I devised a swarm of drones which buzz around me like electrons around a nucleus, weaving an interference pattern and rendering me invisible to any form of detection. I watch the decoy drone which mimics my transmitter spin away from me and continue to the east. Much depends on it. If it should malfunction I will pay dearly for my folly.

My scanner shows that Father is moving quickly so I must hurry, else he may escape the range of my crude tracking device.

I do not know how an old man who is dying can move so quickly. My own fitness is not in question but I had to take this moment's rest. My legs feel like lead weights. Nevertheless I confess I take a certain pleasure in this reckless course I have set myself upon.

A most unusual thing has occurred, one which even now causes me such inexplicable terror that I can barely gather my thoughts. After chasing my father for two days he suddenly stopped moving onward and at last I was able to close the distance between us. I came into a clearing in the certain knowledge that he must be very close now. My scanner has no great directional capability at such close range so I could not be sure exactly where he was.

A voice came from behind me calling, "Who is there?" It was a guttural sound, more like a snarl than the distinguished tones I know so well. I turned and saw my father, perhaps fifteen strides away. I said nothing and he asked again, "Who is there?" Then he raised his head and sniffed, and in that moment I believed that he knew of my presence by the scent of me carried on the wind.

Something happened to me then. A primal phobic response that caused me to flee from the clearing. I ran for many minutes then collapsed sobbing. I do not know what is happening, either to my father or to myself.

"Hello Ballette," he says. I virtually jump out of my skin as I wake to that same guttural voice I heard in the clearing. The leaves rustle under me as I push myself back from him. He sits cross-legged on the ground just a few steps away from me. He inclines his head to the sound of the leaves. "I know you're here. Speak to me."

"Father."

He smiles then. "Foolish, foolish child," he says gently. "Show yourself."

"I cannot, Father. If I make myself visible to you, I open myself to detection by the Preservationists."

"I see. Then you must remain as you are. But go home child, go before you're discovered."

"But what is happening to you?" I said. It was the first truly foolish thing I had done since setting out on this endeavour.

"Oh, child. The changes are well advanced now. You know what is happening to me."

"How can you bear it?"

"When the change starts to come, it feels natural. Suddenly, all repulsion at the idea melts away. I'm quite looking forward to becoming a Haal."

"It is not possible. You despise the Haal as we all do. How can you stand to become one of them?"

"Just a few days ago I thought I was going to die. This is not only preferable, I welcome it."

"This change, it comes to us all?"

"Yes."

"And the Preservationists know of this?"

"Of course they do. Poor Ballette. It would be better if you had not learned of this. You have perhaps three more summers ahead of you as a Yanintow."

"How much longer will you live as a Haal?"

"They tell me that in the Haal form I will almost certainly survive the first winter, but probably not the second. When I am fully changed I shall forget my former life as a Yanintow."

Angrily I said, "There is no dignity in it."

After a moment he said, "It is not the sophisticated, cultured existence to which we aspire, but there is dignity to be found in it. When the change began, all my senses became heightened. I experience the world about us on so many new levels. It is wonderful."

"Then, perhaps, people should know."

"A short time ago I would have disagreed with you. I would have said people must never know. But now, if I could make them understand that it is a good thing, not something they need to be afraid of or protected from, yes it would be good for them to know."

He stood up anxiously and his thoughts seemed to drift away in the direction we had been travelling. "But you must not tell, unless you wish to spend the remainder of your Yanintow days in a cell."

"Father . . ."

"Go back now, my Ballette. Do not follow me anymore."

He ran then, and I knew that he would run all the way to the southern coastline, there to spend the rest of his days amongst his own kind, the Haal.

3

The setting sun paints all the shades of red across this southern sky. I remember there were raised eyebrows when I unceremoniously abandoned my studies in Engineering, and switched to a course in Zoology.

I studied long and hard through the wintertime. I studied the Cantan Gulls who fly away from the Yanintow tribe-lands during the wintertime, always to return the following summer. I studied the Ice moles who bury themselves deep under the ground when winter comes, some say burrowing to the ferric core of our world. And I studied creatures such as the Gabblefly, born into one form then metamorphosing into another.

Along the way I quietly took an interest in the Haal. Just one more creature among the many I studied. I keep up the pretence that the Haal and Yanintow are different species, since I would not lightly destroy everything my people believe in. In that sense, I suppose I have become a kind of preservationist myself.

My knowledge of the truth brings me a profound sense of worry for us. I find it astonishing that this deception has persisted for so long. That no one about to metamorphose has ever revealed the truth to those close to them. That no one before me has ever successfully evaded the Preservationists and learned the truth. Perhaps though, there have been many who have known, and like me they have all chosen to remain silent.

And what of the Preservationists themselves? Father said they knew. There is therefore a hierarchy of knowledge among the Yanintow. Those who know hiding the truth from those who do not. This seems like insanity on a colossal scale.

When they asked me where I should like to travel for a zoological study I suggested the southern coastline. When I listed my personal objectives for the expedition I did not mention the Haal. There was some resistance from the Preservationists. As a rule, the Yanintow stay close to the tribe-lands, and they expressed concern for our safety. They eventually approved the petition, though only with the proviso that a Preservationist accompany us.

Having travelled on foot for thirty days, I look forward to our arrival tomorrow with great anticipation. There have been many interesting zoological finds along the way. Now we have begun to sight Haal. They sit together in small groups beside tributaries flowing to the shore. They seem to do little other than clean each other, eat sugar cane, and occasionally sip water from cupped hands.

My father believed that he would most likely perish during his second winter as a Haal. I have succeeded in coming here before that time. I realise that I may never find him again, and that even if I do, in all likelihood we will not recognise each other. Still I have hopes that I may yet sit beneath the stars with him once more, that time will slow to a halt, and the winter snow will seem far, far away.

Something is very wrong. We have come at last to the coast-line and I cannot believe my eyes. Between ourselves and the ocean there is another sea. A sea of Haal. Vast numbers of them, perhaps two hundred deep and stretching as far as the eye can see in either direction along the shoreline. I have given up all hope of ever finding my father.

They sit lazily, seemingly having no particular reason for being here, as opposed to staying further inland. But it is not their location that is significant, it is their numbers.

I turn to Maritan, the leader of our expedition, "It is staggering."

"How wonderful," he says. "And strange. Why are they here?"

I glanced at Preservationist Gort then, Maritan did not see the look of horror on Gort's face. He seems as shaken by this as I. If the life expectancy of a Haal is only two winters, then there cannot be so many of them. I think there are more Haal here today than there are Yanintow in the tribe-lands.

Where can all these Haal have come from? Perhaps other colonies of Yanintow exist. It is possible I suppose, but although it is rare for us to travel there have been expeditions on occasion. We have journeyed far to the east and west and no one has ever reported other colonies. No, I do not believe there are other Yanintow.

Then how? Perhaps the Haal live much longer than my father was led to believe. There is subterfuge upon subterfuge here if this is so. If it is true, then each of us must live longer as Haal than as Yanintow. I find it hard to take in, these thoughts come to me in such a rush.

There is excitement all around us amongst the study team. Only Gort and I are subdued. He must know the true nature of Yanintow and Haal. I wonder if the Preservationists genuinely believed that the Haal lived only two winters. If so, I wonder how they will react when Gort returns with the news that they are badly mistaken. I fear I may have made a grave mistake in bringing us all here.

Gort has vanished. What am I to do? The Preservationists have a fragile hold on a system of untenable values. They must relinquish it and tell our people the truth. Yanintow and Haal are one, and the Haal state is not some demeaning final moment in our lives to be hidden away and denied.

Gort will make much swifter progress in returning to the tribe-lands than we made in coming here, without the regular stops we made for study. Even so it will take him perhaps half the time to return home, and the same again for the round trip should he return.

I have decided to tell my tutor Maritan everything I know. Perhaps we can use the time we have here to good effect, learning more about the Haal. Are they truly as lacking in mental faculties as we believe? For what purpose are they crowding together along the shoreline? I have thirty days, or thereabouts, to find some answers. If I am forced into an argument with the Preservationists, I would prefer to be able to argue my case from a sound basis in fact, rather than the nest of hollow eggs I have at present.

We have been studying the Haal for eight days now. Maritan is a good friend. I'm not sure he believes everything I have told him, but he is happy to study the Haal. He is well aware of the impact upon our society if it is all true.

A Haal has been friendly towards me, more than once approaching me and sitting with me as if I were a Haal. Naturally I wonder if he might be my father. If only the Haal could communicate with us.

We decided to sedate him so that we could run some medical tests upon him. He seemed perfectly fit and healthy. His heart beat strong. A blood sample we took was generally compatible with mine, further evidence that he may be my father. Yet we found many strange elements present in the blood, and hormone levels that would be strange in a Yanintow. We could find no indication of any carcinogenic factors or infections of any kind.

He recovered from the sedative without any discernible detrimental effects. I begin to wonder whether the Haal might be immortal, and we are all standing on the shore of eternity.

I have discovered something so unexpected I do not know how to assimilate it. I feel as though everything I have ever known is spinning away from me like dirge down a waste disposal pipe.

The Haal are breeding!

Today I travelled inland to study the few Haal who stay away from the coastline. I found a female Haal suckling a baby Haal. Fortunately I was alone. I do not know if I dare reveal this even to Maritan.

It cannot be. Gabblefly do not give birth to baby Gabblefly, they give birth to worms which later metamorphose into Gabbleflys. If the Haal were to give birth at all I would expect them to give birth to Yanintow.

Who knows how long the Haal live, they're breeding, and the Yanintow are becoming Haal. All roads lead to the Haal. The Yanintow are being cut out of the loop.

When Father was changing he came to welcome it. Perhaps I should too. Let us all wear our mourning clothing. It seems our civilisation is no longer required.

Twenty-eight days have passed. Maritan enters my tent, sees the scanner held in my hand, hears it beeping. "That looks like something a Preservationist would have," he observes.

"I set up a scanner to track Gort. It wasn't difficult."

"Resourceful aren't you. He's back then?"

"Not yet. About midday tomorrow I would think. It looks like they have camped down for the night."

"They? He's not alone then?"

"No. I have about a hundred other signals in close proximity to his."

"Oh."

We sit solemnly for a while, the candles failing to cast much light upon us. "We're not getting anywhere," I said dejectedly, "and we've almost run out of time."

"What do you think the Preservationists intend?"

"Damn the Preservationists. Change is coming whether they want it or not. We have to understand what's happening with the Haal. That's what's important. That's all I wanted."

"You're convinced they'll shut us down?"

"Oh yes. They'll storm in here with their big boots and trample over everything. I wouldn't be surprised if they shoot the lot of us. Us and the Haal together."

"Nonsense."

"Perhaps."

"We've got nowhere in twenty-eight days."

I had to agree. So we stayed up all night talking about Cantan gulls and Ice moles and Gabblefly. And slowly we began to hypothesise a relationship between Yanintow and Haal which was a combination of migration and metamorphosis. A relationship from which fables and myths could be derived, telling of death in the winter and rebirth in the summer. I do not think I shall ever face another day with such a mixture of excitement and dread as I experienced that morning, as the first rays of Cal's light entered our tent.

The transfusion flows from me to my fath … to the Haal. We give him as much of my blood as I can stand to lose. All we can do now is wait.

"They're almost here," I tell Maritan, "we must wake him."

Maritan nods agreement and administers the antidote to the sedative.

Gort enters the tent. "You're going home," he says.

"We have important work here," I argue.

"A team of Preservationists will continue the investigations into this Haal infestation. It is not a task for a novice student."

Maritan says, "I wouldn't class myself as such."

"No, no of course not," Gort concedes, "Nevertheless you will return home with your students. The decision is made. We would be most grateful for any notes or journals you may have prepared."

Maritan and I glance at each other uneasily. The silence is broken by another voice.

"Ballette?"

I spin around towards the Haal and my heart fairly leaps from my chest. He is in that in-between state, half-Yanintow, half-Haal, as he was that fateful day when we last spoke to each other.

"Father."

"I . . . told you to go back."

"What?"

"I asked you not to follow me."

"Father . . . I did as you asked. Much time has passed since then."

"Has it? Oh."

Gort steps forward, "Kalin?"

My father's gaze moves from myself to Gort. "Preservationist," he says slowly, still groggy from the sedative, still in that in-between state.

"Why do the Haal congregate along the coastline?" Gort demands.

"We're just waiting."

"Waiting for what?"

"For summer to return. It won't be long."

Gort turns to Maritan, "What nonsense is this?"

I step forward, "Can't you see? The Haal state was meant to be a winter form, the Yanintow a summer form. But for some reason the change back to Yanintow isn't happening. We're missing some catalyst for that change. Perhaps there has been a change to the climate. Or . . . no, I can't begin to speculate on the reason. But we triggered the change in my father by giving him a transfusion of my blood. We hoped that by changing the balance of his blood, hormone levels, that kind of thing, we could trigger the change back. And it worked.

"All these Haal are just sitting around with no concept of the passage of time. Waiting for a summer that has never come."

I saw a look on Gort's face then that I will never forget. I think it was a realisation that, if this were to become known by the general populace, there would be no need of the Preservationists. People might not mind spending their winters as Haal, safe in the knowledge that they would be reborn in the summer as Yanintow, the winter seeming to have passed in the blink of an eye.

4

Father's transformation continued and he was fully Yanintow again after two days. We talk constantly between ourselves of the changes that will come to our society. We do not have the infrastructure to support the vast numbers of Yanintow we will have.

There will be much work to do, building new towns for them to dwell in. We feel very excited about the possibilities of this expansion. And we imagine what it will be like to talk with Yanintow from so many generations ago. How many of the famous artists, scholars, philosophers of the past will be returned to us? Perhaps all of them. Just imagine it!

The food panel is drawn aside with its familiar clanking sound and our evening meal is pushed through the slot. I pick up the two trays and pass Father's to him. We're like the Haal, I often say. Trapped in a prison cell, waiting for the wintertime to end.

SNARE

By John Grant

Every year — for, let's see, it must be fourteen years now — on the 17th of September he's made a solitary pilgrimage down to the river, and this year is no exception. And, again as always, you'll be going with him.

He's married now, of course. His wife's a sales executive for Wellington and Sons, where he's second in charge of the accounts department — the friendliest accounts department in the South West, as they like to boast to their trainee recruits. He wasn't much more than that — a recruit — when the dashing Miss Thomas, rising star in sales, the secret torrid dream of the spots-and-lunchtime-sandwiches-in-clingfilm brigade, staggered the offices by announcing that henceforth she and young Mr Doremus in accounts were to be considered as an item. David himself could hardly believe his luck: perhaps Carol was a groupie manqué, or something, with a penchant for retired minor members of unsuccessful seventies rock bands; the thought occurred to him the first time she allowed him to undress her, and it came near to unmanning him. But she went through with the wedding, and until the kid was rising two, by which time it was too late, the sleekness of her body and the size of her salary distracted his attention from the fact that he didn't like her very much.

Mr and Mrs Doremus live in a converted Georgian house in the right part of Exeter in a state of perfect connubial contentment. They have sex once a month because, as she puts it, that's often enough for anyone. She drives the kid to school each term-time morning in the Volvo and then, stereo blaring, carries straight on to Wellington and Sons to get stuck into work early, as she always has. He takes things a little more slowly, pottering about the house for half an hour, making himself one Marmite and one peanut-butter sandwich for lunch before travelling in on the minibus to start work at 9.29-and-not-a-moment-later.

Except that once a year, on the 17th of September, he takes a day's leave — or, when it falls at a weekend, is 'phoned by a friend who's just passing through and wants to talk about the old days over a pint — and goes down to the river.

No Carol. No kid.

He goes on his own.

Except for you.

There's a precise ritual that he follows. Today, like last year, the year before, and the year before that, he waits until he's certain that Carol and the kid have really gone, and then he reaches to the very back of the tools drawer, trying not to get stray tacks under his fingernails as he scrabbles around looking for the C90. He pulls it out and blows twelve months' dust from the box; then he fastidiously wipes off the stickier grunge and the desiccated moth with a couple of sheets of peach-coloured Andrex and flushes the grimy package down the apricot lavatory, watching as it's sucked away with an expensively near-silent gurgle. The ball-point writing on the cassette's insert has faded into brownness now, of course, but that doesn't matter because he knows exactly what it reads. He smiles at it sadly — hello, too-old friend — and stuffs it into the right-hand front pocket of his least uncomfortable trousers.

Finding the Walkman inevitably takes a while longer, because the kid borrows it most of the time. Finally he discovers it in the Lego box; he puts Madonna to one side and hums to himself — homespun biofeedback — as he untangles the earpiece flex from the uprights of Sindy's en-suite dressing-table. The batteries are dead, of course, so he leaves everything where it is and pops along the road to the corner shop to buy a fresh packet of four, two of which he puts into the machine and two of which he sets to one side to be lost. He tests the player, pressing the button so that the little red light comes on and the spindles turn; he doesn't put in the C90 yet, of course, because he still has to get lunch organized.

No sandwiches today.

The would-be model in the shop smiles at him and makes her engagement ring very obvious, so that he's reminded to look but not touch. Yes, he forgot — as every year he does — when he was in getting the batteries that he also wanted a single green apple and a large can of Carlsberg Special. She gives him a second admonitory flash of the ring and bends over to get the beer so that her tight jeans say "F.U." at him, except that he's discourteously forgotten that he's supposed to be looking-without-looking and is staring at the video-game in the corner instead. Back home he washes the apple carefully under the cold tap and dries it on a flannelette kitchen towel. Apple and can go into a Dingles carrier-bag; the Walkman is clipped to his belt; he throws on a brown leather jacket that Carol doesn't know he still has; he checks that he's put his change and his keys in the pocket without the hole; he checks that the snugly fitting windows and the back door are closed and locked, and that the cat-flap is swinging freely.

There are seven songs on the cassette. There were many more songs than that, of course, but only seven were ever recorded, the last of them in the drawing-room on a little mono portable.

At last, just as the two of you go out the front door, he pauses to put the C90 into the player. He fiddles with the flex and then sets the earpiece over his head. As his right hand gives the door a little shake to make sure that the lock's caught, his left reaches blindly for the play button.

It's only about a hundred and fifty yards to the bus-stop, but if he dawdles along the way the first track will last just exactly long enough.

\#

there's a place just down the road
where they're selling souls in celluloid —
you know, the kind that your mother used to make.
they're bribing girls in pinafores
to stand half-naked in the doors
of cars that use more petrol than a starving child can take . . .

\#

It was a joke song, of course, made up for a joke band in the back of a joke pub (ye olde leatherette and die stamped horse brasses) by Alyss and me when we were pissed and giggling. The Satin Shirts had just finished yet another bloody gig for another bloody bunch of rat-arses. We'd sung the usual mixture of Beatles and Stones standards, plus a couple of Engelbert Humperdincks for the mums; anything more modern was unpopular with the punters. The four of us had been bored as hell. As usual no one had noticed that our performance was as flat as a sheet of cardboard — flatter, in fact, because earlier on Alyss, peckish, had absent-mindedly eaten the banana she'd been supposed to toy with during our rendering of "Satisfaction". Satisfied in the warmth of a bad job badly done, we were in the process of drinking our fee.

Everything as usual.

Chris and Bri were off fighting with the scrum at the bar to get the next round.

Not everything. Alyss was letting me hold her hand; maybe she just hadn't noticed that I was.

She was laughing about something that I'd said, and then she stopped. With her free hand she began to draw a pattern in the spilled beer on the veneered table, her long black fingernail (she was very into black nail-varnish at the time) moving with a quick precision that wasn't reflected in her voice.

"What do we do it for, Dave?" she said, quietly enough that I had to lean forward to hear her. There was a sheen of sweat on her face but she managed to smell like talcum powder.

"What do you mean?"

"This." Hand taken out of mine. A sweep of the arm to embrace a hundred purple faces. Hand dumbfoundingly returned to mine. "The Exeter pub circuit isn't exactly paved with gold, is it? No need to fret about whether the latest platinum disc would look better in the sitting-room or the hall, is there? We're playing shit for shits and getting paid shit."

Alyss swore quite often, but it was always a surprise when she did.

"We have fun," I said, shrugging. "The money's not much, but it helps pay the bills, lets us have a good night out . . ."

"Yeah," she said, her yellow-green eyes suddenly focused, suddenly filling mine, "and that's all there is to it. In a few years' time we'll all have our degrees and our secure, regular jobs except me because I'll have 2.4 babies and be married to rather than doing a secure, regular job like you guys, and if people ask us over the cocktails if we're into music we'll tell them that we like a bit of everything and not say that at university we bumped out our grants by setting Mantovani to music for the benefit of the wives and girlfriends of the Duke of York's Darts B Team. God. The Satin Shirts. Even the name makes me want to puke."

"Well . . ." I said, looking on the bright side. After a couple of silences I said it again: "Well."

"Don't pay any attention to me, Dave," she said. "It's the Guinness talking. I've just got into one of my what's-it-all-for? moods, that's all."

There wasn't a lot I could say. Luckily Chris and Bri came back with the drinks a few moments later, so I could drink instead of think. Alyss's hand was gone from mine, now; it was resting in her lap, the fist tight clenched so that her knuckles were red blotches against the paper-white of her fingers. She didn't say much, even when Bri started doing his Sherlock Holmes act and joshing her about the Case of the Missing Banana. She looked at me a couple of times, and her eyes made mine sad-feeling. Maybe I was wrong to think that she was doing any more than glancing in my direction.

"Alyss's a bit low because she thinks we could be doing more than pub gigs," I said when there was a space to say it in.

Bri began to laugh but Chris, more perceptive, looked at me earnestly, then at her, then back at me, then nodded, telling me to carry on. So I said the gist of what Alyss had been saying and then I began to expand on it, because the words I was speaking were persuading me as well, so that now I was on her side. After I'd finished none of us said very much for a bit. Alyss had both hands curled in her lap now, and she was watching the fingers flex and unflex. Chris was staring at his half-empty pint. Bri was smiling, bright and cheerful, sitting on his hands and looking backwards and forwards around our faces.

"Look," he said eventually, "there's crap and crap, you know. We play good honest crap — everybody knows it's crap, including us, and everybody's happy, because that's all they want." He took a couple of slugs of his Strongbow and then sucked his upper lip briefly to get rid of the fizz. "You come down to the boozer on a Friday night, you don't want to have to stretch your brain too much: you're looking for crap, and that's exactly what the Satin Shirts serve up for you. OK. They're doing a good job — Purveyors of Good Honest Crap by Appointment to Her Majesty kind of thing. No shame in that. But ninety per cent of the bands in the charts aren't doing that: they're supplying *bad* crap, *dis*honest crap. Why? Because it's pretending to be something better than it is — maybe the bands even believe it themselves. Certainly the kids do. A bunch of prat-heads hire a synth that plays itself, call themselves — oh, I dunno, the Flaming Goolies or something — sing a song about teenage angst and the unreliability of underarm deodorants and whazzo! They've got a hit on their hands, the wrinklies shake their heads and call for Peregrine Worsthorne, Robin Denselow tells us in the *Grauniad* that it's the voice of a new generation, and the kids have another Statement, another Testament. Day after tomorrow it's a different band and no one remembers the — what was it? — yeah, Flaming Goolies any longer but the Flaming Goolies don't mind because they've earned enough to live in the Bahamas for the rest of their lives. That's what I mean by *dis*honest crap. Everyone's deceiving everyone else; they don't give a fuck that they're deceiving themselves, too. Deceiving themselves all the way to the bank."

Chris swirled the rest of his bitter around in the bottom of his glass.

"I like the name," he said at last.

"What d'you mean?"

"'The Flaming Goolies.'" He grinned suddenly, digging out his roll-up tin. "Only you'd want to give it a touch of class, you know. Spell the `Goolies' bit g-h-o-u-l-i-e-s, so it'd be a cunning pun, like."

Alyss's face was getting animated, too, as if she'd suddenly decided to throw off her moroseness like winter mittens — to hell with whether her hands got cold, this was the official proclamation that spring had started. "We'd all have to have new names, too," she said. "I mean, `Alyss Henderson' doesn't have much of a pelvic thrust to it, does it?"

The green eyes had melted.

Within half an hour a new band was born. Yeah, lessavverbighan, ladles and jellyspoons, for

THE FLAMING GHOULIES
line-up
Fallopia Green (lead vocals and banana)
Crotchy Thumbstrangler (lead guitar, synth and vocals)
Buster Blancmange (bass guitar, axe and vocals)
Dave "The Beast" Dormouse (drummer, inaudible backing vocals)

I was the lucky one, I guess, because I didn't even have to change my name. If your surname's Doremus (my father reckoned Sinclair Lewis must have been sleeping with a distant relation of ours when he was writing *It Can't Happen Here*) it's pretty obvious what people're going to call you. Chris — sorry, Crotchy — told me that it was my job to write the songs, because drummers always wrote really crap songs unless they were called Kevin Godley, which I wasn't, and the Ghoulies needed nothing but the crappiest, so I said fine, my fee was only a couple of pints, guv'nor, and Alyss said she'd help me with the lyrics.

While Crotchy and Buster — see, I got it right this time — were up at the bar again getting my fee, Alyss and I set to work with a felt-tip pen and the blank pages at the back of her White/Handler/Smith *Principles of Biochemistry*. We sat side-by-side on the tackily upholstered bench so that her shoulder rubbed warmly against mine through the various layers of cloth between us.

Crap we were able to manage, all right — a few pints and that's easy enough. Buster had told us to make it good and pretentious, too, and that was a bit more difficult until Alyss remembered "Windmills of Your Mind" and began to hum it. We weren't quite able to match it, but we came pretty close with "Hill Snow and the Day of Peace". Call it my talent for titles. Alyss put an arm round me and kissed me on the nose when I thought of it, and her breath smelt of beer and warmth, and her eyes were speaking to me because there were only the two of us, you see, in the little cocoon we were spinning with the lyrics.

Then it was a while later and I was sitting in the kitchen of the house we'd all shared since the start of term. Crotchy had lent me his "other" guitar so that I could work out the tune. He wasn't going to be needing it because Fallopia — maybe it was the booze — had finally, after all these weeks, said he could share her bed and he'd tell me about it in the morning. I wasn't too upset, of course — why should I have been? Just a little surprised, that's all, but after all she was a fully grown adult. I was happy for them in their happiness as my fingers picked out the chords; the tap in the sink served as my rhythm track.

#

He's timed things perfectly, as he always does, and the pair of you reach the bus-stop at the very moment that the final mutilated chords echo away and there's nothing but the tape's dispassionate hiss. He clicks the stop button firmly; there's the air about him of a man who's just performed a difficult job very competently. His eyes are quite bright and alert as he surveys first the two old bags waiting there ahead of him and second the road to the right of him, checking that there aren't any minibuses in sight.

He nods to himself, pleased.

Nothing.

With luck there won't be a minibus for at least two minutes and thirty-six seconds, which is how long the second track lasts. If one does come before then it won't be a disaster, of course — he'll just wave it on impatiently as if it's not going to the right destination for him — but he always hates the times when that happens, resents the momentary intrusion.

You don't resent it yourself — not directly, anyway. It vexes you only at second hand, as it were, because it annoys him. You're glad it's such a short track, so that there's every chance he'll have time to hear it the whole way through. One year an old guy tapped him on the shoulder and shouted through the muffling earphones for the price of a cup of tea, and you thought there was going to be murder on the street. You look backwards and forwards anxiously with your not-eyes, but there's nary a drunk in sight.

Dave presses the "start" button and leans against the Adshel, feeling its hard plastic give slightly against his back. He's excavated a battered old Boar's Head tin from a pocket of his green corduroy jacket, and he's rubbing some of the powdery-dry black dust into a slightly clammy-feeling Rizla blue. The roll-up'll ignite like tinder when he's finished making it, but that's all right because you're not allowed to smoke on the minibuses anyway.

\#

<blockquote>
when I came down from Bristol town
I was utterly alone.
I spent my days just wandering round
through streets I'd never known,
and when at last I found someone
who seemed to care at all,
I said, "please, please, please, mister,
let me punch your wall"
</blockquote>

\#

The tune came out better than it had been intended to be, even though there were only five chords in it. It wasn't exactly Beethoven or even "Roll Over, Beethoven", but it was good enough to tap your toes to if you didn't have anything better to do with your toes at the time. I sung the thing through the following day after we'd all got back from lectures. Crotchy and Buster were reasonably take-it-or-leave-it — it was "adequate", said Buster, which just about summed things up (he got really bad hangovers, and the Ghoulies joke hadn't seemed so funny today, especially not during Soviet macroeconomics, whatever the hell that was) — but Alyss, who'd very sensibly stopped off at the chemist's on the way home, said she liked it. She grabbed her White, Handler, Smith off me and we did the thing together, and with her singing it sounded a lot better than it had when it had just been me, so Crotchy got his plank and Buster, a bit reluctantly, his bass. I drummed on the kitchen-table, marvelling as always about the nice sound thick-gravy-stains-on-fablon produces. Crotchy and Buster plugged themselves into the little amp-speaker unit they kept beside the toaster and we ran it through a few times and it sounded . . . yes, adequate: Buster had been right.

Next Friday's revellers at the Double Locks thought it was pretty good, anyway. Since Jamie took the place over they get a lot of younger people down there, but back in those days it was one of those pubs where the landlord scours the obit columns in the local paper to see if it's worth opening up that evening. Well, not quite. Some of the people there might have been under forty. The guy who was running the place was trying to make it appeal a bit more to yuppies, and we were part of his grand, failing campaign. I think half the punters thought it was an old Gerry and the Pacemakers number they couldn't remember having heard before; the other half had never heard of modern stuff like Gerry and the Pacemakers. (My dad used to play Gerry and the Pacemakers to me — them and the Swingin' Blue Jeans and Freddie and the Dreamers. Then he had the nerve to tell me Genesis sucked.)

Since no one had actually thrown anything at us, we started to include "Hill Snow and the Day of Peace" in our regular act. It was about the only change we made all that term and halfway through the vac. (We stayed on in Exeter, none of us having anything we particularly wanted to go home for except money, and you can post money, can't you?) Oh, yeah, there a few things. Crotchy and Buster got themselves bow ties, because the guy who ran one of our nicer venues suggested it would make us look a bit more upmarket; they wore the things everywhere else, too, for a piss-take that no one noticed. Alyss only slept with Crotchy a couple of times before returning to her nunnishness; it suited her, for some reason I couldn't fathom. Buster got seriously involved with some girl from the poly who later proved to be under-age, which made for a lot of moist eyes in the starlight and crossing-off of days on the calendar. I just drifted along, the way I've always been so good at doing, quite enjoying *Piers Plowman*, quite enjoying *Beowulf*, quite enjoying *Sir Gawain and the Green Knight* . . .

The funny thing was that none of us ever thought of writing any more songs to go with "Hill Snow". We'd written it as a joke, but those few headbangers who listened to the lyrics in between the scrumpies seemed to take them perfectly seriously. I mentioned this to Crotchy one time, and he laughed. "Buster was right," he said. "Make the crap pretentious enough and people'll think it's for real."

Then there was the night we were playing the Drunken Driver, a not-bad pub (you've guessed it) just opposite St David's Station. After we'd finished and were tucking into our post-gig on-the-house pizza marinara and chips, a young, thin-faced bloke in a jockey cap came over and asked if it was OK to join us.

We got to know Jaques (spelt that way, no "c", and pronounced "Jake") quite well over the next few weeks. He was an all-right person — very straight unless you were the SS, in which case I'd guess he'd have been about as honest as a magpie, with his six kids, invalid grandmother and mortgage repayments. His mum was nice, too, when we met her. She'd allowed him to rig up the garage as a sort of rudimentary recording studio — egg-boxes, ancient four-track, remember that Concorde goes over late afternoon — and he'd managed to con a couple of relatives into "investing" enough in him so that he could press a couple of singles a year. So far Scrubbadubba Records hadn't precisely recouped its capital, but the bands he'd recorded were slowly selling their way through his stocks at their gigs.

That was Jaques's resumé, as he told it to us in the Drunken Driver. His proposal: if we wanted to cut a disc of "Hill Snow", which he didn't much like himself but thought was commercial enough to outweigh his more worthy enterprises, he'd take a gamble. He'd only just got round to telling the SS that his uncle had contracted chronic diarrhea six months ago and moved in, so he had some back-pay to play with. He couldn't offer us anything but a share of the profits.

Well, why not?

We didn't have a B-side, that was why not.

We couldn't do one of the other numbers we regularly played, because that'd have got us all into copyright hassles.

No problem, said Alyss, smiling at me the way she smiled only at me: we can write another song together, can't we, Dave?

Two days later we had "Let Me Punch Your Wall". Alyss wrote the lyrics all by herself this time; and, although she meant them to be funny the way "Hill Snow" was, I could hear the sad little yearning voice that was hiding away behind their smothering shield. In her first year at university in Exeter, I knew, she'd been pretty lonely; all her Bristol friends had scattered to their different universities up and down the country, and she was having difficulty making new ones who didn't want to feel her up the whole time. I hadn't realized this, of course; I'd seen her across the Drum Bar a couple of times, sitting on her own with a book, and wished I'd had the courage to go and say hello to her, but I'd assumed she was waiting for some handsome, intelligent, athletic hunk bastard of a boyfriend. It's funny how prettiness can be a burden like that for women. They never know if men actually like them or are just hoping to get to bed with them, which most of them are; while the people like me who'd like to make friends with them as people are frightened off by the nonexistent competition. And she was very pretty — more than pretty. She was only small, and had very pale skin; her eyes were yellow-green. She wore her hair short in what I later learnt was called a gamin cut; it was that kind of coppery red that the bark of silver birches can sometimes be. It sounds a cliché, but she had an elfin face: pointy little chin; small, expressive mouth; cheekbones tinged with pink.

Anyway.

I tried to get as much of her remembered solitariness into the tune of "Let Me Punch Your Wall" as I could, and though I say it myself it turned out a very, very lovely little song. Even Buster thought it was good: "haunting", he called it in an off-hand sort of sarcasm when he first heard it, but often enough later I'd hear him whistling it. It'd have been all wrong for an A-side, of course, but it was just right for the flip of "Hill Snow". That was just about the end of the period when people bought singles for their A-sides and ended up playing the B-sides instead.

As I say, Alyss wrote the lyrics all by herself. She was to do the same for our next three songs, too. I wrote the last one in its entirety — words and music both.

But that wasn't to be for a while.

#

Someone — presumably God — must be orchestrating your journey today, because the minibus arrives just as Dave's thumb presses the "stop" button again. He looks satisfied, as if there isn't any luck involved, as if things are working out just exactly the way they were planned to be.

Politely he gestures to the two bags, who're still talking like geese, up the steps ahead of him; neither of them pauses in their logorrheic spate to acknowledge the courtesy, which is about par for bags. He has his exact fare ready for the driver; he takes his ticket and pushes up the narrow, shopping-littered aisle to a vacant seat at the back. A couple of other people clamber on, one of them a young mother with an unbelievably tiny alabaster child clamped against her chest in a sling; he half-rises, but someone nearer the front of the minibus has already stood. The driver lets in the gear with a groan.

It normally takes about seven minutes to get to the High Street, where he has to change buses for the river. In the rush-hour it can take a lot longer, of course, but this isn't the rush-hour. Anyway, delay's not the worry. Mid-morning, like this, the road's pretty clear and, if there aren't many people wanting to get on or off and the driver's in a rush, the trip can take only three or four minutes — which is cutting things fine. The next track on the C90 lasts just over four minutes.

The whole journey becomes quite exciting for you. You're not listening to the tape, of course; instead you alternate your not-gaze up and down between his digital watch, where his hand rests on the rail in front of him, and the road ahead. It seems to take forever for the numbers to change, and the vehicle is whipping along merrily, skipping right past the stops because it's already full.

Dave notices nothing of this, of course.

Fortunately a child's been run over in Sidwell Street, so the traffic's being diverted round by the bus station. That'll add at least a couple of minutes to the journey time — more than enough.

How kind of God to maim a child especially.

\#

all the other women they got stockings and tights
but when I snuggle with my lover that just doesn't seem right . . .
so I'm a little looker wantsta turn back all the clocks:
when I strip off for bedtime I just strip on my socks,
'cos I got socks
socks
yeah I got socks
I ain't got the measles
I ain't got the chickenpox
I got socks . . .

\#

Devonair, the local radio station, played "Hill Snow" quite a lot, but for a while that was the only airtime it got.

We weren't too worried. Our finals had suddenly stopped being in the infinite future and started being nine months away, so all four of us were spending most of our time working: although of course we were living in the same house, we only really saw very much of each other on Friday nights, when we'd get all the gear together and trundle off in the back of the old banger Crotchy had bought himself to whichever pub reckoned it needed us. Jaques popped around from time to time to tell us gloomily about all the copies the single wasn't selling (the half-dozen or so we were getting rid of at each gig was about the extent of things), but soon he saw that he was just interrupting our studies and he stopped coming.

Buster split up with his polytechnic girl; or, at least, she split up with him — preferring, as she apparently explained to him, someone younger. He was pretty fucked up about it for a while, but then Fallopia very sweetly took pity on him and, as it were, screwed him back to sanity. It was an act of genuine friendship on her part, she told me, but I was unconscionably relieved when the arrangement fizzled out. Shared houses can be a bit of a strain at the best of times; sex between the occupants can so often lead to emotional tensions that can shatter the whole precarious edifice. The same applies to bands, of course.

What I couldn't get over — still can't — is the way that Fallopia and the two guys could carry on afterwards living in apparent perfect amity as if they'd never been anything other than good friends who happened to live in the same house. It wouldn't have been possible for me to act that way. To me, lovemaking involves the complete disrobing of the soul, the unveiling of one's innermost self so that no blemish, no failing, is left uncovered. When you're making love with someone you're allowing yourself to be seen completely without pretension; you're saying to the person you're with: "Look, I trust you enough to see me totally raw. Will you trust me that much?"

Don't get me wrong. I'm not necessarily talking about love and devotion here. Well, love maybe. I could quite understand Fallopia having enough love-of-friendship for Buster that the two of them could trust each other sufficiently to be soul-naked with each other — and, anyway, Buster was so fucked up then that he was soul-naked in front of everyone, all the time, so the sex part of it must have been purely a technicality, a symbol of the everyday reality. But it's the afterwards that baffled me. I could have come to grips with it if he and Fallopia had thereafter become sort of brother-sister close, or even if they'd been occasional lovers when one or other of them needed the comfort; but instead they were just back to the way they always had been, good buddies, nothing special, a whose turn is it to go to the launderette type relationship – as if they'd both suffered some kind of joint amnesia. And the same went for Crotchy and Fallopia.

I was alone in the house one afternoon when Jaques 'phoned up. He was in a cal-box, as usual, so the first thing I did was jot down his number and ring him back.

Great news, great news! As always when he was excited it was a bit hard to work out exactly what the great news *was*, but I made myself appropriately jubilant anyway and then tried to worm it out of him.

Actually, as news goes it really wasn't bad.

Some pinstripe from Floozy Records plc (Jaques was quite meticulous about including the "plc" every time he mentioned the company, and later the rest of us got into the habit, too) had been driving back home from his hols in Cornwall with the wife and kids, and had caught a bit of Devonair while passing through. One of the DJs had stuck on "Hill Snow" as a golden oldie – six months is a long time in the pop biz – and the pinstripe had rather liked it. Liked it enough to 'phone Devonair on the Monday to get the details; liked it enough to get Jaques to sell him a copy (possibly a unique experience for our youthful tycoon); liked it enough to start making noises about it being time for us to take the next step towards (yawn) stardom . . .

The next few weeks were hell, and the direct cause of the fact that I don't have a degree. Because I was the band swot, I was regarded as the one most likely to sail through the finals without further work being needed, and so I was selected to go through all the business mill. I got us an agent in faraway, exotic Bristol – Hawkeye Poulton – and he negotiated a contract for us with Floozy Records plc on terms that were so favourable to us that we only ever saw about ten per cent of what we earnt. I went up to London a handful of times to have my hand bathed in the pinstripe's moist grasp and get taken to L'Escargot. I agreed the dates when we could go into the studio to recut "Hill Snow" and "Wall" as well as a couple of other tracks which Alyss and I would write. I did everything for the Flaming Ghoulies that needed doing, because the other three just didn't have the time; I tried to keep my own studies up to date as well, of course, but it just wasn't possible.

"I Got Socks" was a nice song. Once again Alyss caught that strange happy-sad emotion in the lyrics. Some of the kids might just be perceptive enough to read into them was what actually there, but I doubted it; I tried to help them through the melody, which was another very delicate one. When I listen to the track now it reminds me a bit of early Kate Bush (say, maybe we're where she got her ideas from) except that Alyss's voice was different — sort of like a virginal Chrissie Hynde might have sounded.

Fallopia and Jaques got something together for a while during my absences, I gather, but it wasn't anything serious.

#

It's a short walk between the two stops in the High Street, but the two of you negotiate it easily enough, Dave dodging among the fixed-eye shoppers and the pebbledash litterbins and the benches. And all of this he manages even though he's temporarily blind. There's nothing in the earphones at the moment, of course; he hears the pedestrians trailing their feet along the pavement and the straining of the minibuses as they trudge away from their stops as a single white noise.

Anyone looking cursorily at him now as he leans against the stop would think that he was either drunk or had been up all night. But someone who peered into his half-closed eyes would see that instead it is a matter of his body being empty: his entity has retreated far behind them into some secret place known only to him. There he is hearing the echoes of a long-stilled voice and the sounds of lilting music; he's seeing the lights, some of them quick-dazzling and others muted; there's the touch of many hands on his body, fingers tugging at him . . .

You — the only one, perhaps, who could join him in that place — choose, by contrast, to drag him out of it. Running yourself down his arm, you make his fingers twitch, then move towards the Walkman's solid box. There should surely be time for him to play the next song before his minibus comes. It's a short song not just in terms of the number of minutes and seconds it lasts; it's the one track that, in the course of his annual pilgrimage, he plays only because it's there on the tape, because it needs to be played if he's going to get from the previous track to the next.

Forcing his fingers to clasp themselves around the Walkman is more difficult — for the first time since the pair of you rose this morning, you feel yourself consciously having to undergo some exertion — but soon they respond to your urging. Then his thumb presses down on the play button and, as the preparatory hiss returns to his ears, his self eases itself back into his body, uniting him once more, like a caveman returned to his cave.

#

and when your bloke has left you
and you're feelin' all bereft'n'you
've discovered that you're out of booze'n'cigs,
don't let your hopes go flaccid
or drown yourself in acid —
there's no need to leave it tacit:
just yell "PIG"

#

I haven't any idea how many palms had to be greased along the way, but somehow the publicity people at Floozy Records plc who'd promised us *Top of the Pops* or at the very least *Old Grey Whistle Test* managed to book us in for a slot on some late-night variety show on Harlech that none of us had ever seen. It was the first time any of us had ever been on television except Brian, who'd inadvertently been A Small Boy Passing By in a commercial when he'd been six, and we were naturally very excited. The Floozy Records plc people had supplied us with some new gear to play — they said it would come out of the royalties of our next disc (or platter, as Hawkeye quaintly described it over the telephone to me); a sign of their optimism was that the pick-shield on Chris's guitar was peeling off at one corner and had to be glued back in place. The other three were too cool to show it — the excitement, I mean — but I know that I was embarrassing. I even 'phoned my mum. The person who really blew his mind was Jaques. Exactly what his financial position now was *vis-à-vis* ourselves I had then and still have no idea — presumably he was getting some kind of a backhander from good old Hawkeye —

but you'd have thought he'd just found the Crown Jewels on his doorstep. Of course, he insisted on coming with us in the van up to Bristol, sitting on the broad front seat between Brian, who was driving, and Alyss, who clearly didn't much like him sitting that scrunched up against her; you could tell it from the too-easy way that she laughed at the rather coarse jokes he told as we belted along the motorway. Besides, that close to him she must have had two nostrilsful of his odour the whole journey: he wasn't a great one for bathing, was Jaques.

Although the programme wasn't to be going on air until half-past eleven, we had to get to the Harlech studios by early afternoon. When we arrived, a little late through having got stuck in Bristol's one-way system for a while, none of us had eaten. To be frank, I don't think I'd have been able to — I was knotted up inside by a mixture of exhilaration at the fact we were making it into the big(gish) time and a dread certainty that something was going to go terribly wrong, like a foot through one of the drums — but the others, excepting Alyss, were making a great song and dance about it. Hawkeye appeared from a crack in the wall and told us that we'd have a chance to grab something in the canteen later on, but to shut up for now.

We were met by *Laugh – I Could Have Pissed Myself!*'s producer, who looked about twenty years older than I'd expected: not at all the type of person you'd think of as running a show packed with alternative comedians. Those were the early days of alternative comedy, when everybody was still getting used to the idea that jokes about tits and bums and bollocks were ideologically sound and acceptable to the radical chic, not just sexist crap like they used to be. It's a style of humour that I've always felt uneasy with, guilt smothering laughter, glancing at the half-open door to worry that my parents might be standing outside it, waiting to pounce.

Nicholas — the producer, and not a Nick — ushered us and our equipment down a confusing selection of brightly lit corridors, pausing to exchange words every now and then with people he didn't introduce us to. Finally we were into the studio itself, where that evening's live edition of *Laugh – I Nearly Pissed Myself!* was going to be presented before an invited audience of a couple of hundred. None of the other artistes had arrived by then: we were the only ones who'd be rehearsing there all afternoon. Nicholas told us that this was because it didn't really matter if the alternative comedians screwed up their acts because that was what the audience expected of them — all part of the fun — but the musical interlude was a different thing. Actually, he went on to unnecessarily explain to us, it didn't really matter all that much if we screwed up as well, because we were the bit of the programme when the audience at home hopped out for a pee, but he had a certain professional pride. I think he was just winding us up, though; I think the point was that the camera crew wanted to get their angles sorted out — zeroing in on Crotchy's nimble fingers or Fallopia's jeans, that sort of thing.

The rehearsals were tedious.

We'd written a special song for the occasion, Alyss and I, so that we could be more in keeping with the spirit of the rest of the show. I didn't rate it too highly, and I don't think even Alyss was very fond of her own lyrics after the effects of the Spanish red she'd drunk to write them had worn off. Unlike our other songs — even "Hill Snow" — "Pig" had nothing at all behind the words and the music: it was just a jolly bellow, something you could hear a couple of times and then be annoyed about, years later, when it popped back unexpectedly into your head.

Nicholas didn't like it very much either. We were only half-way through the second verse — because of the way they were working, it took us about an hour and a half to get that far — when he began shouting that we should be doing something else. Him and Hawkeye went into a huddle, from which we could hear nothing but grunts, so we ended up playing "Hill Snow" that night because it was the only one of our songs that Nicholas had heard before.

The audience was about the same as the ones we'd got used to when playing pub gigs, only bigger. There was about the same distribution of ages, and the same lack of real interest in and expectation of the fare that was being presented in front of them. They laughed at all the jokes they were supposed to laugh at, which was more than we did, standing waiting with the less famous comedians in a small sound-proofed room at the rear, watching and listening to the whole horrendous palaver on a small colour television set in the corner. There was a fridge in one of the other corners stocked with beers and miniatures, and all of the comics plus Fallopia and Crotchy laid into it with a will; I told her that she was being foolish, what with this being a big opportunity for us and all, but she was too overwhelmed by nerves to listen and just snapped another ring-pull.

And then it was the time for us to be lugged on stage, just before the second commercial break ("They run the two of them together," Crotchy whispered, "just in case it's a crap the folks at home want"), trying not to make any noise because there was one of the comedians at the far side of the stage, spotlit, still going through his patter to the delirious yells of the mob. I felt as if we were the next load of Christians just about to be shovelled into the arena after a spectacularly good gladiatorial contest, and wondered why still nothing had gone wrong with the gear. A couple of technicians bustled around us, plugging little black insectile mikes onto and into our instruments and our bodies. I adjusted the spiral-winding stool they'd supplied me with until it was the right height — someone must have been fiddling with it since we'd finished rehearsals, I guess, but at the time I reckoned it was that I must have got smaller while waiting in the anteroom.

Then I was swallowed up in light and noise, alone except for the moving silhouettes of Fallopia and Crotchy and Buster in front of me.

She'd forgotten her banana, of course. I'd known something would go wrong. But I only realized that later, when all of us — the comics and Hawkeye and us, the Flaming Ghoulies, and Jake and the production guys and even Nicholas were getting thoroughly pissed at Harlech's expense. It didn't cost them much, in our case, because we were halfway high already on the experience of having done the gig, and anyway we'd never had the chance to find the canteen. I hit the crudités and the mixed nuts for as long as they lasted, and tried to make sure that Fallopia ate some of them as well, but she was glistening with sweat and the flattery of one of the alternative comedians — who was apparently very famous for his shock of frizzy hair, but he's forgotten now — and she didn't pay me too much attention.

I didn't mind, of course. Often we don't pay very much notice to the things that are dearest to us in our lives: we take them for granted, is the hack phrase, but that's not quite it. They're the stable rocks that we know will always be there for us to cling to if the seas of our existence for any reason get too dangerously stormy. Like dogs and spouses, armchairs and Winnie the Pooh. We're much too deeply fond of them to need to think about the fact that we love them. I was proud that Alyss loved me enough to rely on me that way, to regard me as her friend in that uniquely special fashion.

Crotchy and Buster eventually vanished with a couple of girls — even Jaques got lucky — which left just me and Alyss, except that, when I hadn't been watching (she didn't like me watching her too much) she'd left as well. Hawkeye put me up for the night on the imitation-leather sofa at his flat.

It was really very comfortable, once you got used to it.

#

The minibus ride down to the river twists and turns and can take quite a while, even though the route is underused at this time of year and there's hardly ever anyone waiting at the bus-stops. You're all eyes, in as much as you're anything, for this is certainly the prettiest part of the journey to the river, and you only get to travel it once a year. The only other people in the minibus are the driver and a man with a beard and the *Grauniad* crossword, so there's nothing to distract you. First there's the bustle of the High Street and South Street, with their traffic lights and their unpredictably crossing pedestrians to be worked slowly through, but then for the latter part of the journey it's down Western Way, which is broad and here curves gracefully, before the minibus turns off to the left into a narrow street whose name Dave can never remember. Now the minibus has to go more cautiously and slowly, giving you time to appreciate the buildings, which are a mixture of late- and imitation-medieval, with the truly ancient remains of the city wall somewhere off to your left.

You have a faint recollection that once upon a time you might have come walking with him here: you can't remember exactly what lies around each next corner, but you're not surprised when you see what's there. Certainly it's as romantic a little street as any can be near the centre of a city. Partly that's to do with the age and style of the buildings on either side of it, and the fact that its quietness is a contrast to the turmoil of the nearby South Street; but it's more because of the street's actual shape. It's unlikely that any medieval town-planner sat down and decided that the street should trace a course whose very bends and inclines would induce a sensation of affectionate security in those who walked down it; perhaps if someone had tried to design it that way the result could never have been achieved. You watch, now, the walls moving past the windows on either side of you and again those tendrils of memory touch you. There's a corner where maybe you stopped to kiss one night. The yellow street-lights wouldn't have obscured the Moon or the edged clouds. You'd have been able to hear the music of the riverside nightclubs from here, maybe, if the wind had been right. But it's hard to tell, because the memories aren't your own, even though they're of you.

He moves his Dingles carrier bag on the seat beside him, obviously not knowing that he's doing so, equally obviously oblivious both to you and to the street down which the minibus is passing: whatever memories that he might once have had of walking here on misty evenings have been erased through overuse, like the songs on the C90 will become in time.

It's a wonder, really, that they've survived these many years. He'll have already, at some stage during the journey, made a resolution to re-record them onto a fresh tape once he gets home, but he'll never get round to it, of course: it would be a breach of the time-caressed tradition if he did.

His lips move as he listens to your voice.

#

when I first saw the cigarette smoke in your eyes
you were wearing your heart on your sleeve,
and when you asked if I were otherwise compromised
I didn't know quite what I was supposed to believe.
but you said you wanted me to be your lover in each and every way,
you said you wanted me to be beside you all of the night yes and all
of the day.
I suggested my place, but you,
you said that you knew this really great café . . .
and now we're out and running down the dawn-dark streets
down all the dark alleys where the sun never stays
watching the paving stones vanishing beneath our feet
as the sky performs its greens and pinks, reds and yellow-greys
and then a tattered canopy and a rectangle of aching light
you touch a door handle and suddenly everything is too bright
as we stand in the doorway our eyes are the eyes of
creatures of the night

#

We can't have been as bad as in the morning I thought we'd been, because a couple of days later Hawkeye gave us a phonecall to let us know that we were wanted for *Old Grey Whistle Test* and also for one of John Peel's Radio One sessions.

"He just wants us because we're lousy," proposed Chris dourly of the latter.

Alyss stopped mid-celebratory pirouette and stared at him. He was sitting with his elbows on his knees on one of the squeaky plastic-covered orange armchairs that our landlord had instructed us were actually very comfortable.

"Why do you say that?" she said. White wine vinegar and lemon juice in her voice and her eyes.

But she knew what he was talking about. John Peel used to play a lot of good music, but then again he liked an admixture of truly outrageously cruddy bands, people that no one in their right minds would ever listen to in the ordinary way. I guess that was exactly why he had them on his show: so that, just for once, they'd get listened to. Something about seeing through shells of ugliness to discover the true, hallowed, unobserved beauty within.

Most of the time, I thought, you did all the picking in-through-the-shells-of-ugliness bit and still found ugliness, but I didn't say anything because it occurred to me that Chris was probably right. And I hated him for saying it out loud. Listen hard to The Flaming Ghoulies, friends: they're the latest freak show in town. Way out and wild they are: you'll never forget Fallopia and Crotchy and Buster and, oh yes, the drummer . . .

Maybe that really was what it was all about, but as things proved it didn't matter. The Peel exercise and *Whistle Test* and an increasing number of others sold records, and all of a sudden "Hill Snow" was in the top 40. Only just. And very, very briefly. In six months' time, Hawkeye assured us, we'd have quite a lot of money coming to us — enough, maybe, to pay off the rest of that crap kit that Floozy Records plc had advanced us for the Harlech gig.

Alyss had got a first-class honours degree. Chris had got a 2/1. Brian and I had got nothing but happy memories, or in his case sad ones because it was splitting up with his girl that had wrecked his chances. There are two sides to every coin, though: at least he was able to blame his failure on her desertion.

I don't know when any of us first realized that this whole Flaming Ghoulies thing was really serious. Not long after *Whistle Test*, I should think. Before then we'd regarded it all still as being some kind of a joke — or, perhaps more accurately, like a peculiarly improbable dream that some time soon we'd wake up from. We couldn't really have been fooling all of the people all of this time, now could we? But then, without us noticing it, we'd become a commercial property — a commercial property of which we were only the part-owners, if in many ways the least important ones. Because there was money coming in from what we were doing, it had become a respectable endeavour rather than a mere self-indulgence, an overextended student prank.

Making Tesco's instant coffee in a cold kitchen on a grey morning, the torn linoleum cold on one's feet, bladder throbbing because Brian's still in the bog, realizing there's no milk in the fridge. All that and the awareness of one's own celebrity stardom, too.

Alyss almost didn't let me set "Vampire Café" to music — in fact, she very nearly didn't let any of us see it at all. I'd known that she'd been writing something that was troubling her, touching something deeper inside her than shouting "Pig!" ever could, but of course the other two hadn't noticed that. For a couple of days she was strangely quiet, keeping herself to her own room a lot of the time, even missing a meal or two, the yellow-green of her eyes looking grey as if I were seeing them through smoke . . . rather the way it says in the song.

She never said outright who the guy was. That irritated me a bit, because I was accustomed to sharing her confidence — besides, it wasn't easy for any of us to keep secrets from each other, living all tumbled in together in the house the way we were. She'd been gone for a week or ten days some time during the summer — nine days in fact — and had never told us exactly where she'd been. I could have asked, but I didn't want to pry. We weren't big enough (would never be big enough, in fact) for the press to have noticed her absence, which was a blessing. She'd been miserable when she got back, and for a time we'd been worried that she might want to jack in the band. I overheard Chris quizzing her about it — typically insensitive — in the kitchen one night when the two of them were doing our weekly washing-up, and all she said was something about having wanted to get away from us all and the whole Flaming Ghoulies farrago for a while, spend a week at home eating her mum's cooking and pushing her dad's wheelchair out for walks along the seafront; that she'd needed to reevaluate herself, and us, and what we were doing, and what we were becoming.

It seemed to be enough of a lie to satisfy Chris.

But it was me to whom she finally showed the lyrics for "Vampire Café", one night when the other two were out and it was just she and I alone in the house. I was in the drawing-room, fooling around on Chris's old Yamaha, trying some improbable chords to see if there was any way they could be run together to make something better. The synergy wasn't working when Alyss came in, very quietly, and settled herself down to watch me. She was wearing burnt-orange jeans, just loose enough so that your mind had to work out for itself exactly what shape she was inside them. Her teeshirt was a washed-out grey, the fabric around the neck so stretched from age that, even though her hand was moving constantly to adjust it, you could still always see one or other of her shoulders. There was a tiny mole on one of them. She was as quiet and as self-contained as a cat as she watched me.

I looked up, at last, letting the final discord die.

"I've got a new lyric," she said, "Dave."

She held out a reporter's notebook — one of those cheap spiral-bound ones you can pick up in any corner shop. She looked as if she were forcing herself to give it to me — as if, if she didn't do it now, she never would.

I moved very gently as I reached out across the wilderness of the carpet to take it from her.

"We can work on it together," she said. "If you'd like."

Then she settled back into the armchair's squeals and yelps and burlesqued kissing noises as I read it.

It was a song that told a lot about her, if you could only learn to read the lyrics right. If you didn't — well, it was saying something else entirely. The first verse seemed to be all about a standard party pick-up; no, maybe something less casual, less dispassionate than that. But then it went on to tell more of the story, of how they'd gone off for a dawn coffee in the Vampire Café of the title, of how they'd talked together in that slow and trivial delaying way that soon-to-be lovers have: a long and erotic foreplay that's carried on beneath sheets woven out of words and glances. Except that this time, you come to realize as you read the lyrics, it hadn't been working out right. The longer they'd dallied over the skinned coffees and the formica tabletop and the obsolete jukebox in the corner, the more she'd realized that it wasn't her affection or even just her fucking that he wanted: he really was a vampire, you see, which was he'd brought her to this café. Not a vampire with long teeth and hidden wings, but a vampire nonetheless. He was drawing the spirit out of her, and he'd go on doing so. He was taking the soul out of the person that she in fact was and trying to jam it into the form of someone quite different, an image of her that he'd himself created — he was trying to make a new person out of *bits* of her, and in so doing was discarding what he regarded as the dross but what she regarded as her core. He wasn't exactly building a tulpa, the way you read about people doing in tales of the Tibetan wilds, but it was something very like it; and the end-product of the process would be the destruction of the original *her*".

But she didn't make her excuses and run: that way he and she would be with each other for ever; she'd never be able to shake herself clear of him. If she were ever to be free of him, she would have to perform an act of exorcism. Besides, the intensity of his desire for her essence was flattering in itself. But it was also that she was being dictated to by his need for her, that it was controlling her actions: she had no choice. There was a whole complex of reasons — many more than these — why finally, after almost one too many prevarications, they'd gone somewhere and screwed, "made love" being distinctly the wrong term. And at the end of the lyric, as you're reading it, you realize that it's not really over, even though there aren't any more words left: that maybe it's never going to be really over. That you don't know if the exorcism has worked or not, because she herself still doesn't.

I didn't speak for a while. It was a good lyric, a great one; but the thing that really enforced my silence was the truth of it. Alyss couldn't have shown more of herself if she'd taken a scalpel and cut herself open, found the part of her that contained her soul and plucked it from its surrounding flesh.

I picked up the Yamaha. I dragged a stool nearer to me and put the open notebook on it. I glanced at her. She was watching me, her eyes seeming to scrape the skin from my face with their intensity.

She cut the stare and uncoiled herself from the armchair.

"I'll make some coffee," she said. "See if it's good enough to set to music."

"I know a really good café . . ."

She held up a hand to stem my nervous joke.

"I'll make some coffee," she repeated.

Left alone there with the lyrics of "Vampire Café" in front of me, I found my mind beginning to fill with swirls of imagery. Maybe some people merely *hear* the music in their head, but for me it's never been that simple. The music inside my mind — whether it's something I'm composing, or just nonce-melodies popping into and out of focus, or even memories of tunes I've heard on the television — isn't purely a matter of sound. There's a lot of colour in it, for one thing, as if my senses were synaesthetically confused; sometimes there are smells as well. There's also something that I can only call "ambience", realizing as I do so that that's not really a very clear description. It's the same sort of thing, I guess, as the way that, when you remember hearing an old String Band track, or something, your whole self maybe remembers everything else about when you were listening to it one time. "There goes our song again" — clichéd but, like some clichés, pointing at a quintessential truth. Except with me — and maybe, for all I know, with everybody else as well — *all* the music that plays itself in my mind is like that: as if the songs I haven't finished composing yet, and even the ones I'll never compose (which are all of them, these days), are predicting the ambience in which I'll one day hear them. Or maybe it's more that they're creating it. They come complete with noises off and the tang of cigarette smoke and the touch of someone's hand. Sometimes the ambience is there even before the song itself, so that the music itself need merely be dropped in as a mechanical afterthought.

"Vampire Café" was one of those songs. Even while I'd been reading the lyric for the first time, I'd felt the finished song all around me, holding me. Sitting there in our drawing-room, I was beside the jukebox of the song, the jukebox whose lights "were the lights of hell". If I said now that I deliberately concentrated on adding in all those apparently pointless embellishments to the melody — the way that Alyss's voice hangs on seemingly too long at the end of every line, until you're almost ready to become impatient with it before it suddenly stops, and you realize that, in retrospect, it was held for exactly the right length of time . . . Or the way that the loudest parts of each verse seem at first to be the wrong parts, the places where the lyric has the tenderness that Alyss put into it so you'd expect gentleness. She'd done the same sort of thing with the words, of course, with that change of tense from the past to the present between the first verse and the second that some pedants objected to so blindly: the point she was getting across was that the past and the present were indistinguishable now for her, the girl at the end of the song. When the second verse starts:

so now we're out and running down the dawn-dark streets,
down the long alleys where the Sun never stays

Alyss was clearly signalling that this wasn't just a song about one set of streets, one early morning — one fixed time. She was still running down those same streets: would always be.

What I was starting to say was that I could tell you about how I cleverly manipulated all of those technical tricks in the music, and how Alyss did likewise with the words, but I'd be lying. I can see the techniques there now, looking back on it after I'd done it; but I knew nothing of them then. I won't say, either, that the tune just came to me naturally, like it'd had always been there and I just happened to be the person it chose to alight on — that's happened to me once, but it hadn't happened to me yet. No, I worked hard on "Vampire Café", maybe five or six hours or so, right through Chris getting home with some drunken girl and Brian 'phoning up to say that he was going to stay out with his. For much of the time Alyss just sat there with me, completely still and soundless except when every now and then she replenished our coffees. She watched as I brought the song into the light.

And then, when finally it was done enough for me to be able to play it to her from front to back, she wept.

I had to sing it again and again for her, until she was joining in with me and then beginning to take over the vocals entirely. Quite often she had to stop singing because of the tears or the way her nose was running. Sometimes I cried, too, I think.

I've never in my life been as close to another human being as I was then. Making love in her bed through the dawn was only a part of it.

#

> *the first wise man produced his gold,*
> *and the angels cried "hurray"*
> *the second brought out frankincense,*
> *but the angels said "no way"*
> *so the third decided "better not the myrrh"*
> *and got his wallet out;*
> *and the angels sang "now there's a man*
> *who knows what it's all about"*

\#

But "Vampire Café" wasn't the next single we released, even though we all agreed — even Chris and Brian, which amazed me — that it was far and away the best thing we'd ever done. We'd been gigging around the country for a solid month since Alyss and I had written it, mixing in a dozen or so new songs (but not "Vampire Café") with all the old junk we'd used to do as the Satin Shirts, and we stopped off in Bristol on the way home. Hawkeye listened to it once in the rough, just me and Alyss doing it together with Chris and Bri watching us, and he pretended to dry a tear from the corner of his eye at the end of it and then told us it wasn't commercial enough for us — or at least not *now.* Maybe later in our career it would be something we could get away with — have a smash hit with, even — but we were as yet still too young a band in the public consciousness to be trying anything experimental, anything *risky* like "Vampire Café".

He'd got a much better idea for our next single. There were still three months to go before a sensible release date, but it was about time we started writing and maybe even recording a Christmas number.

Me and Alyss wrote it in the back of the van on the way home from Bristol. The four of us thought "Spend Spend Spend" was hilarious, but there was a lot of bitterness in our laughter on the motorway.

A week later we recorded it and forgot about it. The same afternoon we recorded "Vampire Café" for the B-side, and didn't forget it.

There was a lot of joy in me in those days. All through the tour I'd found myself smiling whenever I was alone. Which wasn't all that often, because Alyss was usually somewhere close to me. No matter how bad the venues, no matter how lousy the grotty B&Bs that Hawkeye had booked us into, I was living in a magical country with her. Most nights the two of us were crammed together into a lumpy single bed, but we didn't need any more space than that. A lot of the time we talked or spent kissing each other everywhere, but we made love often as well, her period no hindrance. The gigs were a part of it all, too. Sometimes they were big halls where we were the support for some other band just as bad as us; sometimes we were the Main Attraction in a pub or a club. It didn't make any difference to me or Alyss: there were only the two of us on the stage, with nobody watching except the spotlights.

But then we recorded "Vampire Café".

She . . . changed.

It was sudden. For a few nights it seemed impossible, for some reason or another, for the two of us to go to bed at the same time. Usually I'd go first, and be asleep by the time she came up. I didn't let myself know that there was anything wrong until one night we walked down by the river. We'd been drinking, both of us a bit too much for what I now recognize were our different reasons, but now the pubs were closed and we needed the air before the long walk home together.

Tonight, with the Moon hanging above the water, she tore her hand from mine.

I reached out for her but she twisted away, avoiding my touch.

"Leave me be!"

"What's the matter? Have I — ?"

"Let go of me. Stop clinging to me. Let me free."

I didn't know what she was talking about.

"What's the matter?" I said again, stupidly.

"I don't want you any more. I don't want your bloody band and I don't want *you*. You revolt me!"

"But I love you," I said, trying to sound soothing. It was all just a thing of the moment. Too much to drink. Gods, but we all go through patches when we can't stand ourselves so we take it out on other people. "And you love me."

"I don't!" Fallopia howled. "I never have! Haven't you got ears to hear?"

I froze where I was. I can remember that my mouth was half-open, and thinking that this was what mouths did in similar circumstances in books but that I'd never before noticed my own mouth doing it.

"I *love* you, Alyss," I said at last.

"You *don't!*" Fallopia shrieked. "Not *me!*"

I still don't understand what she was trying to say, then. Anyway, it all seemed insignificant in the light of what she said next, which was something too horrific to be remembered. I find myself unable to force myself to try to remember it. I think this is because it was something very trivial — a gratuitous insult, however close to the quick it must then have cut me.

What I *can* remember is realizing that Alyss would not wish to say such things, and putting my hands around Fallopia's throat and squeezing until she couldn't foul the air with any words any longer.

It meant, of course, that neither could Alyss speak her thanks to me for the service I had rendered, but that didn't matter. I could, anyway, feel her gratitude in the weight of her shell in my arms.

I waded out into the river until its water was up around my chin before I let the current gently remove the shell from my embrace.

I was dry by the time I'd walked home. Crotchy and Buster were either out or long ago in bed — certainly they didn't disturb me as I set up the cassette recorder on the coffee-table and tucked in a cassette and put Crotchy's old Yamaha — he never used it any more, now that he'd graduated to posher equipment — across my knees and sang into the cheap little inbuilt mike the song I'd composed in my head during the walk home.

That's the only recording there's ever been of "History Book", the last and the best of all the songs I ever wrote for the Flaming Ghoulies. I was able to keep my voice unchoked throughout it.

Then I pulled the cassette out of the machine, kicked in the back of Crotchy's cast-off — I enjoyed that in a grim sort of a way — and went up to my doubly empty room and packed those few of my things I wanted to hang on to.

I didn't leave a note or anything for the other two. There wasn't anything I much wanted to say to them. If they needed me, they knew my parents' address, so they could get in touch with me that way.

Which they never did.

Now here's a funny thing: in fact, no one at all from those days has ever contacted me. Maybe no one noticed that Alyss had disappeared, as if she'd never been. I can hardly credit that, but it seems the only possible explanation. Maybe Buster and Crotchy just thought the two of us had gone off together — we'd been so close the past month or so that it wouldn't have been surprising if we had. Perhaps they tried to keep it a secret, because a couple of times over the next few months I saw the Flaming Ghoulies on late shows, and they were using old videos of the band with her still singing up front — and, I couldn't help noticing ruefully, with never a close shot of me, the drummer. It was always that way. Always that way for drummers.

Yes, I can think of reasons Crotchy and Buster might not have raised a hue and cry when we both went. But you'd have thought that her parents must have . . .

I don't understand it. Sometimes it's as if it was me, not Alyss, that never was.

In my life now there is no Alyss, and all that are left to me of the Flaming Ghoulies are memories that I resent whenever they attempt to intrude. At least, that's true three hundred and sixty-four days of the year (and three hundred and sixty-five in each leap year). Annually, however, on the 17th of September, the day of the night she died and I recorded "History Book", I remember a little more. I experience again the pain, but I experience again also the ecstasy — for there was a lot of ecstasy we shared in those days, and I was able to feel it. As I still can once a year, today.

Oh, and sometimes briefly at Christmas. I don't know if it's Crotchy or Buster — I suspect Crotchy, because he's always been the more sadistic of the two of them, and besides I don't know that Buster would have the brains — I don't know which, but one or other of them sends me an annual Christmas card, with her name written on it, "Alyss", like a signature, and a cross to mark a loveless (maybe jeering?) kiss, and sometimes the single word "Sorry".

But I chuck it on the fire before Carol or the kid can see it.

\#

when Alyss awoke she was all alone
and past all hopes of caring.
the train rattled through a country station or two
with empty houses staring.
she wanted to move, walk up and down for a while
but found that she could not stand.
her sight fastened for a winter's moment or two
on the lifeless hook of her hand
(and who could touch her
and who could teach her
that time lies in confusion?
conviction, knowledge and understanding
are all parts of its illusion.)
that's when she saw in her leathery palm
the reflection of an angel
its hand upon her shoulder . . .

\#

He's walking along the side of the river, looking for all the world just like someone else who's out for a stroll on an autumn day. There are ducks on the Exe in profusion, and some swans: if he were down here with the kid they'd have bagfuls of bread to throw to the birds, the kid tossing the pieces high to watch the gulls swopping down and plucking them out of the air. Carol might be with them, watching, eager to leave, wanting to *do* something. Carol fills her days with *doing* something.

Today, of course, he doesn't see the ducks and the swans, and nor the way the sunlight makes the disturbed waters look as if they were, each instant, new-formed from sharp-edged glass.

But you see all of this.

Soon the shops and the pubs are far behind. There are still too many people on the towpath; after he's passed the Double Locks it'll get quieter, and eventually he'll reach the stretches where people hardly ever go.

You don't know why it is that you're singing, but you are. No one can hear you, of course: most certainly not Dave. It's "Vampire Café" that you're singing, but he's hearing "History Book". He recorded it over and over again onto the rest of this side of the C90, and he covered the whole of the other side with it as well. It was the song he wrote for you, he said; you'll never be able to make him listen to you telling him that it was the song he wrote so that he wouldn't be able to hear "Vampire Café".

At long last a place where the estuary is broad and where the only signs of other human activity are on its far side. The ducks gave up following him hopefully along the bank some while ago, the swans even before that.

He spreads out his old leather jacket on the coarse grass and sits down on it. He's been curbing his desire all this time, knowing that he's not allowed actually to *play* "History Book" until he gets here. But it's all right now: it's permitted; indeed, the rules are that he *must* play the song.

He presses the play button, then pulls his knees up to his chest and puts his arms around them. His eyes close as he listens to himself sing.

But now he can see the chopped surface of the water in the unwarming light. This is the way that it's been all the other years, even those times when it's rained or the mist has been opaque. He knows what is about to happen.

And so do you, for you pull yourself free of him, as you do every year, and you sweep out over the river, playing with the air in front of him, drawing threads of sunshine and hues of breeze in towards you until, fifty or a hundred yards from the bank, rapidly weaving your body for yourself, you touch the water.

He sees that touch, watches as the surface is struck by a gust of wind that causes it to start swirling in upon itself. Reeds are torn from their place along the riverbank and are dragged, accelerating, across the oblivious face of the water. There are autumn leaves around him, and now the breeze picks these up from the grass and carries them out towards the place where you're troubling the water. You need the leaves for the colour of your hair; the yellow-green of your remembered eyes exists nowhere in nature and so you have to create it specially.

Your body, rising from the brown water, is still not fully formed; the arms and thighs are irregular columns of bundled reeds, the head a blurred, eyed mass. You teeter like an unstrung puppet. But now you are pulling to yourself strands from that ancient recording of "History Book". The plosives of Dave's frenetic voice, exaggerated by the tinny crystal mike built into the cheap cassette recorder he used, become your joints and vertebrae; the stretched penultimate syllables at the ends of alternate lines are appropriated as your fingers; the inadvertent taps of his fingernails on the guitar's soundbox swiftly paint in the details of your face and the lines of your ribcage showing through your smoothing skin; once, twice, there is the sound of his indrawn breath, and your small breasts are pinkly present; his slurred sigh each time your name occurs becomes the v of your pubis and the roll of your hips cradling it; his clumsy strumming is your feet.

Your body finally bound together by the lines of chord progressions, the corners of your mouth quirked into a smile by a D-minor played where there should have been a D-major, you walk towards him across the powerful, ponderous flow of the river's current.

Time passes. Now you stand, naked and dripping, beside him. You put the palm of your hand on his forehead, and the two of you exchange the substance of yourselves. He can feel you and see you very clearly, even though his eyes are still firmly locked closed, as if shut against a spotlight. His lips are moving soundlessly to the only song he now knows:

> *and who could touch her*
> *and who could teach her*
> *that truth's no one's dominion?*
> *there are no such things as facts any more*
> *(well, that is my opinion)*

And all the rest of the afternoon the two of you are together, talking and singing together and making love in the warmth of the past.

Here in the place where, fourteen years ago, you lost your life and were born. Here where Dave will never remember the words you screamed in your fury and your despair and your revulsion . . . and your pity:

"You *can't* love me. You're not *allowed* to love me."

And:

"I exorcized you."